MURDER IN VIENNA

MURDER IN VIENNA

E. C. R. LORAC

Edited and Introduced by
Martin Edwards

Poisoned Pen
PRESS

Introduction © 2024, 2026 by Martin Edwards
Murder in Vienna © 1956 by The Estate of E. C. R. Lorac
Cover and internal design © 2026 by Sourcebooks
Front cover image © Hi-Story/Alamy Stock Photo

Published by Poisoned Pen Press, an imprint of Sourcebooks,
in association with the British Library
1935 Brookdale RD, Naperville, IL 60563-2773
(630) 961-3900
sourcebooks.com

Murder in Vienna was first published in Britain in 1956
by Collins, London, for The Crime Club.

Cataloging-in-Publication Data is on file with the Library of Congress.

Printed and bound in the United States of America.
VP 10 9 8 7 6 5 4 3 2 1

For
DAPHNE,
with love and gratitude

Trauttmansdorffgasse
Wien 1954, 1955

INTRODUCTION

Murder in Vienna, first published in 1956, was one of a number of British detective novels from that period which were set in enticing overseas locations. Crime writers were responding to the desire of readers, wearied by years of domestic post-war austerity and keen on escapist fiction, to enjoy a vicarious sense of the glamour of foreign travel.

In the early 1950s, Agatha Christie published *They Came to Baghdad* and *Destination Unknown*, two stand-alone thrillers quite distinct from her detective puzzles as investigated by Hercule Poirot and Miss Marple. Other authors had their series detectives investigate crime overseas— sometimes during the course of a holiday interrupted by murder. Examples in the British Library's Crime Classics series include *Tour de Force* by Christianna Brand, *Death on the Riviera* and *A Telegram from Le Touquet* by John Bude, and *Crossed Skis* by Carol Carnac (another pen-name of E.C.R. Lorac).

In the opening pages of this book, Superintendent Robert

Macdonald of the C.I.D. is flying from England and has "an odd feeling that he was reliving his own past, slipping through the years as imperceptibly as the Viscount slipped over the North Sea." He too is in the mood to escape from reality: "he didn't want to think about Occupying Powers and the turmoil of East-West power politics." Lorac was, of course, writing in the era of the Cold War, and one can readily imagine that the author felt much the same as Macdonald when she flew off on holiday.

Macdonald observes his fellow passengers with interest, and talks to a number of them. As well as striking up an acquaintance with a young woman called Elizabeth Le Vendre, who is travelling to Austria to take up a secretarial role with Sir Walter Vanbrugh, a veteran diplomat who is working on his memoirs, Macdonald also chats to a free-lance photographer called Webster, whom he finds loquacious but rather endearing.

Macdonald is paying a visit to an old friend, a psychiatrist called Natzler, whose son is also a doctor. He is keen to see the Viennese sights and soon finds himself bumping into some of his fellow passengers from the trip, including Elizabeth, but although the story is a slow-burn, a number of incidents take place in the early pages which will later prove to be highly significant. And when, during a thunderstorm, the Natzlers receive a call from the Vanbrugh household that Elizabeth has gone missing, the plot begins to thicken.

Lorac's great strength as a writer was her ability to evoke place, and the setting of this novel is especially interesting. It's also worth bearing in mind that, in 1956, Vienna was a cutting-edge choice for a background. Over the years, the city's history has been turbulent, and the period after the end of the Second World War was particularly dramatic. What happened during those years would have been fresh in the minds of readers of the first edition, especially given the success of *The Third Man*, the wonderful film noir written by Graham Greene and released in 1949, which captures the seedy, menacing quality of the city in the wake of the conflict. But it may be useful for readers of this story if I provide a brief outline of the historical backdrop.

Shortly after the end of the war, Austria's independence from Nazi Germany (of which it had effectively been part since the Anschluss of 1938) was proclaimed. For the next decade, Austria was occupied by the victorious powers. British, American, Soviet, and French forces divided the country into four zones, and there was a similar scenario in Vienna, which also had a common, inter-allied zone. It is easy to imagine that country and city might have suffered long-term division, like Germany and Berlin, and tensions ran high in the early stages of the Cold War.

However, western diplomacy seems to have been highly effective so far as Austria was concerned. After a decade of occupation, the Austrian State Treaty was signed on 15 May 1955, paving the way for the creation of a free, independent, and democratic Austria. Occupying troops had to leave over the next ninety days, and Austrian neutrality was established. This was the situation that existed at the time when Macdonald's plane lands.

As is often the case with Lorac, the fact that one of the characters—a man named Walsingham who writes under a pen-name—is an author gives her the opportunity to make passing comments about the literary life and the publishing world. "Because he was a popular writer, his picture appeared on the jacket of his books" is a line that suggests Lorac's wry humour and awareness of her place in the hierarchy: as far as I know, none of her detective novels ever carried a picture of her. Macdonald himself, we learn, reads Ezra Pound from time to time.

Lorac gives us something rather more, I would argue, than a mere travelogue. She was fascinated by "human geography" (rather like one of today's leading crime writers, Ann Cleeves) and the way she presents the characters in this unusual time and setting means that this novel, like so much of her fiction, offers something more than a competent mystery: it's an intriguing slice of social history.

E. C. R. Lorac was the principal pen-name of Edith Caroline Rivett (1894–1958), who was known to her friends as Carol Rivett. My own copy of this book was inscribed by the author in her elegant hand as follows:

To Miss Grace West
from a grateful author who will always remember the trouble you took in reading the proof sheets of this book— you were the perfect proof-reader!
With love from
Carol in the Looking Glass
E C R Lorac

The good-natured tone of this inscription reflects the character of a woman who was popular in her local community and further afield; she was a strong-minded individual but with a warm and generous nature. It is sad to think that, just two years after she wrote that inscription, she died from lung cancer. But it is wonderful to reflect on the renaissance of her reputation as a result of the successful revival of her work in the Crime Classics series.

Martin Edwards

www.martinedwardsbooks.com

A NOTE FROM THE PUBLISHER

presented as it was originally published with two edits to the text and minor edits made for consistency of style and sense. We welcome feedback from our readers.

I

1

AS THE AIRCRAFT CHANGED COURSE, HEADING A POINT east of south, it seemed to pivot on a wing-tip, smoothly and effortlessly, like an albatross whose glancing wings plane delicately to win advantage from an air current.

Far below—so very far below that visibility had a ghost quality—the crazy patchwork of English fields faded out, to be replaced by a shot-silk effect, vaguely bordered by a drift of golden-brown.

The man who was looking down through the oval window of the Viscount, watched fascinated as the English coast slipped away. He had often seen all this before, but never wearied of it. Nothing here of the famous white cliffs which board-ship passengers sentimentalise over, he pondered: no white headlands outlined proudly against a pale English sky. There was hardly any shape at all; just a gradation of colour blurred by chiffon trails of low tenuous cloud, a mingling of earth and strand and sea, like interwoven scarves of colour changing imperceptibly from pale gold to paler aquamarine, as the shallow waters deepened and earth and sand faded out. The shipping away below looked no more important than sardines—very slender sardines—gliding over a shimmer which was more like light than sea.

"Dungeness," thought Robert Macdonald, "with Romney Marsh behind, and Rye and Winchelsea away back, but it might be anywhere in the world: elements of geography misted over into a dream."

It was very tranquil in the aircraft on that sunny September morning. There are many ways of travelling from London to Vienna, and those who love roads and seas wax scornful over the lazy unintelligence of air-travel; but for a tired man, intent on a comfortable holiday, there is a lot to recommend the ease of flying. From the passenger, no effort is demanded: once his baggage has been checked in, he is taken in hand by benevolent authority. He becomes freight—human freight, handled with care—and there's nothing he need do about it: only watch a silver wing-tip describe an arc over the land he is leaving, and enjoy (if he is wise) the blended colours far below.

As the English coast slipped away and the blurred out-line of the Continent took its place, the aircraft bumped a little in the air-pockets which often signal an aerial "land-fall." Macdonald had an odd feeling that he was reliving his own past, slipping through the years as imperceptibly as the Viscount slipped over the North Sea. He had travelled overnight from Inverness (where his forebears had lived) to London (where he had spent his boyhood). Now he was somewhere above northern France and the Low Countries, where he had fought in the London Scottish between 1914 and 1918. Names came back—names never forgotten by Englishmen of Macdonald's age—Amiens, Abbeville, Ypres, Passchendaele: the Aisne, the Somme, the Marne. Was that the valley of the Marne, away below there, with Rheims to the north and Vitry to the south? After the Armistice of 1918, Macdonald had gone on into Germany with the Army of Occupation, marching eastwards, as the Viscount was bearing him eastwards now—into another zone of "Occupation."

With a sudden sense of repugnance, Macdonald decided his analogy had gone too far: he didn't want to think about Occupying Powers and the turmoil of East-West power politics. He thanked his stars he had never got involved in what is generically described as "Intelligence"—M.I.5, Special Duties, Counter Espionage and "Security." His passport described him as a Government Servant, and that was true enough, but his job was, of its very nature, blessedly unpolitical: it gave a man leave to be himself when on leave, not binding him to Intelligence with a capital I.

With acknowledgments to Robert Graves in the long ago, Macdonald said "Good-bye to all that," turned from the window and its reminders of the war-to-end-war, and considered his fellow-passengers instead.

The white-haired man of ambassadorial aspect he recognised: an ambassador of commerce this one, a V.I.P. in one of the great chemical combines. The stout lady was French, her complexion and closed eyes denoting that she fought an internal battle with air sickness.

Immediately across the gangway from Macdonald sat a

fair-haired girl, neat as a daisy in a nicely-tailored suit, with a demure little wing of a black hat on her shining hair. She was doing her best to look out of the window, but she had been unlucky in not getting a window seat. Beside her, blocking the window as he leaned over a book, was a young man to whom Macdonald took an immediate dislike. Hunched up in a most superior top-coat of the "camel" variety, he leant over his book so that only his unruly dark hair and outsize horn-rims were observable. A blasé young man, obviously quite uninterested in aerial views: he didn't want to see the world below, or the incredible shining cloud-scape which occasionally obscured that world. "He might just as well let the lass have his seat," thought Macdonald. "He's seen it all before and he's bored in advance. She's never seen it and wants to."

Inevitably he began to place his fellow-passengers: the girl, he guessed, was not merely on holiday. She was so neat, so soignée, so businesslike, despite her chic. "Going to a job, and all kitted-up to look efficient as well as attractive," he hazarded. And the young man? Something self-consciously artistic—but his artistry appeared to pay. That coat had cost a lot of money. "Architect, doing nicely out of the dehumanised school?" thought the Scot, "or a designer... book production... going to the Vienna Trade Fair as representative of some precious bindery or pure-fount type. And the stout merchant might be encouraging the sales of Scots whisky—if it needs any encouraging."

Coffee was brought to the passengers by the inevitably charming stewardess: newspapers were offered, but Macdonald turned to his window again. Chalons-sur-Marne was away behind: Switzerland was coming up, and Switzerland brought wholesome memories: the Wengen Scheidegg ski-run: climbing Mont Blanc (not nearly so difficult as some of the lesser peaks), driving over the Simplon—and the view from the hospice. Switzerland… a sane, safe wholesome country: alpen-sport and the best watches in the world.

When the Viscount began to circle over Zürich, Macdonald observed again the astonishing contrast between British and Swiss systems of land tenure. The English land-scape, "… plotted and pieced, fold, fallow and plough" was a patchwork quilt—crazy patchwork, no modern geometry of hexagons or such like: every field a different shape and size, a jig-saw of individual eccentricity. Below him now, in Switzerland, striped ribbons curved over the rolling land-scape, each strip of exquisite precision: vivid green of mown meadow, gold of stubble, brown of ploughland, blue green of root crops; border and headland as precise as if measured by a foot-rule. It had an astonishing look of ordered virtuosity, an economy both beautiful and efficient.

The plane swung lower and lower, the white buildings of the airport came into view, as tiny as a child's toy, and then the long white runways. The plane swooped gently, lined up on its own runway, touched down without even a bounce and taxied towards its place, between a K.L.M. and a T.W.A. Macdonald glanced at his watch: they were ahead of sched-ule: the following wind had added an unofficial quota of m.p.h. That meant a good hour in Zürich airport—a pleasant prospect on this sunny morning: air travellers frequently say that if you have seen one airport you have seen them all, but the Swiss had done an out-of-the-way good job at Zürich and it is a pleasant halt.

The passengers all left the plane and were shepherded to the airport building, cards thrust into their hands: "Those leaving the plane at Zürich this side, please. Those going on to Vienna, this side. Thank you: you will be called when the plane is due to leave."

With smiling courtesy, repeating their injunctions in other languages, the Swiss airport hostesses dealt kindly yet firmly with their little flock, encouraging the passengers for Vienna to walk on into the main hall of the airport. Macdonald went downstairs for a wash, finding the Swiss version of the international word "Toilet" catered for in thoroughgoing Swiss fashion (baths, barbers, and toilet articles all laid on).

When he returned to the main hall (where nationals of seemingly every variety were eating, drinking, buying and chattering), he walked across to examine the display of Swiss watches at the farther end and found himself standing beside the fair girl whom he had observed in the plane. She looked a little lost and uncertain, but her face brightened as she saw Macdonald.

"Please—are you going on to Vienna?" she asked.

"I am—B.E.A. flight 265; and you?"

"I'm going there, too. I'm terrified of missing the plane. Sorry to sound so feeble, but I've never done this before. I tried to keep in sight of some of the other passengers, but they've all melted away and I wondered if I'd got stranded."

"It's all right," said Macdonald. "We shan't be called for over half an hour. We got to Zürich early because of the northwest wind. It's all a bit bewildering the first time, isn't it? But I'm certainly not going to miss the plane, so freeze on to me if it'd give you a feeling of confidence."

"Thanks awfully! It would!" she replied promptly; "it's terribly kind of you not to mind. I'm pretty good at trains and buses abroad, but I've not developed the right sort of attitude to all this."

"Would you like some coffee?" asked Macdonald, "just because it will be Swiss coffee and therefore different?"

"I should love some—but I haven't got any Swiss currency."

"I've got enough for coffees. Say you go and sit by the window and I'll see about it."

When he returned with a waiter, carrying the little cups piled high with cream, he asked, "Will this be your first visit to Vienna?"

She was very young—not more than twenty-one, he guessed—and she was looking around happily now.

"Yes," she replied. "I've got a job there. Isn't it marvellous?"

"I'm sure it is," he said. "Jobs in Vienna can't be very plentiful."

"I was lucky, a friend put me on to it because I talk German. I'm going to be secretary to a V.I.P. who's writing a book—or oughtn't I to have said that? Everybody warned me not to talk too much."

He laughed. "I don't think it matters saying it to me. I'm so obviously British. Anyway, I won't quote you."

She turned and looked at him, her face dimpling. "When I saw you in the plane, I decided you were a doctor. Are you?"

"No—no doctorate of any variety. It's my guess now: you read Modern Languages at…Oxford, was it? and then you had a secretarial training, and since you spell correctly and talk German, you seemed to be the right person for this job."

"You're very good at it, aren't you?" she said. "When I put

you down for a doctor it was because you look observant and analytical—used to diagnosing: and I knew you'd be helpful."

"Thank you: that's very pleasant and quite acute," said Macdonald. "Is your father a doctor?"

"No, but my uncle is. Daddy's a Civil Servant—poor dear."

"No poor dear about it. I'm one myself—of a sort."

"I didn't mean to be rude," she said hastily. "We always tease Daddy because the Civil Servants get all the abuse and can't answer back. Do tell me, what did you make of the young man next to me in the plane? I've developed an allergy to him."

"He takes up too much window space, doesn't he?" said Macdonald. "When we get in the plane again you may be able to get a window-seat: several passengers were only travelling to Zürich."

"He was reading Ezra Pound," she said, "and *The Pisan Cantos* at that: or if not reading, going into a trance over."

"One does, over the *Cantos*," said Macdonald.

She dimpled at him, her curving cheeks as charming as a child's. "If you read Ezra Pound I shall have to think again. Not a don, surely..."

"Definitely not a don," said Macdonald. "Commonplace people like myself do sometimes read Ezra Pound, though perhaps he's more a poet's poet."

"My allergy isn't a poet: he's only trying to look like one," she said. "Poets are always poor and that coat of his cost the earth. He wears suède shoes. I had a bet with myself they would be suède and they were." She turned and looked out at the planes, all colours and shapes and sizes, lined up on the airfield.

"Isn't it marvellous: you could go anywhere in the world—just like the magic carpet. But I'm terribly thrilled to be going to Vienna. It must be lovely. Have you been there before?"

"Once, a very long time ago: travelling 'hard.' It was hard, too. It's a perishing long journey in a third class railway carriage, when you haven't much money to buy food. But it was worth it. Hallo, they're calling us. Listen."

The Tannoy blared out: "Attention, please. Passengers for Vienna by British European Airways, flight 265…"

"You see, it's as easy as that," said Macdonald. "They never let you get lost. Come along—only ninety minutes and you'll be circling over the Danube and humming Strauss to celebrate."

She jumped up. "The Danube! How superb—and thank you very much for being so kind to me—and won't you tell me your name? Perhaps Daddy knows you."

"My name is Macdonald. Your father doesn't know me; he's in the Home Office, isn't he?—and your doctor uncle, too. You see, I couldn't help seeing the nice new name-tape on your handkerchief, and your name is rather an uncommon one. Perhaps that's cheating, but that's how it was."

She laughed. "You ought to be a detective! Anyway, thank you again. The coffee was marvellous."

2

Within a few minutes, the passengers were settled in their places in the Viscount again. Much to Macdonald's amusement, the dark young man in the camel coat collected the papers he had left on his seat and moved to another place in the rear of the plane, close to the door. The fair girl (whose name Macdonald had learnt to be Le Vendre) now had the window seat, and she laughed up at Macdonald as he passed her. "Allergy mutual—and he hadn't—" He lost the final words of her sentence and went on to his own place. The plane circled over the airport again, the striped ribbons faded out as they gained height, and lunch was served with the dexterity of a conjuring trick as they rose above the clouds and floated over a shining white floor of cumulus. It was after lunch that the white-haired man moved across the gangway.

"Am I right in thinking that your name is Macdonald?" he asked, speaking with almost apologetic courtesy.

"Quite right, Sir Charles."

"I thought I couldn't be mistaken," said the older man. "On holiday—or on a job, like myself?"

"Holiday, sir."

"I hope you have a thundering good one. May I sit here for a moment? I've got a story that might amuse you."

"Delighted," said Macdonald.

The silver-haired man sat down in the gangway seat beside Macdonald and said, "You met my daughter not so long ago—Mrs. Nigel Villiers. You may remember they'd had a spot of excitement over a burglary: I've no doubt she told you about it, it was her chief topic of conversation for days and we all got a bit tired of it."

"I remember. She lost a fur coat."

"That's it. I gave her the coat when she got married. A silly business: a mink coat is just asking for trouble—but all the girls want one. Well, to cut a long story short, the coat's been found."

"Well, the insurance company will be delighted to hear it," said Macdonald. "Where did she find it?"

"She didn't. Some workmen found it—on the roof."

Macdonald laughed. "That's an even better story than the original burglary," he said.

"Quite a story. The roof leaked, and they had the builders in to see to it and they found a small suit-case tucked away by the chimney stack. In the suit-case was Val's fur coat. It was her own suit-case, too. Now the interesting point is that the trap-door leading to the roof was bolted on the inside: the police had a look at it—careful chaps, take nothing for granted. The trap was secure—and it's a foolproof fitment. Access had been gained to the house by a lavatory window—but I've no doubt she told you all that. She told everybody."

Macdonald chuckled. "Yes. I remember."

"Well, the great idea now is that the burglar didn't want to be seen leaving the house carrying a suit-case or parcel, so he went up to the roof and hid his loot—to be collected at leisure later—rebolted the trap-door and left the house with no incriminating parcel or what have you. You may remember, the house they live in is one of a terrace—like so many of the houses round the Park."

Macdonald nodded. "Yes. A common roof, so to speak."

"That's it: and one of the other houses is in the hands of builders—being modernised—so it may be the thief was looking out for a chance to get up to the roof that way."

"I've no doubt he'll find a reception committee waiting if he tries that on," said Macdonald. "All the same, he's left it quite a time. It's over a fortnight, isn't it?"

"Yes. I admit that occurred to me: still, I can't see any other explanation. There wasn't anything else missing. The young folks are a bit casual, as all youngsters seem to be these days, but I think they've checked up by now."

Macdonald sat silent for a moment, and Sir Charles Bland added, "I thought you'd be amused to hear the upshot of the story—now I'll leave you in peace again."

"Don't hurry away, sir. I've enjoyed hearing a story off the record, so to speak, and I agree with you it's an odd story. What you might call a new technique. Your son-in-law is a publisher, isn't he?"

"It'd be more exact to say he's in a publishing firm—Barrards. How far he'll get, I don't know, but they say he's a flare for spotting winners. However, there weren't any price-less manuscripts stolen, or anything of that kind: and from what I've seen of the scripts he brings home, a burglar who stole one would be madder than the chap who wrote the script—if possible. Well—there you are. You showed a kindly interest in the original story, so I thought you'd be interested to hear the upshot."

"I am—very much interested, sir."

Sir Charles chuckled. "Forget it—as the young say—and have a good holiday. How long will you be in Vienna?"

"Three weeks."

"Fortunate you. I have three days, and conferences every day. But it'll be too bad if I don't get to the Opera—and a *Heurige*. Good luck to you and the best of holidays." And with that he went back to his own seat.

3

Macdonald laughed to himself a little. He was pretty certain that no one had overheard Sir Charles Bland's story, but if they had done so, they would have taken it for nothing but a casual anecdote—the sort of story which travellers tell to pass the time. Nothing in Sir Charles's approach gave any inkling that the man he spoke to was a Superintendent of Scotland Yard, or that that same Superintendent had gone to the Villiers' house when the mink coat had been stolen. The Divisional Police had been bothered by a series of burglaries in the big houses round the Park, and the C.I.D. from the Central (or Commissioner's) Office had been brought in for consultation. Macdonald thought back to his inspection in the Villiers' house: it had been an amateurish sort of burglary to his mind. While Nigel Villiers and his wife were out, and the two maids immersed in television, someone had climbed up to a lavatory window at the side of the house, forced the window-catch and gone upstairs to the Villiers' bedroom and removed the coat. The wardrobe and drawers had been left open, as though the thief had been disturbed, and nothing else had been taken (except the suit-case found on the roof). The job had nothing in common with the more carefully organised burglaries (all on a much larger scale) which the Divisional Police had been investigating.

Sitting in the Viscount, aware from the changed note of the engines, that the long run-in had begun, Macdonald said to himself, "Reeves can cope with all that." But because no man can entirely dismiss interest in his own profession from his mind, the C.I.D. Superintendent could not help listing the points which would be of particular concern to Chief Inspector Reeves.

One was the trap-door to the roof. It was, as Sir Charles had observed, a very efficient fitment, with good bolts: and it had certainly not been opened since it was last painted, six months ago. The burglar had not used the trap-door to get access to the roof. That brought up the second point: the builders in a house farther along the terrace: a builder's man might well have been concerned in this—and other burglaries. Finally, the two maids: they were both foreign girls, but girls with very good characters. Macdonald suddenly remembered that they were Austrians, from Wiener Neustadt, a few miles south of Vienna.

"That's a bit odd," he thought. "Surely a man of Sir Charles's intelligence doesn't think I'm out for a busman's holiday...or did he think the 'holiday' was a put-up job? If so, he's wrong for once in his life. But why tell me the additional items at all? He has the reputation of being a man who never says anything without a reason... Glory! There it is..."

"It" was the River Danube: a sight of which it might be said "Once seen, never forgotten." Whether from the air or from ground level, from the heights of the Wiener Wald or from the bridges, the Danube is unforgettable.

II

1

AS THE AIRCRAFT LOST HEIGHT APPROACHING VIENNA and the world below gained definition, it was not the city which claimed immediate attention, but the river. Vienna is not built "on the Danube," as London is built "on the Thames." The city was established well away from the flood-plain of its tremendous river: at first Macdonald saw the city as no more than a shadowy blur, while the great ribbon of the Danube itself showed strong and dark and clear, right across the endless plain. To the west, the bastions and foot-hills of the eastern Alps had levelled out: to the east, the plain stretched away to the limits of visibility, to continue, far beyond, to the unseen Carpathian Mountains. As he watched, Macdonald pondered over that vast level expanse of eastern Europe: that was the way the Mongol hordes had come galloping in, Attila and his Huns, the Turks, and all the other invaders from the east, he meditated. Vienna was, for them, the gateway to central Europe and the cross-roads to north and south.

Slowly the Viscount lost height, banking almost silently, the aircraft vibrating a little, pulsing like a live thing, the wing-tips describing great arcs across the sky, right above the city. Staring down, trying to pick up remembered landmarks, Macdonald saw the Danube Canal, then recognised the green dome of Karlskirche and the long roof ridge of St. Stephan's Cathedral before they flew on, south-east of Vienna, to the airport of Schwechat. He had seen Vienna and the Danube long ago, from the heights of the Leopoldsberg and the Wienerwald, but there was a sense of drama in seeing it thus from the air—the river, the city, the plain.

They flew east of Schwechat, and then swung round, up-wind, and approached the airport, whose undistinguished shed-like buildings stood no comparison with Zürich. Taxiing in on the runway, Macdonald saw the fair girl smiling at him as she collected her belongings.

"Wasn't it marvellous?" she said. "I'd no idea the Danube was so terrific."

"It's a wonderful sight," agreed Macdonald. "I was as thrilled as you were. Are you being met at the airport, or do you go into Vienna in the B.E.A. bus?"

"I'm being met here: at least, I hope so! Isn't the airport quite a distance from Vienna?"

"I believe so—but I shouldn't worry. I expect there's a reception committee laid on for you. Good-bye—and good luck!"

"Good-bye, and thank you again—and a lovely holiday!"

As Macdonald left the plane and went down the steps behind her, he saw that there was indeed a group of people

on the tarmac, come to welcome those who were distinguished—or fortunate—enough to merit this privilege.
Members of the Embassies were allowed to greet their
guests as they stepped from the plane, and a man of Sir
Charles Bland's standing would certainly be accorded this
courtesy, but the majority of passengers had to wait until
Customs and passport formalities were over before meeting
their friends. To Macdonald's amusement, Miss Le Vendre
was greeted and escorted to the buildings by an elderly man
with "diplomat" written all over him: it was the assurance, as
well as the smiling courtesy, which marked out the Embassy
official. Queueing up with the rest of the commonplace
travellers (and enjoying being one of a crowd for once), the
C.I.D. man found himself waiting at the Customs counter
beside the young man in the camel coat and was able to
have a good look at him. His name was Charles Stratton—it
was boldly printed on his handsome pigskin suit-case—and
he was somewhat older than Macdonald had guessed—
probably about thirty. He certainly spoke excellent German,
and he was let through without being asked to open his case.
Macdonald's German was rusty, and he answered the routine questions in English. The Customs officer gave him a
deliberate stare and then asked him to open his suit-case.
Macdonald obliged, and his innocent belongings were carefully investigated, while the stout man who might (or might
not) be associated with Scots whisky, watched proceedings
with evident enjoyment.

"This'd be jam for some folks I won't mention," he said.

"Why?" asked Macdonald.

"I happen to know your dial—known it a long time, too,"

chuckled the stout man, "and I enjoy a joke as much as the next chap."

"Delighted to give you pleasure," rejoined Macdonald, as he closed his case. "I don't remember your face, though."

"You wouldn't. No one remembers us—I'm a camera man. If you look, all you see is the camera. I've often wondered some folks don't use that—just the ticket on certain occasions."

Macdonald moved on to the final passport officer, and again the stout man stood behind him.

"Name of Webster," he said affably. "I got a lovely shot of you outside C.O. not long ago. Having a little vacation?"

"That's the idea," said Macdonald. "I've got enough sense not to argue with a camera man, but if you'd keep your lens off me while I'm on holiday, I'd be grateful."

"You needn't have said that, sir," said Webster, sounding quite hurt. "A job's a job, whether it's yours or mine, and you're not my job in this city."

"Thanks. No offence meant," said Macdonald. "Who're you after—or would that be telling?"

"Well, you might have guessed that in one, sir, with all the ballyhoo over the reopening of the Opera House. I'm not doing anything official, you know—free-lance stuff. Celebrities in Vienna—shots outside the Opera House, outside the Hofburg, at Schönbrunn and all the rest. And if I'm lucky, a nice picture of the grand old star—that wonderful old singer, Hedwige Waldtraut Körner. She's been a singer, she has: the Scala at Milan, San Carlo at Naples, Bayreuth, New York, Covent Garden—the whole caboodle. And now she's in the news again along a different line—but you'll know about that."

"I'm afraid I don't," replied Macdonald. "Operatic celebrities aren't my long suit."

"You're kidding me," replied Mr. Webster, but Macdonald moved up to have his passport stamped and did not reply. Before he moved on, however, he turned to say good-bye to the stout camera man: there was something endearing about Mr. Webster.

"Well, good luck to the picture making," he said.

"Thank you, sir: very kindly said. And you needn't do the right about if you happen to see me around: I'll not get you in the viewfinder, not even by mistake. I've got more sense than you might think and I wouldn't cramp your style for words."

He slapped his passport down on the counter and winked at Macdonald. "You to your job and me to mine," he said.

"I'm not on a job. I'm on holiday," said Macdonald.

"O.K., sir. Have a good one!" replied the other.

2

"Robert Macdonald—welcome to Vienna! I've waited a long time to say that, my friend. It is ten years since you said 'I'll see you in Vienna some day.'"

Franz Natzler stood beside his car, smiling up at his tall visitor. Natzler was white-haired now, and his blue eyes were misty with genuine feeling. As Macdonald shook hands, memory took him back in a flash to London during the blitz, and Franz Natzler fire-watching beside him. Natzler was a doctor and a practising psychologist, highly esteemed in Vienna, but he was partly Jewish in descent and he had managed to get his wife and himself out of Vienna before the declaration of war in 1939 and had arrived in London as a penniless refugee. It was in London that Macdonald had met him, working at a first-aid post in a bombed area, and the two men had started a friendship which had endured—and now they met again after a lapse of ten years.

"It's good to be here, doctor. It's twenty-five years since I was in Vienna and I've always promised myself I'd see it again. To see it with you is best of all."

Natzler opened the door of his car. "Get in, my friend. Vienna's not quite what it was, but the worst of the damage is made good. Now do you remember the district where I live—Hietzing?"

"Not far from Schönbrunn Palace—I remember that all right, and the Tiergarten…and the Gloriette. It's to the west of Vienna, isn't it? Near the woods."

"Quite right. Pretty good after quarter of a century, my friend. Now would you like a quick drive round the city before we go home—to see the Stephansdom and the Karlskirche and the Opera House?"

"I should indeed."

"We've got to get across Vienna anyway—and if Herr Vogel would only move on, we'll get cracking—as the English boys say."

Looking ahead at the car which stood in their way, Macdonald suddenly saw the camel coat again: he was sure there couldn't be two coats like that in Vienna. The owner of it was in the Volkswagen ahead, talking to the driver.

"Is Herr Vogel a friend of yours?" Macdonald asked. "His passenger was on the plane."

Dr. Natzler sounded a tattoo on his horn. "Hardly a friend:

a patient, at one time. You helped me to read Shakespeare when I was in England, Macdonald. 'One man in his time plays many parts.' Certainly Vogel has done so. If that young man is a friend of yours, a word of warning might be reasonable. Ah—he moves, at last he moves."

Natzler turned his car neatly and shot ahead of the Volkswagen and turned west towards Vienna. Macdonald answered his last comment.

"The young man is no friend of mine: I just happened to see him in the plane, and wondered about his occupation in the idle way that travellers do wonder."

Natzler chuckled. "*Kultur,*" he said. "Something to the arts pertaining. That coat, it is *fantastisch.*"

The approach road to Vienna on which they were driving was a dull road with nothing to occupy the attention, and Natzler went on: "I, also, wondered about that young man. I had seen Vogel, pottering about, all agog—is that right, yes?—to meet a passenger on your plane: when the young man appeared it was quite a pantomime. They did not know each other by sight, and they circled round like two dogs, until at last Vogel saw the name on that beautiful suit-case, and then all was well. Although they had quite a little argument, as you saw, before they got away."

The doctor chuckled and then added: "A nice little mystery for you: is that young man, Herr Stratton (I also read his name), being taken 'for a ride,' as they say. Friend Vogel had the look of a cat approaching the cream."

"You seem to have a poor opinion of Herr Vogel," said Macdonald.

"Myself, I would have nothing to do with him," said

Natzler. "He…how do you say it, my English to the dogs has gone…he makes opportunities."

"An opportunist," said Macdonald: "a snapper-up of unconsidered trifles, if you remember your Shakespeare."

"Ach—that is very apt: and the young Herr Stratton, he looked to me a wealthy trifle."

"He looked to me a nasty bit of work," said Macdonald. "Too mannered and no manners."

"Mannered and manners," said Natzler. "That is very English: a crossword language if ever there was one. See, we approach our city. That is—"

"It's the Cattle Market," said Macdonald promptly. "Even I can remember that…and ahead on the left, beyond the railway, is the Belvedere and the Botanic Gardens."

"So…very good, and beyond that, my friend, is Stalin Platz—a new one for you. See, we will go up to Karlsplatz, and then see the Opera House, and up the Kärntnerstrasse to the Stephansdom—and you will have made your bow to Vienna, old and new."

For the next half-hour Dr. Natzler drove Macdonald round the complex crowded streets in the heart of Vienna, until the C.I.D. man began to get his bearings again. He remembered the centre of the city as "the Gothic Kernel"; narrow streets, with no great boulevards laid out as in Paris or Munich. The streets crowded round the great spire of St. Stephen's—as unforgettable as the Danube. It was the containing Ringstrasse that opened up vistas of wide tree-lined streets, of parks and open spaces, and the glorious baroque riot of domes and elaborately decorated façades which make Vienna a delight and a bewilderment to learn. Some buildings Macdonald did remember—the enchanting green dome of Karlskirche and the twin columns in front of it: the Opera House, now once again superb and renewed after its wartime destruction; the Albertina, where he had once rejoiced over Dürer's drawings: the Hofburg, which had been the Imperial Palace (with yet another dome), and Peterskirche (another dome).

"You remember it all?" asked Dr. Natzler anxiously, and Macdonald laughed.

"You're asking something, doctor. Remember it? I never learnt it properly. After all, the Romans began it, and it was the seat of the Holy Roman Empire for about eight hundred years, and they all did something to it. But I remember the core—Stephansdom, and the Ringstrasse around it and the trees and the colour and the gaiety and the baroque exuberance. It still is exuberant—despite Stalin Platz and the Occupying Powers."

"Good, good. Vienna has had its effect, it has made you talk. That is Viennese, to talk exuberantly as you say. Now we will go home. Ilse will be impatient to see you. She will ask you one thing—did you remember the Opera House?"

"Yes, I did. It looks just the same, except that it's cleaner."

Natzler laughed. "Just the same—you should have seen it after the bombing. And you must go over it while you are here. It is now the finest Opera House in the world."

They left the heart of the city, and presently were driving along a wide boulevard, westwards, towards the Schönbrunn Palace and towards the Wienerwald—Vienna woods. Dr. Natzler was almost penitent.

"It is too much, that I should demand of you 'do you remember' after so long…"

"What's a quarter of a century?" asked Macdonald cheerfully. "You were in London in 1945. If you're still alive in 1970—and I see no reason why you shouldn't be—and you go to London, you'll still recognise St. Paul's Cathedral and Westminster Abbey. But you'll have forgotten how to get from one to the other. That's how it is with me, but it'll come back."

"What a sensible fellow you are!" said Natzler. "That is as I remember you: first kindness, then good sense: common sense, as you call it, though I myself should not call it so common, not even among Englishmen."

"I'm not really English. I'm a Scot," retorted Macdonald.

"Ah ha: but I remember you once described yourself as a London Scot," replied Natzler. "In short, you are a Londoner, as I am Viennese." He drew out to pass another car, with a "C.D." plate above its registration number, and he raised his hand in salute as they passed. It was a chauffeur-driven Daimler, and in the back seats Macdonald saw Miss Le Vendre and her silver-haired escort. She saw him, too, and waved to him.

"Sir Walter Vanbrugh," said Natzler, "you know him, hein?"

"No. I've heard his name—he was in the Foreign Office, until he retired. The fair girl with him was on the plane with me."

"Yes. I saw them drive out from the airport. He will have been to the Embassy on his way home. Sir Walter also lives in Hietzing, in Trauttmansdorffgasse."

"And is Sir Walter also a patient of yours?"

"Quite right. All sorts and conditions of men I attend (that is classical English, *nicht wahr*?)—from Sir Walter to Herr Vogel. And the devil of it is a doctor can never forget he is a doctor."

"You're not alone in that," said Macdonald. "It's a failing which develops with age. Last time I was in Vienna I was in the C.I.D.—as I have been ever since. I was only an Inspector then, and I swear I never gave my job a thought. I only wanted to enjoy myself—and I did."

"And it's harder now," said Natzler. "You can't get away from your work: your mind still works on detecting. But that, my friend, is because you are tired. I knew that when I first saw you. You're tough, as the Americans say, and you don't look any older than you did last time I saw you, but you look tired. We will change all that! We will have a holiday together, you and Ilse and I—and Karl. Did I tell you that Karl also was coming home for a holiday?"

"Good!" said Macdonald. "I shall be glad to see him again, he's a fine lad. So he's taken to doctoring too?"

"Yes: he specialises—tuberculosis. He has been working with Köch in his Clinic near Lucerne, and he will be flying from Zürich, as you did. He hoped to be able to get away to-day and so arrive with you, but it was not possible. I shall be glad for you to see Karl again. He has done well in his work… *Sehen Sie!* You remember that?"

He slowed down and Macdonald caught a glimpse of the Schönbrunn Palace among the trees. "Yes. I remember that. It's a lovely sight. It's one of the greatest palaces in Europe, though I always enjoyed the gardens and the Gloriette and the clipped trees more than the amazing galleries and the porcelain room and all the rest. I wonder if the old Emperor used to enjoy his gardens."

"Franz Josef: he lived there and died there and they took him thence to the Capuchin Crypt—the last of the great

Hapsburgs, the end of an era. We have seen some thrones tumble in our lifetime, Macdonald—though the British throne seems more stable than ever. There's something about the British that stands firm."

"Is it because they recognise the need for change and change in reply to the need?—and the royal family changes to meet altered circumstances? There's a difference between Victoria and Elizabeth II—God bless her."

"Amen. A difference and yet a sameness. How can I say it? Sir Walter Vanbrugh—we saw him just now: he's nearly eighty years old. He was in the Foreign Service when Victoria was Queen. Has he changed? I think not."

"Well, he's retired," said Macdonald. "I'm not going to get involved in foreign policy, so I won't say 'a good thing too,' as I might have done. Is he living in Vienna?"

"He is. His son-in-law—Gore Spencer—is in the Embassy here, as Sir Walter was himself once, in the time when Franz Josef was still Emperor. There's a link with the old days for you. The young girl he met at Schwechat would be his new secretary, I think. He is writing his memoirs, he tells me."

"Another edition of 'A Diplomat Remembers,'" observed Macdonald dryly. "I often wonder if the diplomats look back with pride over the results of their activities in this century."

"Ach—you may well ask: but let us not ask. 'Throw physic to the dogs'—I remember that one—and diplomacy with it. Foreign policy, it is *verboten* during your holiday. See, here we turn, away from Schönbrunn to our quiet streets. Altzaugasse, where we live, is quite near the woods, up from the Hietzinger Hauptstrasse—you must learn your way about. Then you can take the car and drive yourself."

The quiet leafy roads of Hietzing were very beautiful on that October day: the trees were turning gold, and their warm colours shone against the stonework and stucco of the graceful houses: houses which had fine doorways and wrought-iron grilles over the ground-storey windows. Macdonald found a resemblance to the Regency houses of London, though in this district of Vienna there was a more spacious air, and the architectural embellishments had something faintly rococo about them. It was difficult to determine exactly what the quality was, for they were reticent houses, yet moulding and ironwork, doorway and shutter, each had a character which made Hietzing quite unlike any corresponding residential area in London or in Paris.

"Ilse will be looking for us," said Dr. Natzler—and Ilse was. The front door of Altzaugasse 25 was thrown open as the car pulled up and Frau Natzler had no inhibitions about welcoming an Englishman. She put her hands firmly on Macdonald's shoulders and kissed him on either cheek.

"You are welcome, dear friend, so very welcome. Franz and I have waited for this day. *Kommen Sie*—I have all ready to make you a good cup of tea. After so long, you have come to us in Vienna."

III

1

MACDONALD SPENT HIS FIRST DAY IN VIENNA BEING
lazy: lazier than he had been for years, for generally when
he was on holiday his questing spirit sent him walking or
driving, intent on enjoying a countryside or staring at buildings and works of art, only too well aware that there were
more lovely and interesting things in the world than he could
ever hope to see. But the Natzlers' house in Altzaugasse was
enough of an experience in itself to keep him happy for a
while. Everything in it was subtly different from the contents
of an English house: the furniture, the pictures, the china,
all had their own quality, and when he had browsed among
the Natzlers' books, studied their pictures, even played their
piano for a while, he went out into the garden with Marboe's
Book of Austria under his arm—and promptly went to sleep
in the mellow October sunshine.

When he woke up, Dr. Natzler was sitting beside him,

studying the *Book of Austria*, and he looked at Macdonald approvingly.

"Good. That was just what the doctor ordered. You have had a good sleep?"

"Very good: two solid hours," said Macdonald, glancing at his watch, "and just before I woke up, I had solved a very complex case. I suddenly saw the answer and everything was made plain."

"Wish fulfilment," said Natzler. "That tells me you rested well. Can you remember your dream?"

"Of course I can't. I very seldom dream and I never remember what I dream about."

"We all dream," said Natzler, "but for those who find life satisfying there is no need to remember the achievements of the subconscious. Nevertheless, if you wished, you could remember your dream."

"I don't suppose I do wish. It was all very unsound—intuition and not evidence. The only evidence was connected with a pair of suède shoes: oh—and that fair girl who was in Sir Walter Vanbrugh's car. That'll please you, you old dream pedlar."

"*Ach, ja...* So you do dream. You have never married, Macdonald?"

"No, I haven't. And I don't propose to experiment in riper years, as the English Prayer Book puts it."

"Why did you never marry?" asked Natzler. "You would have made a good husband."

"No, I shouldn't. I like my job too well: and on various occasions when my job has brought me face to face with a sticky end, I have found time to thank God that I didn't leave an indigent widow in the offing."

Natzler chuckled. "My English will improve during your visit. A 'sticky end'—is that English?"

"No, but it's very expressive, and you know just what I mean. I'll say bloody if you prefer it, but the word has lost its meaning."

"*Gewiss*...and 'indigent'?"

"Penniless. Like most widows. See *Traum*, likewise *Alpendruck*, if I remember aright. You have turned my dream into a nightmare. I will go indoors and wash it away."

Natzler chuckled. "The man of action...but why suède shoes? Did the *gnädiges Fräulein* wear such shoes?"

"I didn't notice, but I'm ready to bet any money she didn't. If you ever meet her, you can ask her if she likes young men who wear suède shoes."

"The plot thickens," chuckled Natzler. "That dream, I perceive it was classical in form, a text-book dream. This book I lent you, it is a very good book. It tells you all about Austria. I lend it to all our English visitors and they say 'That is just what I wanted,' but they never read it, not to the end."

"Have you ever read it to the end, doctor?"

"No. But I have no need. The Pragmatic Sanctions of Maria Theresa—"

"No," said Macdonald firmly. "I did Pragmatic Sanctions in the sixth form at school and decided I never wanted to hear about them again."

"And me, with your Wars of the Roses. We will leave all that, and this evening we will go to a *Heurige* in Grinzing. You remember the *Heurige*?"

"We will go to a village inn, and it will have a bunch of green branches over the door, which means that we can taste the wines of this year's vintage—which I shall much enjoy. And I hope there will be a zither player and that everyone will sing."

"So…" replied Dr. Natzler.

2

The next morning Macdonald "turned tourist" on his own: with a map and a guide-book he walked round the city and sorted things out. He sat in an "Espresso" and drank black coffee and listened hard to the conversation around him, trying to "get his ear in." He found again the church he liked best—Maria am Gestade—and staring up at its vaulting and slender apse, decided that he belonged to the Gothic school rather than the Baroque—though when he went back to look again at the oval dome of Karlskirche and its flanking columns he concluded he was moderately heretical in his convictions, like the Lamas of Shangri-La. Later he met Dr. Natzler and stood him lunch at Sacher's—that most famous of Viennese hotels.

In the afternoon Macdonald strolled over to Schönbrunn Palace, to renew his acquaintance with the gardens and fountains: it was another lovely sunny day and the warm coloured stones of the palace looked almost golden in the October sunlight. ("Maria Theresa yellow," the Austrians called that subtle gold of the masonry.)

It was while he was standing by the garden front of the palace, looking up at the arches and colonnade of the Gloriette on the rising ground to the south that he saw Elizabeth Le Vendre again. She also was looking at the Gloriette, and as she turned and saw Macdonald her quick smile flashed out.

"Hallo! Isn't that lovely? I've just been over the State Apartments and all that splendour got me down—but it's perfect out here. Those arches against the sky are sheer fairyland."

"Yes, I feel rather the same. The palatial tends to pall, but the Gloriette is always enchanting. You should go up there, the view is grand."

He turned and looked at her: she was bare-headed to-day and her loose cream coat blew away from her slim figure, so that Macdonald thought she looked as young as a schoolgirl. "Are you enjoying the job?" he asked.

"Yes—or I think I shall when I get into it. It's all a bit overpowering to begin with. I must tell you—Sir Walter told me who you are. We saw you in Dr. Natzler's car."

Macdonald laughed a bit. "Was it a shock?"

"No, not a bit. It may sound silly, but it made me feel safe. You see, it's so different from London here, and I can't talk to everybody as I do at home, and when I saw you I thought 'I can speak to him. He's quite safe.'" She broke off, and then added, "You see, I told Sir Walter I talked to you at Zürich, and he laughed and said 'Oh, he's quite safe.' I haven't got used to thinking of people as perhaps 'not safe.'"

"I'm glad I was given a good character," said Macdonald, "so would you like to climb up to the Gloriette and see the view?"

"Love to—if I'm not being a nuisance. When I came here, I expected to find Clare von Baden here. I knew her at Oxford, and she's related to Sir Walter in some remote way I haven't sorted out. It was because of Clare I got this job: she gave me a 'good character,' as you put it. She's in quarantine for scarlet fever and she can't come home until she's clear. So that means I haven't anybody to go out with just at the moment."

"It'll be all the nicer when she does come," said Macdonald consolingly.

"It'll feel more homely," she said. "I find it difficult to be dignified all the time."

Macdonald laughed. "I think I know what you mean. Very few English homes are formal these days. The passing of the domestic servant has done away with the formality laid down by Mrs. Beeton in her chapters on Household Management."

It was Elizabeth's turn to laugh. "Did you ever read that? 'The lady of the house receives the guests.' I used to read Granny's copy, it's marvellous. But you've hit the nail right on the head. You know how almost everybody lives in England now: we all help in the kitchen, and we often have meals in the kitchen, because it saves bother, and if we have a reliable charlady who really does come every day, it's heaven."

"And the household in Vienna is quite different?"

"Goodness, I'd say it is. You ring bells for everything, or else bells are rung to indicate what you do next, and the servants are so superbly dignified I hardly dare smile at them. It's fun in a way—but I can't tell you what a relief it is to talk to somebody who's accustomed to kitchens—or perhaps you're not…"

"But I am," said Macdonald. "I'm very competent in the kitchen. I cook my own meals when I've time."

"And eat them in the kitchen?"

"No, but only because there isn't room, unless you stand up. My kitchen has 'ette' on the end. Here we are. It's worth the climb, isn't it?"

"It's lovely!" she cried.

They stood on the rising ground opposite the garden front of Schönbrunn. Above them, the arches of the Gloriette were open to the sky: at their feet the arches were reflected in a formal pool. To the east and north, Vienna was stretched out below them: to the west the Wienerwald climbed to the heights of Leopoldsberg, and to the south, beyond the Gloriette, the ground fell away to open farmland towards the hidden castle of Hetzendorf in the distance. Elizabeth stood facing south, with the keen wind whipping her fair hair back from her face.

"It's lovely," she said again, "and I'm glad it's near where I'm living. It's a good place to come to blow the dignities away."

"Isn't there a dog to take for walks?" asked Macdonald. "Dogs can be very companionable."

"Of course they can. I adore dogs. There is a dog, but he's terribly old—a fat dachshund. It would be a dachshund, wouldn't it? He belongs to Miss Vanbrugh. I asked if I might take him out—he's called Fritzel—and she said yes, if he'll go with you. But so far he won't, he waddles under the sofa and trembles when I touch him." She broke off, laughing, and then said, "Oh, I must tell you. I saw my 'allergy' again, still in his camel coat—on a day like this. He was in the palace, in the Chinese room, and when he saw me he just turned on his heel with an expression of pained disgust."

"Had he got his suède shoes on?"

"No. They were new and they must have pinched, because he changed them at Zürich. I know he did, because when we got back in the plane he'd got leather brogues on."

Macdonald laughed. "Are you sure you didn't imagine the suède shoes?"

"I'm quite sure. He sat in front of me in the bus from the Waterloo Air Terminal, and I particularly noticed his shoes because he stuck them out in the gangway: they were so snappy—quite new, rather long and narrow. What my young brother would call 'spiv shoes.' He really is pretty ghastly— but not so ghastly as he thinks I am."

"Perhaps he is a poet, after all," said Macdonald. "They're very shy birds."

"I'm certain he isn't. He may be a novelist. He'd got a great slab of typescript in his brief-case. I saw him toying with it."

"You're a very observant person, aren't you?" said Macdonald.

"Not really. I only note things in bits. I notice clothes; I'm used to men's clothes because I've got two brothers and they're frightfully fussy. They spend much more on their clothes than I do on mine." She broke off and then said, "May I ask you to have a cup of coffee with me? They serve coffee in the court-yard down there, and you gave me some coffee at Zürich."

"Thank you very much. That would be most agreeable," said Macdonald. "Perhaps we shall see Dr. Natzler. He had to see a patient this afternoon, but he said he'd come along to find me here."

"Oh, I do hope so. I thought he looked a dear, and Sir Walter thinks the world of him."

"Well, we'll keep our eyes open for him, and if I see your 'allergy,' I'll speak to him and try to find out what he is."

Her eyes danced with amusement. "Say if he knows you by sight! Wouldn't he be shattered?"

"That'd make it all the more interesting. He's no business to know me by sight. But he doesn't, anyway. I had a good look at him while we were in the Customs, and he had a look at me and was quite unimpressed."

"Isn't it odd that we've all come to Schönbrunn this afternoon, after travelling in the plane together."

"No," said Macdonald prosaically. "Every visitor to Vienna comes to Schönbrunn, it's one of the show places. I haven't got a Baedeker, but I'm sure he gives Schönbrunn all the stars in the firmament, and to-day is just the right day for it."

"Baedeker," she said reflectively. "Do you know what he said about Oxford and Cambridge?"

"Yes, I do. 'If you have not time to visit both universities, Cambridge may be omitted.'"

"Then you were at Oxford."

"Why the assumption?"

"The complacent way you quoted old Baedeker. No Cambridge man ever quotes it without going pale in the face."

"An unwarrantable assumption," said Macdonald. "Look, there's Dr. Natzler. Now we can all have coffee together."

3

The old Austrian greeted Elizabeth Le Vendre very charmingly, in his own language, and bent to kiss her hand, and she replied in German, speaking with an ease and fluency which betokened real familiarity with the language.

"And now we will talk English, because Macdonald's German is still hard work to him," said Natzler, as they went on to the sunny terrace against the old stables, and sat down at a small table. "It was Macdonald who made me talk English, when I was in England during the war," went on Natzler. "You see, he taught me his language much better than I taught him mine."

"It's terribly difficult to learn a language unless you live in the country where it's talked," said Elizabeth, and Dr. Natzler nodded.

"*Schon*: and you have lived in Germany, *Gnädigste*: I knew that the moment I heard you speak."

"Yes. I was in Germany when I was a schoolgirl. After the war, when everything in Germany was at sixes and sevens, some English officials were sent out to get things going again and sort things out, and my father was one of them. We lived with the Army, more or less, but I had my lessons in German, and I just got to talk it quite easily."

"So. Sixes and sevens," said Dr. Natzler. "Why sixes and sevens?"

"Goodness knows!" said Elizabeth. "There must be a reason, but it's just an expression you use without asking why—English is a most unreasonable language. Oh, do look! Isn't she wonderful? She looks as though she ought to live in Schönbrunn. Erzherzogin Maria Theresa…"

An old lady, superbly clad in a sable coat, topped by an immense picture hat, strolled slowly past them escorted by an even older gentleman in a silk hat, and followed by a severe-looking elderly maid carrying a parasol, a bunch of flowers and a tiny dog.

"Ah…look well, *Gnädigste*," said Dr. Natzler. "You are fortunate. That is Hedwige Waldtraut Körner—one of the great singers of all time: perhaps the greatest operatic soprano

Vienna ever produced. She was indeed great! How many times she sang my heart away when I was a young man."

"Oh…of course I've heard of her," said Elizabeth, "but I didn't realise she was so old. She was in Germany during the war, wasn't she? English people who knew about her didn't like her very much."

"But must we perpetuate our hates?" asked Natzler sadly. "For me, I will only remember her singing. Music overrides national bitterness. Did they cease to play Bach and Beethoven in England during the war? No. I rejoiced to hear German music in London, even though it was the Germans who had driven us from our homes." He bent across and patted her hand "What was it your poet said… 'Old unhappy far-off things.' Let us forget them, *Gnädigste*. See, the sun shines, the world is beautiful—and you are beautiful, too. Our old singer was once young and beautiful, and her singing was divine. It took me up to heaven, and I have never forgotten."

"Forgive me!" said Elizabeth. "It was a silly thing to say. Of course you're right. I'm glad you told me how you loved her singing. I shall always remember you talking about her."

"I am a sentimental old man!" chuckled Natzler. "And now tell me, what are you going to see in Vienna?"

"All of it!" she laughed, "the great palaces and churches— and the Opera House, of course, and the little house where Schubert lived and the house where Beethoven lived— and Strauss. And I want to go up through the woods—to Leopoldsberg, is it? And the Kahlenberg."

"Ach—you have been reading about it all?"

"Of course I have, and talking to everybody who knew Vienna. There's one place I'm longing to see, a village with a monastery and a wonderful church—we should call it Holy Cross in English."

"Heiligen Kreuz—yes, that is most beautiful. But you will need a permit. Sir Walter will see that somebody takes you to Heiligen Kreuz, or he will take you himself. But if you want a guide, to show you your way, remember I shall be happy to take you, *gnädiges Fräulein*. Perhaps I know Vienna even better than Sir Walter does!"

"That's very very kind of you, Dr. Natzler—but I know you're very busy, and it will be good for me to find my way about. And now, will you forgive me if I run away home? I told Miss Vanbrugh I would be in at four o'clock. She is rather old, and she might worry if I am late. She wanted me to take one of the maids with me when I went out—but I couldn't bear it!"

"We will walk home with you," replied Natzler. "Our houses are not far apart. Then we shall know that Miss Vanbrugh has no cause to worry."

4

Having escorted Elizabeth Le Vendre to the Vanbrughs' mansion in Trauttmansdorffgasse, Natzler and Macdonald strolled back to the more homely house in Altzaugasse.

"It will be a little lonely for that child until Clare von Baden returns home," said Natzler. "The Vanbrughs are both aged. There is a nephew living with them—Mr. Anthony Vanbrugh, but he also is mature."

"I expect she'll soon find some young friends," said Macdonald. "There must be several families connected with the Embassy who will take her in hand. I can't imagine that a youngster like that will have a dull time in Vienna." He broke off, obviously considering a different topic, and as they turned in to the Natzlers' house he said, "I was interested in seeing your old opera singer. Can you tell me why an English cameraman should have told me she is in the news? Is her return to Vienna 'news' in the international sense?"

"No, it's not as simple as that," said Natzler. "Come into the garden and I will tell you."

They went and sat on the grass, under Frau Natzler's beloved apple trees, and Natzler began:

"Waldtraut Körner always loved Germany and the Germans. True, she was almost worshipped in Vienna, but her heart was given to a German very long ago. She gave her farewell performance in Vienna in 1935—she was then fifty-five years old, but still beautiful, and her voice was a miracle. She retired to live in Salzburg, but on the outbreak of war she went to a *Schloss* in the Bavarian Alps and lived, under the protection, one might say, of Graf Steinadler."

Macdonald put in a word here: "Steinadler—one of Hitler's generals?"

"Yes. Steinadler was shot after the attempt on Hitler's life. It is now said that the Waldtraut Körner is in possession of Steinadler's diary and private papers. She inherited his property—according to the terms of his will."

"You mean that she has papers of General Steinadler's which have never been published?"

"Just that. I do not, of course, know all the circumstances, but I do know that there was great excitement in publishing circles in Vienna when the news leaked out that Waldtraut Körner was negotiating the sale of some important papers to Probus Verlag. 'Probus' is a post-war publishing firm, and they have produced one or two travel books and escape stories which have had international fame."

"Do you know how the story leaked out?"

Natzler shrugged his shoulders. "There is no one answer. You must realise that Waldtraut Körner is still a great name in Vienna. It was known that she had come on hard times: money will not now buy what it once did. Perhaps some men in the newspaper world always believed that she had a story to tell if she could be induced to tell it. But the Schloss Steinadler was hidden away and difficult of access, and newspaper men could not contact her, as they say. But when Waldtraut Körner came back to Vienna and lunched at Sacher's with Herr Schwarzdorn of Probus Verlag—well, that was news. And as to the rest, if anyone overheard a word about Steinadler, a guess was not too difficult."

"Good lord, no. Steinadler was said to have been behind that plot to kill Hitler—but I should be very much surprised if the Nazis left any documents for future publication at the *Schloss*."

"But they left Waldtraut Körner alive: and if a woman like herself wanted to hide something, I would say the Schloss Steinadler was rich in hiding-places. It is a Gothic castle, with walls ten feet thick, up on the hillside. Steinadler—a black eagle: that *Schloss* is like an eagle's eyrie, for all that the General made it snug enough to live in."

"Well, it's quite a story," said Macdonald, "and so Probus Verlag will put their imprint on another bestseller."

"Not so," said the doctor. "It is said that 'Probus' did not offer a large enough sum. If gossip is right, the General's papers still await a purchaser."

"If it comes to bidding, it's the Americans who can generally outbid the rest of the world," said Macdonald. "I hope the old lady has got her papers in a safe place. They would be worth the attention of certain expert thieves. Where does she live?"

"She is staying in a hotel on the Kärntnerstrasse, but her papers, I do not doubt, are in the strong-room of a bank. Here is Ilse—she has news, I think."

"It is from Karl," cried Frau Natzler, waving a letter. "He comes to-morrow. That is joy for us, dear friend! Two weeks he can stay."

"That's grand!" said Macdonald and the doctor chuckled.

"We should put the flags up," he said. "This is an occasion. I must order some more wine."

IV

1

THE WEATHER CHANGED ON THE DAY THAT KARL Natzler arrived in Vienna. Macdonald drove with Dr. Natzler to Schwechat to meet Karl, and the doctor had some misgivings as to whether the Viscount would be able to land, for the cloud ceiling was low. It was still warm, but heavy purple clouds had been massing overhead and then a mist seemed to settle below the clouds: there was no wind, and to Macdonald's mind it looked as though the fine weather was going to break up with a thunderstorm.

They heard the plane approach and circle overhead, but it did not break the cloud ceiling, and from the sound of the engine they knew it was receding again.

"I am glad Ilse did not come," said Natzler. "She gets nervous. If it's too difficult to land here, they may have to try Munich."

"It's coming back," said Macdonald. "They're still trying."

The Viscount circled three times altogether before it succeeded in coming down to the runway, while all the personnel of Schwechat listened and watched, and the fire-engine
crews stood by in the manner so nerve-racking to the inexperienced. Then the great aircraft touched down and taxied
in sedately.

"*Gott sei Dank*," exclaimed Dr. Natzler. "It comes in safely
every day—and every day it seems a miracle."

For a moment Macdonald found it difficult to recognise
Karl. In 1945 he had been a thin leggy schoolboy: now, at
the age of twenty-six he was as tall as Macdonald, well built
and well poised, looking older than his years, and exceedingly good-looking. It was when he smiled and his dark eyes
gleamed with pleasure that Macdonald saw again the schoolboy he had known in the wartime years.

"This is grand!" said Karl. "We have so often said 'When
Robert Macdonald comes to stay, we will do this that and the
other,' and now you're really here. You haven't altered a bit: I
should have known you wherever I'd seen you."

"You've altered quite a lot," said Macdonald. "You're as
tall as I am—just—and you probably weigh more than I do."

"I probably do: you were always lean—'long and lank and
brown,' as I learnt at school in England. What weather for
Vienna! I thought we should have to give up and land somewhere else, but the B.E.A. pilots are marvellous chaps."

They drove back to Hietzing and sat in the white-walled
sitting-room, while Karl told his father about the clinic where
he was working, and Frau Natzler pressed upon them the
Viennese "sandwiches" and pastries which are the delight
(and despair) of all visitors. It was when all the professional

news had been exchanged that Dr. Natzler said, "Now I am going to leave you and Macdonald to gossip, Karl. I have a patient to see—a friend of old Weinberg, I gather."

"And I am going to the kitchen to see that Margret has got everything in order," said Frau Natzler.

"Well, that will give me a chance to discuss a point with you, Macdonald," said Karl. "It pertains to doctoring, but it's one on which you may have had more experience than I have. Have you ever known a case of a head injury which subsequently proved fatal when the injured person was able to get up and move and speak normally after the injury?" He held out a box of cigarettes to Macdonald (Player's No. 6, bought in Switzerland).

"There are a number of such cases on record," rejoined Macdonald, "as you probably know from the text-books." He lighted his cigarette and went on: "I take it you want to know if I have met such a case personally. I once worked on a murder case where a man—a farm labourer—was found dead in his own cottage kitchen, having been seen to walk indoors, take his boots off and ask for a cup of tea before he died. Death was due to brain injuries, caused by a blow on the temple. The confusing part of it was that this man had been attacked outside the cottage, and presumably left for dead. He recovered consciousness sufficiently to walk indoors, where he sat down in a chair and died an hour or so later."

"Well, I'm interested to know you've met such a case," said Karl, "because old Zeiss met me at Zürich on my way through, and told me about a similar case which happened at the airport on the Monday you came to Vienna. About half an hour before your plane arrived, a young chap in hiking kit

went to the Toiletten and slipped on the flight of steps leading down from the main hall. He went a proper purler on his
back and bumped from top to bottom, hitting the back of his
head as he fell."

"Was he drunk?" asked Macdonald promptly. "I should
say those were very safe stairs."

"If he was drunk, nobody noticed, but there's no evidence
to show he was; but he'd certainly got nailed boots on, and
nailed boots are inclined to be treacherous on stairs. He was
also clutching a parcel—a cuckoo clock he'd bought as a
souvenir—and apparently he clutched his parcel trying to
save it, instead of dropping the parcel and saving himself,
silly cuckoo! The attendant saw it happen, and the chap was
knocked right out; by the time he got to the bottom he just
lay there—semi-conscious, I gather."

"It sounds a bit odd," said Macdonald. "Was the attendant
certain the chap wasn't pushed, or tripped?"

"The attendant was perfectly certain," rejoined Karl.
"As it happened, there was nobody else on the stairs at all.
The attendant—Stein—rushed to help the chap up, and
after a few seconds the latter recovered, sat up, collected his
parcel and laughed at himself for being such a clumsy idiot.
He spoke both French and German—he was a Belgian, I
think, and was on his way home to Brussels after a holiday
in Switzerland. He had over an hour to wait for his plane,
because he'd been driven to the airport by a friend, and said
he wanted a shower. I'm giving you all the details, because
it shows that he talked quite collectedly: Stein said he never
thought for a moment the chap could be badly hurt: he said
baths in Switzerland were too expensive and he wanted a

shower and a clean shirt before boarding the plane—all perfectly sensible."

"And you're going to tell me that this chap died from injuries received in his tumble?"

"He died of cerebral haemorrhage some hours later, after being admitted to hospital. The rest of the story is as follows. He went into the shower-room, and the attendant being busy with other customers coming in, didn't give the clumsy chap another thought, until he went to tidy up the shower-room best part of an hour later. He found the chap—Welsbach his name was, I think—unconscious on the tiled floor. A doctor was sent for, the patient was removed to hospital and died there. The injury to the base of his skull set up haemorrhage and he must have fallen a second time, this time on the tiled floor of the shower. It was an odd case, but from the medical point of view consistent with what was known to have happened."

Macdonald sat and pondered. "I take it the police were informed?"

"Certainly they were. I know what you're asking yourself—was Welsbach robbed? The answer is that he was not: his purse, wallet, passport, plane tickets, watch—everything was safe, including the broken cuckoo clock. The authorities found his address, notified his people and somebody came along in another plane and identified him. It was all quite straightforward—but it demonstrates again the incalculable nature of head injuries. Moral, never move a patient with a head injury until a doctor has arrived."

"Very sound—in theory," said Macdonald. "If I'd stayed put and waited for a doctor every time I've been bashed on

the head, I should have been dead long ago. My general preoc-
cupation is to get my head out of the way before the next bash.
But come to think of it, I was lucky on Monday. Presumably
the unfortunate young man was lying unconscious in the
shower-room when I went down to the lavatories at Zürich
Airport. If I'd seen him tumble, or found him unconscious,
professional probity would have forced me to stop and say
'What's all this about?'—just as you would have done if you'd
found him. And I should probably have missed the Viscount."
He paused and then added, "My guess is that the chap had put
down a couple of cognacs, or what have you, and was dizzy
before he tackled the stairs."

"Well, it's an idea," said Karl Natzler. "Eaten something
which disagreed with him, had a couple of drinks to steady his
stomach and it didn't work. Biliousness can make any chap
see double, even without the brandy... Hallo! You said it was
going to thunder, and you're right! It's going to be a terrific
storm."

"We'd better move those deck-chairs in," said Macdonald,
"it's going to pour."

They rushed outside to the garden, moved the chairs and
hurried back indoors to hear Frau Natzler exclaiming to her
husband:

"But she will be sheltering from the storm. No one would
walk through a storm like this."

"But English girls never mind storms," said Dr. Natzler.

He turned to Macdonald. "Miss Vanbrugh has just rung
up. She asked if Miss Le Vendre were here with us. The young
lady went out for a walk with the little fat dog, and the dog has
gone home alone, all trembling and frightened, and the young

lady has not returned, although it is past the time she promised to be home. Miss Vanbrugh is worried about her, and as we are the only people Miss Le Vendre knows in Vienna Miss Vanbrugh rang me up to inquire."

"I expect the dog smelt the thunder and rushed home on its own account," said Macdonald, "and Miss Le Vendre may well have taken shelter. At least, that's what I should say if I were in London," he added.

"Perhaps you can't say it quite so comfortably in Vienna," said Karl. "Who is the young lady?"

"Sir Walter Vanbrugh's new English secretary," replied Dr. Natzler. "She has only been in Vienna a few days. She came on the same plane as Macdonald."

Karl turned and looked at Macdonald. "A sensible girl?"

"Quite sensible—but very young. Still, I don't think she'd have done anything silly, like accepting a lift from a stranger."

"Sir Walter Vanbrugh," said Karl thoughtfully. "He was a V.I.P. in the Foreign Office at one time, wasn't he? Is he in Vienna officially?"

It was Dr. Natzler who answered. "No. He has retired, and is living in Vienna as a private resident. His son-in-law is in the Embassy, of course, and it may be that Sir Walter acts in some advisory capacity. It is not for me to say—and one does not inquire."

"How does an Englishman contrive to live in Vienna in a private capacity these days?" Karl asked Macdonald. "I thought your currency regulations were binding on everybody, high and low alike."

"I don't pretend to know," replied Macdonald. "Ex-Foreign Office eminences are not the concern of my department, unless they are given police protection, and even then they're not my cup of tea." He turned to his host. "About this girl," he said. "Do you think there is any reason for disquiet?"

Natzler shrugged his shoulders. "I should have said not, especially in this sector of Vienna. It is as safe as your Hampstead Heath…generally speaking."

"But there have been exceptions," said Karl.

"Not in Hietzing," said Frau Natzler firmly. "In any case, if Miss Vanbrugh is worried, she can let the police know. We have police in Vienna," she added to Macdonald, rather indignantly, but her husband replied:

"Sir Walter is out, and Miss Vanbrugh did not wish to raise an alarm unnecessarily. She is an old lady," he added to Karl, "and she is of a nervous disposition. She never ventures out alone herself, and she did not feel happy that this young girl insisted on going out alone—as all English girls do, of course."

"And Austrian girls also," said Frau Natzler. "It is ridiculous to imagine a young girl is not safe in Vienna: there are university students, music students, art students—and of all nationalities. It is only the Russians who do not go out alone," she added severely.

"But that doesn't help Miss Vanbrugh if she is troubled about Miss Le Vendre's absence," said the doctor. "As I have said, Miss Vanbrugh is old, and she tends to exaggerate her troubles: if she is worried she gets a migraine, with a *tic douloureux* which is most painful. I think I will just drive round and see her. I can at least reassure her."

"But, Franz—look at the rain! It is a deluge, it is like a wall of water! Would any girl walk through such a downpour?"

"I think this one would have," said Macdonald. "Miss Le

Vendre wouldn't be frightened of a thunderstorm, still less of a downpour, but I think she would be very unwilling to cause Miss Vanbrugh distress. I don't like it very much."

"I will go round to the Trauttmansdorffgasse," said the doctor, "and I will let you know if the young lady has returned."

"I'll come with you," said Macdonald, and Karl said:

"I'll come, too—and then we can all take counsel."

"Do not be late for supper," said Ilse. "My chicken, it must not be spoiled."

2

It was nearly dark when they dashed across to the garage through torrential rain, and lightning was fairly crackling across the sky in blinding spasms.

"We have not had a storm like this for years," said the doctor. "It is indeed fierce. Perhaps Ilse was right—no one would walk through this."

"You're worried, Macdonald," said Karl, "and that is not like you. What are you thinking?"

"Simply this: if that child—and to me she's no more than a child—if she took the dog for a walk, she would have gone up towards the woods—it's the obvious direction to take a dog for a walk, especially in Vienna, where leads and muzzles are demanded. Accidents in thunderstorms aren't very frequent, but they do happen, and when they happen, it's generally under trees."

"True enough. I wasn't thinking of the woods," said Karl. "If she did go through the woods, she probably walked up to the old anti-aircraft-gun emplacement. It's the obvious place to walk to, because it's something definite, and being high up you get a good view on a fine day. But perhaps we shall find she's got home again. Otherwise," he added resignedly, "it looks as though you and I are going to get very wet, and the chicken is going to be ruined."

Dr. Natzler drew up outside the imposing front of the Vanbrughs' house. It did not stand in a garden, as the Natzlers' house did, but straight on to the pavement, with wrought-iron grilles across the lower windows and great double doors closed before the carriage entrance. It was so built that cars could be driven in under cover before the occupants alighted, but Natzler drew his car up at the kerb and stood in the rain and rang at the formidable-looking gates.

Karl whistled to himself as they sat in the car, and Macdonald said, "This seems rather bad luck on you—and on your mother. You've only just got home for a holiday, the fatted calf is being prepared, your mother is rejoicing, and then the whole time-table is upset because an English girl goes out and gets caught in a thunderstorm."

"But that's nothing," said Karl, "or one might say it's in character with family habits. Hardly a week goes by without my parents being involved in somebody else's crises. Anything from a lost dog to a runaway husband, a premature birth or a sudden death—and I might tell you my mother rushes to the rescue also, *presto, con brio, sforzando, agitato*. I am used to it. Had it not been the English young lady, it would have been the little fat dog. If I have to get wet to the skin, I would rather it were the young lady… Ah, here is my father."

Dr. Natzler reappeared to tell them that Miss Le Vendre had not returned, and that Miss Vanbrugh was still unwilling to inform the police without her brother's permission. "She does not wish to make 'an international situation,'" said Natzler. "She is foolish—but then she is very old. Now Schmidt—the old maid, thinks that Miss Le Vendre went up into the woods with Fritzel—"

"I knew it," said Karl. "Macdonald and I will go up to the old ack-ack site—and there, while he and I are soaked to the skin, we shall find a sensible English miss keeping dry in the lee of the emplacement. Have you a torch in this car? It is nearly dark—good, here is a torch."

"Take the car—it will save you some walking," said Natzler, but Karl retorted:

"No. You may need the car yourself. The little dog may get lost next—or Sir Walter himself. And ring the police, Father: report on your own authority. This is not really funny."

"How long has the girl been out?" asked Macdonald.

"Nearly two hours. She started before there was any thunder at all."

"Then it's quite time she was found," said Macdonald.

Dr. Natzler went back into the house, and Karl and Macdonald turned up the collars of their raincoats and set out in the pouring rain through the quiet shadowy streets. It was not more than ten minutes before they reached a hilly road which led to the open woodland which lies to the south and west of Hietzing, adding great charm to that pleasant district. Soon the road became a track, down which the rain-water poured in runnels.

"There are dozens of these tracks," said Karl. "She may have taken any of them—and there are small houses, châlets and gardeners' shacks where she could have sheltered. I'm only guessing at the route she took, on the supposition that she's more likely to have made for the high ground and a definite point. Then it's possible the dog chose the way: Fritzel may be old and fat, but all dachshunds are intelligent."

"It's a wild goose chase anyway," said Macdonald. "At least you have an idea, so we might as well follow it."

They trudged on through the rain: in the gloom it was impossible to tell if the woodlands were of large or small extent, but at least there were definite paths and they climbed steadily until they were clear of the trees and approaching a sort of plateau. It was less dark here, and Macdonald could see the line of a building against the sky—not a house, but a wall of some sort whose ridge was clearly perceptible.

"That's the gun-site," said Karl. "I often thought of this place when I used to go for a walk on Hampstead Heath when we were in London during the war. The distances in London are much bigger, of course, but Hampstead Heath gives a view over London as these hills do over Vienna. Let's walk right round the emplacement to begin with, and then go up to the gun-site."

The thunder had almost ceased: only an occasional distant rumble sounded now, and the lightning flickered sporadically behind the heights of the Leopoldsberg away to the north. The rain still fell, not in the storm torrents of half an hour ago, but steadily, and a wind was blowing through the rough herbage and undergrowth. Through the curtain of rain Macdonald could see the blurred lights of the city far below, and the heavy clouds reflected the lights in a sullen glare. The C.I.D. man walked on beside Karl Natzler, who was swinging his torch and whistling cheerfully: the tune he had chosen sounded incongruous to Macdonald in this place, but he joined his whistle to Karl's, feeling that if an English girl heard "The bonny bonny banks of Loch Lomond" in the hills above Vienna she would surely be encouraged to find out who was whistling it. The two men walked round the rampart, and then Karl said:

"There are some steps up here to the gun platform: there'd be shelter of a sort under the walls…"

It was there that they found Elizabeth Le Vendre: she was lying at the foot of the steps, as though she had fallen down them. In the beam of the torch, her fair hair shone a little, as the runnels of rain-water shone: she lay face down in a pool of water and her light woollen coat lay in sodden folds on the saturated ground.

3

"She can't have drowned…not in that puddle…she can't." It was Karl who muttered, as he bent and lifted the girl, very slowly and gently, while Macdonald held the torch. "No… She's not dead, either, but she's deadly cold." He laid her on her back and his hands moved round her neck, under her head, and then the careful skilful fingers felt over her skull, under the sodden fair hair which still shone pathetically round the grey-white face.

"It's here—the hell of a bump: she must have fallen backwards… Well, it's your drill again, Macdonald—be careful how you move a head injury. We daren't risk carrying her. A stretcher's the only way."

He stood up and took his raincoat off and bent to wrap it round the girl's body. "I'll run to the nearest house that has a telephone and call an ambulance. Then I'll come back here with blankets. I won't be long. If we try carrying her we may kill her."

"Yes. All right. I'll stay here."

Karl pounded off down the slope, and Macdonald added his own coat on top of Karl's. He knew well enough that cold following a head injury and shock might weigh the balance on the wrong side. Then he stood beside the prone body and sought to penetrate the gloom around him: he could see the steps, and could believe that it might have been possible for the girl to have been half stunned or stupefied by the lightning and to have crashed down the steps. His eyes picked out a lighter patch on the dark ground and he found her bag, a white leather satchel: it was closed and the contents were still in it. Not robbed, then: though robbery in this place did not seem very likely.

Macdonald felt uneasy and unhappy about the whole business: when he and Dr. Natzler had walked back from Schönbrunn with Elizabeth Le Vendre the doctor had talked about the walk through the woods, and Macdonald had said, "When you have made friends with Fritzel, you must take him up there for a walk. I remember the view from the top, though it's years and years since I was there."

"I told her to come here," he thought, "and this is the result."

He bent down to listen for her breathing, aware that her face had looked so much more dead than alive—and then he heard running footsteps and Karl's breathless voice.

"I've called an ambulance: they'll bring the stretcher up here. With any luck she'll be all right…and perhaps the chicken will still be edible after all."

V

1

"AND I ALSO RANG UP AND INFORMED THE POLICE THAT an accident had occurred," said Karl, as he bent and tucked a blanket round the girl's body. "And the police will be annoyed, Macdonald, as they are the world over, because we have moved the body. Not that the patient is dead, but police prefer the evidence to be left undisturbed."

Macdonald was aware that Karl found an element of the bizarre in the present situation—which was in itself cheering, because if the girl were dead or dying, humour would have had no place, for Karl was a kindly young doctor.

"You'd better make up your mind," went on Karl. "Do I present you to the Herr Rittmeister (the police officer) as his English colleague? Or do I explain that you are my father's guest who kindly co-operated in the search for the missing lady? Are you, so to speak, 'on' in this?"

"Not if I can help it," said Macdonald. "I am on holiday. I have no official standing—*Gott sei Dank*, as your father says."

"I should keep out of it if you can," said Karl. "The Herr Rittmeister is certain to smell his private rat if he knows you are an English detective. After all, if you were called to a casualty on Hampstead Heath and found an Austrian girl unconscious on the ground and an Austrian detective beside her explaining he happened to find her whilst he was on holiday, would you not say 'this is too apropos'?"

"I probably should," replied Macdonald, "but London is simpler than Vienna. I don't want your Herr Rittmeister to get it into his head that I am over here for any other purpose than for a holiday."

Karl chuckled. "He's almost bound to let his imagination loose on you once he knows your status: being a Viennese he will approach the matter with more élan than an English policeman: he will say 'He is here on a private mission connected with these English high-ups'—private missions always crop up in Vienna—and laughing apart, I regard this situation as an accident. The poor child has not been robbed. It seems to me that she just fell and stunned herself."

"In the main I agree—and in any case, it's the business of your city police to sort that one out," said Macdonald. "If they're not satisfied and think there's any mystery about it, I will discuss it with them willingly, but I feel a bit like the aged Miss Vanbrugh—I don't want to cook up an international situation. Listen! That will be the ambulance men."

"Yes—and my father. I told them to ring him. He will go in the ambulance with the patient and see her suitably accommodated in hospital. You and I are on holiday, Macdonald. All we have to do is to answer the questions of the Herr

Rittmeister. Are you prepared to enjoy that? How long is it since you were interrogated by a policeman?"

"I can't remember that it's ever happened," said Macdonald, "but I know the drill—and you have to interpret for me. If I try talking German I shall perjure myself. Here they are."

It was the ambulance men who arrived first, with Dr. Natzler just behind them. They laid the stretcher on the ground and with great skill and care lifted the girl on to the stretcher, steadied her head between pads and strapped her firmly. They had good torches, and the two Natzlers superintended the operation. It was just as the ambulance men lifted the stretcher that the police arrived—a Chief Inspector and a constable. Dr. Natzler spoke to them with the firm authority of the medical man in charge of a patient.

"It is your duty to ask all the necessary questions about this accident, Herr Rittmeister. My son and my English guest will answer your questions. It is my duty to get my patient to hospital without delay. So—forward."

The ambulance men went off with the stretcher and Karl began his statement: he spoke simply and clearly, and Macdonald followed his German without much difficulty. In Vienna, as in London, the police drill was straightforward. Names, addresses, times, essential evidence—all were entered in the official note-book. The Chief Inspector was sensible and considerate: it was not necessary to stay here in the rain, he said. Any further questions could be asked later: all he wanted to know now was if, in the opinion of the two witnesses, this incident had the appearance of an accident only. Karl gave his own answer and then interpreted for Macdonald:

"Judging from the evidence, Macdonald, have you any reason to believe that this was anything but an accident?"

"The only thing against the accident theory is that she fell backwards and not forwards," said Macdonald. "It was the back of her head that was damaged, yet she was lying face downwards when we found her: but she was not robbed. Her handbag had not been emptied, and the pearls round her neck are real pearls—I think."

The Chief Inspector grunted, thoughtfully. "Yes. Yes, that will be considered. You believe that she would have fallen forward if she had been blinded by the lightning and had slipped?"

Again Karl interpreted, and Macdonald, who had followed the German, had time to check his natural response which would have begun "In my experience…" Instead he said, "That is for you to decide, Herr Rittmeister."

The Chief Inspector looked at Macdonald in the gleam of the torch.

"You are acquainted with this lady?" he inquired.

"She travelled from England on the same plane as I did, and we talked during the journey," said Macdonald. "I had never seen her before."

"And I had never seen her at all," concluded Karl.

The Chief Inspector nodded. "Very good. I will not keep you here. We will examine the ground, and I will call on you later if any further questions present themselves. Ach! Who is there?"

Even as he spoke a light blazed in their faces for a split second, leaving them momentarily blinded.

"A cameraman," said Karl. "Who told them to come here?"

The Chief Inspector was angry and he shouted, first to the unseen operator of the flashlight to halt, then to the constable to pursue the man. The constable leapt forward obediently, but being still half blinded by the flash, he promptly took a header as his foot caught in a trail of bramble. Macdonald's German was defeated by the Superintendent's outburst, but the police whistle spoke for itself. Reinforcements were being called up.

"This is your affair, Herr Rittmeister, not ours," said Karl firmly, when he had a chance to get a word in. "It was not I who informed the press there had been an accident. And we are both wet through: with your permission we will go home and change our clothes."

The permission was gruffly accorded, and Karl Natzler and Macdonald trudged away down the track. It was not long before Macdonald realised that Karl was shaking with laughter.

"It is a long time since I featured in a performance so bizarre," said Karl, when he could control his voice sufficiently to speak, and even then his English sounded markedly un-English.

"I'm glad you didn't tell the Herr Rittmeister I was an English colleague," said Macdonald. "He was angry enough with that unfortunate constable as it was: had he known a London C.I.D. man was watching, the Herr Rittmeister (as you insist on calling him) would have had a seizure—but can you explain what a cameraman was doing up here?"

"Of course I can. If there's nothing else on hand, pressmen haunt the local police station in the hope of a scoop. When the patrol set out, the press hound followed, though he was too late to get much in the way of a picture—unless he synchronised with the ambulance down below there. We'll try to get a copy of the picture for you, Macdonald—your first public appearance in Vienna. Let's hope it won't have a caption saying 'English ace detective co-operates with the Herr Rittmeister Brunnerhausen in a mysterious affair in the Hietzing Woods.' These newspapermen are devils at smelling things out. Here is Father's car: we can drive home and investigate the chicken."

"The cameraman incident still seems a bit odd to me," said Macdonald a moment later. "Why did he do a bolt when challenged? Our chaps don't do that—they brazen anything out: and it's not an indictable offence to take photographs of policemen in conclave—or is it?"

"I suppose things are a bit touchier in Vienna," said Karl. "We have all suffered from 'Occupation Nerves.' It's a malaise which makes people do unpredictable things. And the Herr Rittmeister is famous for his severity: when he bawled Halt! I expect the cameraman lost his nerve."

"In that case, cameramen in Vienna have their nerves much nearer the surface than the same breed in London," said Macdonald.

2

Frau Natzler rendered praise and thanks to God with enthusiasm when Karl and Macdonald reappeared: during the absence of her menfolk she had imagined every sort of tragedy and crisis, and Karl reassured her with affectionate exuberance. The *gnädiges Fräulein* had been taken to hospital after an accident in the thunderstorm: Dr. Natzler had accompanied the ambulance and would soon be home again. Karl himself and Macdonald had covered themselves with glory. "And we are both wet through," concluded Karl. "Can the chicken wait until we have had hot baths and put on dry clothes?"

"Go, quickly! The water is hot, the bathroom awaits—and I will bring you up some hot spiced wine to check the chill," said Frau Natzler, and upstairs they went to the tune of "*Nun danket alle Gott*" (which took Macdonald back in retrospect to the great hall of the City Scriveners' School on the last day of term).

It was not very long before they were all assembled round the chicken (from which issued a spicy fragrance never experienced in the more modest English style of cooking). Dr. Natzler had returned home, having seen his patient handed over to a colleague of whose skill he could not say too much.

"The child should be all right," he said. "She has a bad concussion, but they think there is no fracture. It was indeed a providence that the two of you found her so quickly." He paused and then added, "I have, of course, informed the Vanbrughs and told them all that I could. Sir Walter is very anxious to see Macdonald—and Karl, too. I said that you would perhaps go to Trauttmansdorffgasse after dinner—"

Frau Natzler interrupted with loud cries of protest. "It is too much!" she declared. "They have their utmost done: they have both soaked to the skin been—and if I my English forget, it is that I am angry. Let the poor fellows have some peace. Have they not enough done?"

"Sir Walter offered to come here, but he and his sister are both old, and they have been very much upset over this accident," said Dr. Natzler.

"Of course they're upset: they bring that young thing out to Vienna, and she nearly kills herself only a few days after she arrives," said Karl. "I'm sure Macdonald won't mind coming in the car with me to see them. After all, they know who he is, and it will console them to have the benefit of his experience."

"Of course I'll come with you," said Macdonald, "if only to assure Sir Walter that I am not butting in as a policeman, and that the Herr Rittmeister accepts me as Dr. Natzler's English guest and nothing more; but when it comes to experience, I think it is Karl's experience which can explain the accident, not mine—if I followed his evidence to the Herr Rittmeister aright."

"Well—it seemed to me to resemble an accident I once saw when some small boys played ghosts on a concrete staircase," said Karl. "My guess is that Miss Le Vendre climbed up to the gun emplacement to see the view over Vienna. As you remember, the storm broke very suddenly: I think when she got to the top of the steps she was blinded and half stupefied by that first flash of lightning—it was terrific. She fell back, struck her head against the masonry and rolled over, so that when we found her she was lying face downwards. That seems to me a reasonable explanation. I do not think it reasonable to assume that she was attacked, because she was not robbed, she was not further—disturbed—as I might say for my mother's benefit, and the little dog ran away home."

"And who would have robbed her, in this district?" demanded Frau Natzler indignantly. "Such things do not happen here in Hietzing."

"There are robbers and maniacs in every city in the world," said Karl, "and I have seen the work of some of them—and

Macdonald has seen much more. Did this look to you like a crime of violence, Macdonald? You remember that it was very quiet in the woods, apart from the thunder. We heard no footsteps—no one ran away. And the girl was lying just as she fell: she had not been placed in that position."

"She had been lying in that position since the rain started," said Macdonald. "The rain-water had collected in a hollow by her face, but the ground beneath her body was dry, so she hadn't been moved."

"When she is better, she will be able to tell you what happened," said Frau Natzler comfortably, "and meanwhile I think Karl's explanation is very sensible. Now let us finish the chicken—it is a good bird and none the worse for its extra cooking."

3

It was just after dinner, when Frau Natzler had brought the coffee into the sitting-room, that her husband came into the room saying:

"Have you seen my keys, Ilse? In the general excitement I seem to have mislaid them."

"Your keys?" she echoed in surprise. "But no, I have not seen them. You never leave your keys about, Franz. They must be in one of your pockets."

"But they are not in any of my pockets," replied Franz Natzler. "It is very strange. I must have put them down somewhere."

"When did you last have them?" asked Macdonald. "If I lose anything I always try to remember the last time I used it."

"Yes. That is sensible," rejoined Franz. "I had them when I saw Herr Pretzel, just before Miss Vanbrugh called me on the phone. I remember now: I unlocked my drug cabinet to get some tablets. I gave the tablets to my patient, and I was going back to the cabinet when the telephone rang."

"I put the call through to you in the consulting room," said Ilse, "but you came to the box to speak."

"Yes, yes. I did not want to talk to Miss Vanbrugh with my patient listening. He had taken his collar and tie off—I examined his heart—and he was very slow getting his things on."

"Then you may have left the keys in the telephone box in the hall," said Ilse. "I will go and look." She hurried out, but Karl said:

"You would never have put your keys down by the telephone. It is second nature to put one's keys back in one's pocket. Are you sure you didn't leave the keys in the keyhole of the drug cabinet?"

"I don't think so—but I may have done," said Dr. Natzler. "If so, they are no longer there. The cabinet is locked, but the keys are not in it."

"What sort of tablets did you give?" asked Karl. "Barbiturates? Sleeping tablets?"

The older man nodded. "Yes. You are right." Then he got up, adding, "I will go and look through my pockets again, just to make sure."

Macdonald had been sitting drinking his coffee, and he glanced up as the older man closed the door. Karl gave his characteristic shrug.

"You will have followed the implications of all that, Macdonald. It happens in London, doubtless, but more often in Vienna, where nerves are nearer the surface—with good reason."

"The drug addict who comes to a doctor for sleeping tablets?" asked Macdonald.

"That sort of thing: in some cases they go from doctor to doctor: they develop a vein of cunning. Of course my father knows all this, but sometimes it is difficult to spot; there may be a long and reasonable case history—an accident, a bereavement, an illness which has left chronic pain, a misfortune which has prevented normal sleep. I may be guessing quite wrong, and the keys may be in Father's pocket, in a drawer of his desk, under his papers—but if one's attention is suddenly distracted, as for instance by an agitated old lady on the telephone, one may omit to do the very thing which has become a habit."

"Perfectly true," said Macdonald, "and if one's habit, or reflex, has not worked, then one's left without a clue. Would it be only the key of the drug cabinet which has gone astray?"

"No, there are a number of keys on the same ring—door keys, desk, medical cases—all his keys except the garage key and ignition key. It's quite a heavy key-ring, you'd hear it if it dropped. I'm sorry this has happened: he's had a long day, and losing things is maddening to a methodical person, but it's no use offering to help; he's more likely to remember if he's left alone. Have some more coffee."

"Thanks. It's very good coffee," said Macdonald.

Karl chuckled a little as he refilled the cups. "You're a very restful person, Macdonald. I know quite well that you have several ideas you're prepared to discuss—coincidence, shall we say. But you don't obtrude them."

"I think you've got enough to think about for the time being," said Macdonald. "If you want to discuss coincidences later in the evening, I shall be quite prepared to do so. Here is your father."

"I can't find my key-ring, but things aren't as serious as I feared," said Dr. Natzler. "I have a spare key for my drug cabinet and I have checked my stock. Nothing is missing, nothing has been moved, so there is nothing to worry about."

"I expect we shall find your keys in the cellar, among the coke," said Frau Natzler. "Margret took your wet clothes down there and shook them all before she hung them up to dry, and Margret is deaf: she would never have heard them fall. We will find them in the morning, so let us not worry any more to-night. And if Karl and Robert *must* go out again, let them go now. The rain has left off and it is a beautiful night."

"I think that's a good idea," said Karl. "Shall we walk to Trauttmansdorffgasse? It's only a few minutes, and I don't think it will rain again."

"By all means," said Macdonald. He turned to Frau Natzler. "We will only stay a few minutes," he assured her, "and then everybody can go to bed early. It's been rather one of those days, as we say in England."

"Indeed, I shall be thankful to have you all in bed," said Ilse, "and if the telephone goes to-night, *I* will answer it! There has been enough of to-day."

4

As they strolled down the steep hill to the Gloriettestrasse, Macdonald said to Karl, "I don't want to bother your father again to-night, but I think it would be worth while for him to find out if his patient—Herr Pretzel, wasn't it?—had really been recommended by the friend your father mentioned."

"Otto Weinberg," said Karl. "Father has already thought of that. He telephoned, but Weinberg is away: he is staying near Graz, in the country, and he is not on the telephone, so that must wait. But since my father is satisfied that nothing is missing from his cabinet, it looks as though my suggestions were ill-founded. All the same, as the keys are still missing, we must be careful to bolt and chain the door to-night, and if the keys are not found in the morning we will get a locksmith to change the locks."

As they turned left into the Trauttmansdorffgasse, Macdonald said, "It's just possible that the keys dropped from Franz's pocket while he was bending over the stretcher up in the woods. In which case the police should have found them."

"There's a chance," agreed Karl, "though I don't think it's very likely. That key-ring is fairly heavy and it would stay in the bottom of the pocket. I think Mother's idea is more likely, that the keys dropped out when Margret shook the clothes. But I'm certain of one thing—Father must have been worried: more worried than he admitted. Otherwise, he would certainly have emptied his pockets when he changed his clothes. To empty one's pockets—that also is so habitual that it becomes a reflex. But we will not tell the Vanbrughs that anybody is worried: otherwise we shall not get home till the small hours, and the worry will be like the 'House that Jack Built.'"

"It's odd that you should quote that," said Macdonald. "It's been running through my head... 'This is the guest who talked to the son who suspected the patient who stole the keys which belonged to the doctor who lost the key which opened the door which led to the house that Jack built.'"

"If that's an improvisation, I give it top marks," said Karl. "Do you still read poetry, Macdonald?"

"Of course I do. It's a habit—you either have it or don't have it. Why do you ask?"

"Only because you can improvise words to a beat...and 'Why?' to you? What's the connection between poetry and all this? I can't see any myself, but I think there is in your mind. Your subconscious is logical—I've noticed it before."

"That's enough," said Macdonald firmly. "I know we're in Vienna: I know your father studied Freud and Jung and Adler. I know you peddle in the subconscious: but I do not. I will oblige with my conscious mind as far as it goes: my subconscious is my private property."

"You're very revealing," chuckled Karl. "This is the Vanbrugh mansion: this is where we both say there is nothing to worry about—no matter how much we worry inside—in our own private property, as you say."

VI

1

Superintendent Macdonald, on what might justly be described as "his lawful occasions," had made many entries into many houses, from mansions to hovels, but he had seldom had the feeling that he had got himself involved in a stage-set. As he walked up the wide red-carpeted stairway in Trauttmansdorffgasse, one side of his mind admired the architectural grace of a stylised interior, the other half asked, "Am I a super on an occasion of state, or in a performance of 'der Graf von Luxembourg'? Is this the ambassadorial or mere Franz Lehar?"

Perhaps it was because he was neither on duty nor yet on a purely social occasion that he was conscious of a sense of incongruity—as though he were making an entrance while still uncertain what part he was cast for.

It was a long stairway and a wide one, with a turn half-way up: the stairs were flanked by a fine balustrade with a velvet covered hand-rail, and great pots of gladioli provided an intensity of colour against dark curtains, so that even the flowers looked dramatic. It was, indeed, "a state staircase," but it had the charming Viennese quality of simultaneously mingling mirth with stateliness, an approach suitable to either carnival or splendour, but not, Macdonald thought, a congruous background for two rather solemn men dressed in lounge suits.

Karl Natzler and Macdonald followed a dignified manservant who led them very slowly and decorously up the stairs and then through a long shadowy music-room where a Bechstein grand gleamed in the half light and made Macdonald wonder who played it: then, through a deep white plaster archway, whose underside was studded with moulded stars, they saw the salon proper through long glass doors. It was a big airy gleaming room, beautifully lighted with many shaded lamps. The lengthy approach to this room (preceded by the solemn manservant) reinforced the first impression of dignity playing hide-and-seek with Franz Lehar—or even Strauss in lighter vein—and it was not until Macdonald was face to face with his host and hostess that the feeling of unreality left him and something quite different took its place. Here, he knew at once, were two very worried human beings, and the concern on their aged faces brought the C.I.D. man into focus again: the operatic staircase faded out and the problems of troubled humanity came to the fore.

Karl Natzler introduced Macdonald, and Sir Walter Vanbrugh shook hands and apologised for having brought him out.

"We are already profoundly indebted to you and to Dr.

Natzler and his son," said the old diplomat. "May I present you to my sister?"

Miss Vanbrugh was seated in a wide graceful armchair close to the fireplace. (An open wood fire in Vienna was a rarity, but it added greatly to the charm of the big room.) She was a very old lady, clad in sweeping black, and her ivory pale face reminded Macdonald at once of a Rembrandt portrait in the National Gallery: the finely wrinkled face and filmy dark eyes had the same sombre beauty and dignity.

"It is good of you to come to see us, Mr. Macdonald. My brother and I are greatly distressed over this matter. We cannot help asking ourselves 'Is this just an unhappy accident?' Now will you sit beside me, here—and you do not know our guest: Mr. Walsingham; Mr. Macdonald, Dr. Natzler."

Macdonald turned to face a tall thin fellow of forty to fifty, who studied him with eyes that were at once interested and amused. Walsingham: the name was unknown to Macdonald (apart from historical connections), but the thin shrewd face and lively eyes were somehow familiar.

"Yes, you've probably seen me before," said Walsingham, guessing the unspoken thought. "I was once taken round your department, and I remember you were pointed out to me—it was when you had just tidied up the Rodney Bretton case."

Macdonald had no time to ransack his memory (though he was sure he had never met a man named Walsingham). Sitting facing Sir Walter Vanbrugh, he gave his mind to answering the inevitable question:

"Are you satisfied that Miss Le Vendre's injury was caused by an accident?"

"I can only say that we found no evidence to the contrary,

sir," replied Macdonald. "She was lying where she fell: she had not been robbed: there was no evidence of malicious or maniacal attack. We heard no footsteps and so far as we could tell there was no one in the vicinity. But all these points will be considered by the Vienna police. I think I should make it quite clear that I have no standing in this matter. While I am most willing to answer your questions personally, I am not here as a policeman. Karl Natzler has more standing than I have and his opinion in this case is as authoritative as mine."

"I can only agree with what Macdonald has said," said Karl. "I think Miss Le Vendre was dazed by the lightning and fell backwards when she was standing on the gun-site. There was nothing at all which suggested a struggle, and I imagine she was a strong healthy girl. I looked at her hands and her neck—there was no evidence which suggested she had been attacked."

"I am indeed glad to hear you say that," said Sir Walter. He turned to his sister. "I think you have been worrying unnecessarily, my dear—though it may relieve your mind to tell Mr. Macdonald what bothered you. Neville—Dr. Natzler and Mr. Macdonald must have a drink."

Walsingham, with a twitch of an eyebrow and a gesture of his hand, tacitly inquired what Macdonald would drink: there was an array of most decorative bottles on a table standing in front of the long faint gold curtains.

"Cognac?" murmured Walsingham. "I commend it as being like wisdom—above rubies—or a whisky and soda? or a concoction?"

"Cognac, thanks," said Macdonald. "Neville," he said to himself. "I remember him now: J. B. S. Neville...what was his last book...it went into edition after edition..."

"It seems a foolish story to inflict on you," said Miss Vanbrugh. She still had a beautiful voice, very soft and deep, with a rare quality of clarity, every vowel and consonant exquisitely enunciated. It occurred to Macdonald that her voice had something in common with the brandy which Walsingham (or J. B. S. Neville) had handed him in a balloon glass—both had aroma.

"I was once a very good housekeeper, Mr. Macdonald," she went on. "I have ordered my brother's households in more places than I care to remember, from Peking to Washington and Madrid to Copenhagen—but I fear I let things slip and take the line of least resistance these days: in short, I leave domestic matters to my good Frau Schmidt." She smiled at him, the least twinkle in her dark eyes, and Macdonald realised how beautiful she had once been—and how beautiful she still was in her old age.

"I am ashamed that I should inflict on you anything so banal as domestic troubles: the servant problem in short—the stock-in-trade of the harassed suburban housewife," she went on. "To talk to you, in Vienna of all places, merits a more intelligent choice of subject—but I will try to be brief. Schmidt consults me about the maids we employ here: you will understand that we cannot be casual in this matter, but generally I rely on her judgment. Recently, however, we made a mistake, and engaged a pretty young thing to work in the kitchen—a lovely fair girl named Clara Schwarz. She was frivolous and lazy, and she has been dismissed. But this morning another of the maids, Greta, told Frau Schmidt a rather disturbing story: last night—or last evening—the two girls went for a walk in the Hietzing woods, and Greta says they were attacked by an unknown man." She paused, and Macdonald asked:

"Attacked in what way? Was either of them hurt?"

"No, I gather not, though Greta was very incoherent: she realised they were being followed and said so to Clara, who laughed and turned round to see who was following them. Greta caught sight of a man with a stick in his hand, and as he raised the stick Clara screamed and called to Greta to run. They were both good runners and they got away and ran home. Now that in itself is a foolish little story, Mr. Macdonald. I can well believe that Clara is a type to invite followers, but there is one thing which made me uneasy. Greta says that as they went out, Clara had the effrontery to borrow a coat from the *Garderobe* in the front hall, and the coat which Clara wore last night was Miss Le Vendre's coat—a loose white woollen coat which Miss Le Vendre slips on when she goes out for a walk."

Sir Walter put a word in here. "This baggage, Clara Schwarz, was sent packing this morning, after Greta had told Frau Schmidt about the coat," he said, "but when charged with the offence, Clara denied it utterly. It is one girl's word against another. My sister, of course, was troubled lest Miss Le Vendre were attacked by mistake for Clara. They both have fair hair, and wearing the same coat it is conceivable that such a mistake might be made."

"I see," said Macdonald. "This story puts rather a different complexion on the matter. I take it you have told the Superintendent of Police about it."

"Not yet," said Sir Walter. "My sister was very anxious not to make any statement to the police before she had consulted me."

Miss Vanbrugh laid a wrinkled white hand on Macdonald's sleeve for a moment. It was a moving gesture from one so old and dignified, like an appeal for understanding and sympathy.

"You may well think I am both foolish and timorous, Mr. Macdonald, but I want you to understand my repugnance to calling in the police unnecessarily. We are foreigners here: I have always followed the principle of being scrupulously careful before complaining to the police of a country not my own. In the first instance, I did not wish to trouble the police without good cause: it is all too easy to get English people a name for being suspicious and intolerant, and I feel this particularly in Vienna, for the Austrians are the most friendly of peoples."

"I understand that very well," said Macdonald. "The London divisional police are quick to resent unjustified complaints from the many aliens who live in London. I don't belittle your scruples, I respect them: but I think this matter has gone beyond the merely trivial—and that the Vienna police should now know about this incident."

"Thank you for your understanding," she smiled. "Now how does the position stand? I take into my household a pretty, frivolous, foolish child. Clara Schwarz is not much more than a child. Her work is unsatisfactory and she is dismissed: so far I am justified. But am I justified in bringing her to the notice of the police when I have no more to go on than the report of another young maid, who may have made an accusation out of jealousy of a girl more attractive than herself? The very fact that we are English, and that my brother has held high office in times past, might cause the police to act with greater severity than the circumstances warrant." She held out her frail wrinkled hands in a troubled gesture. "I do not know for certain that pretty, silly Clara is involved in this at all, but if I report her to the police, involved she will be."

Macdonald smiled at her. "Are you not worrying too much, madam, and being over-scrupulous about this 'baggage,' as Sir Walter calls her? Why not trust the discretion of the police? I can only give you my word for it that the police are generally discreet in such matters, and I have no reason to believe that the Vienna police would fall short of the English in their investigations. I do advise you, very strongly, to tell them the whole story."

"Mr. Macdonald is perfectly right, Miss Vanbrugh: the police must be told," put in Walsingham. "They will probably get the truth out of young Greta in a matter of minutes and then deal with Clara. Does she live in Vienna, by the way?"

"No. She came to Vienna to find work, and stayed with a married sister. I think she has gone back to Wiener Neustadt. My good Frau Schmidt will know," replied Miss Vanbrugh. She looked at Walsingham with some severity. "You say the police will get the truth out of Greta: my own fear is that the police will terrify her. I have seen this very thing happen before." She turned to Macdonald. "If I were in London, I should not feel like this, Mr. Macdonald. I wish there were a kindly sensible London police constable here—I have a great regard for our London police." She smiled at him. "You talk German yourself, I am sure."

Macdonald laughed back at her, replying to her underlying thought. "I'm very sorry, madam, but I cannot help you over this. My German was never fluent and I have forgotten most of what I did know, but apart from that, I cannot interfere. Police rules are as exact and punctilious as diplomatic ones."

The old lady sighed. "I knew you would say that—but I regret it. Nevertheless, you did say quite explicitly, both of you and Dr. Karl Natzler, that you thought that Elizabeth Le Vendre was injured in an accident, not by an assailant. With all my heart I hope that that is true, and that she herself will be able to reassure us on that point when she recovers consciousness."

2

Ten minutes later, Macdonald and Karl Natzler were strolling back towards Altzaugasse in company with Neville Walsingham, who had said that he would enjoy a walk. The evening air was sweet and fragrant after the storm, the rain-washed earth and trees giving out a scent which was at once tonic and sensuous.

"I have a certain amount of sympathy with the old lady over this business," said Walsingham abruptly. "There was some wretched story—in Germany, I think—when a young maid employed by the Vanbrughs killed herself rather than face the police when she had been caught stealing—or snooping—or both. The circumstances here are different, of course, but Miss Vanbrugh was immeasurably distressed over the other business."

"That explains her present attitude," said Macdonald. "It occurred to me that there must have been a reason, for common sense dictates that all the facts should be put before the police."

"How thankful she would have been if you and Natzler had undertaken to interrogate Greta, poor old lady," chuckled Walsingham. "An English C.I.D. man on the spot was like an answer to prayer. But it's quite a conundrum, isn't it? Assuming that the blonde baggage did borrow Miss Le Vendre's coat, who is to say whether Clara Schwarz was attacked because she was mistaken for the English girl, or the English girl was attacked because she was mistaken for Clara Schwarz? And believe me, in the gloaming it would have been quite easy to have mistaken one for the other."

"But why should anybody have attacked the English girl?" demanded Karl. "She has only been in Vienna a few days: and I agree with my mother that things like that are not characteristic of Hietzing."

"I can't tell you," said Walsingham, "but I do believe it's true that there is an aftermath of wartime distrust in Vienna. By and large, the Viennese have liked the British, even in conditions of the Occupation, but there is a small minority, especially among the pro-Germans, who hate us. And I think Vanbrugh is a man who has made enemies as well as friends. He's unconsciously arrogant, you know."

"Even though that is all true—and I don't admit it—why attack an English girl from the Vanbrugh establishment?" demanded Karl indignantly.

"Again, I don't know," said Walsingham, and Macdonald put in:

"You may not know, Mr. Walsingham, but it occurs to me that you have some ideas on the subject. If that is so, I hope you'll give the police the benefit of your ideas."

"I haven't anything as definite as ideas, and certainly

nothing that I could tell the police," said Walsingham, "but I sense a tension of sorts between Vanbrugh and some of the Austrians who are ultra nationalists. It's difficult to put into words, and I shouldn't attempt to do so if it weren't that you were here, Macdonald. You know, you're bound to get drawn into this, however rigidly you try to keep outside."

"I don't propose to argue on that point," rejoined Macdonald, "but I should be interested to know what you mean by a tension between the Austrians and Sir Walter Vanbrugh."

"Again, I'm not prepared to give you chapter and verse," said Walsingham, "but I have known Vienna most of my life and I pick up the feelings of people I knew in the long ago. I'm a writer and my friends are mostly in the bookish line. It's known—how, I can't tell you—that Sir Walter is writing his memoirs, and I think that a number of people in Vienna would be happier if his script remained unpublished." He paused, and Macdonald put in:

"All this is no business of mine, whether you are right or wrong in your surmises, but I should be interested to hear if you, in your own mind, connect an accident to Sir Walter's secretary with the apprehensions (of persons unspecified) concerning Sir Walter's memoirs."

Walsingham laughed, quite good humouredly. "Oh, I know my suspicions are nebulous—without form and void as the Scriptures put it—and it's because I do know that, that I should decline to give any opinion to the police even if they asked me to do so. But one can't help being aware that certain results may follow from Miss Le Vendre's unfortunate accident. I think, you know, that she will be sent home to England after she has recovered. Not that she isn't an excellent secretary: I'm told she is very good indeed. But Miss Vanbrugh will plead that she does not care to have responsibility for a young English girl so far away from home: and Sir Walter has got to a stage in what some might call his 'literary labours' when a trustworthy and competent secretary is needed. I'm sure he was a most distinguished diplomat, but as an author he is a fine old muddler. I've seen his script—holograph, with addenda, footnotes and corrections *ad lib*. In short, in the absence of a secretary, the great work will falter: especially as Miss Vanbrugh, who has previously co-operated, finds this work too wearing." Walsingham broke off, and there was a note of amusement again in his voice when he added, "It's a pity that you insist on the formalities of police procedure so firmly, Macdonald. I think there might be a number of points in this problem on which your opinion might be of great value to your Austrian colleagues. And this business of pretty lazy Clara intrigues me quite a lot. She may not have been so foolish as Miss Vanbrugh assumes."

"Well, I admit that you have put forward some fruitful suggestions," said Macdonald, "but I think it not improbable that the Vienna police will envisage all the possibilities which have occurred to you without co-operation from either you or me."

"Even so, they'll never get beyond the façade in the Vanbrugh mansion," said Walsingham. "You would see through it. But to consider the simplest elucidation of this story: Dr. Natzler, what are the chances, in your opinion, that Miss Le Vendre will remember exactly what did happen to her just before she fell off the gun-site?"

"My opinion is of no value," said Karl. "It's not a subject on which there can be any certainty: some concussed patients remember events in detail, some suffer a complete black-out. The most I can say is that I should expect Miss Le Vendre to remember if there were anybody near at hand immediately previous to her accident."

They had reached the gate of the Natzlers' house, and Walsingham bade them good night adding to Macdonald, "I shall hope to see you again while I am in Vienna. Admittedly I may try to cadge some information from you—writers are shameless cadgers of information—but it's just possible that I may be able to reciprocate with a *quid pro quo*."

"That should be very interesting," said Macdonald dryly. "Incidentally, when did you yourself arrive in Vienna?"

"Yesterday; I left London on the same plane as yourself, oddly enough. I don't think we noticed one another—or at least, I didn't notice you. I put in a brief visit to some friends in Zürich and then came on here." He broke off and then asked coolly, "And you maintain that you are in Vienna on holiday, having no ulterior motive?"

"I am on holiday, having no other purpose of any kind," replied Macdonald. "I thought I had made that clear."

"Abundantly clear," chuckled Walsingham. "Well, I respect a man's holidays—so I'll leave you to yours. Nevertheless, I doubt if a specialist of your calibre is any more capable of ignoring detection than a medical man is capable of ignoring diagnosis."

"I leave you to your doubts," retorted Macdonald, "only reminding you that detectives observe professional etiquette as doctors do. In other words, we don't butt in on other men's cases."

Walsingham laughed a little. "Very high-minded. I'm a writer—perhaps not a very high-minded one. I take an interest in anything interesting that comes my way. Good night."

3

Karl Natzler paused in the hall. "What did you make of that chap?" he inquired.

"I didn't like him too much: but he has a capacity for fitting together the bits and pieces he has observed, and I think it's probable that he has more powers of exact observation than you might imagine from his conversation," replied Macdonald. "In fact, I know he has: he's a pretty able writer—J. B. S. Neville. You've probably heard of him."

"I know his name—but what does he write?"

"Travel stuff, generally with a political angle. Between the wars he wrote up his travels in Eastern Europe: in 1945 he published *Wings over the World*—an assessment of aerial attack in the future. His last book dealt with the north polar regions, a medley of exploration, adventure and future air bases on the polar ice cap. It sold in thousands."

"What's he doing in Vienna?" demanded Karl.

"*Ça, se voit*—getting material for yet another book. Perhaps he thinks he's found it. A lot of writers are cashing in on the popularity of the intellectual 'blood.'"

Macdonald paused for a moment before entering the sitting-room. "I was interested in the fact that Walsingham thought out for himself the two possibilities—that Clara Schwarz might have been attacked because she was mistaken for Elizabeth Le Vendre, or vice versa. And he produced a reason of sorts to account for an attack on the latter."

Karl nodded. "Wouldn't it have been more logical to attack Sir Walter himself, though?"

"More logical but less easy," said Macdonald. "Vanbrugh doesn't go for solitary walks in the Hietzing woods, and I expect he's driven to all his appointments, with a chauffeur to see him in and out of the car. He couldn't be got at 'accidentally' in short. If Vanbrugh were attacked there would be an uproar."

"Then you think this man Walsingham may be right in his ideas?"

"I've no means of knowing—and anyway it's not my business," said Macdonald firmly. "The Vienna police don't butt in on my preserves and I'm not poaching on theirs."

VII

1

Neville Walsingham, known the world over under his pseudonym of J. B. S. Neville, had all the qualities which make a successful writer. He wrote admirable prose, lucid, rhythmical, shapely, with a real understanding of words and a capacity to use them in a forcible and original way. Perhaps his outstanding quality was controlled dramatic emphasis: everything he wrote was exciting—and at the same time highly literate. Someone had once said of him: "He's a common denominator between the Royal Society and the twopenny libraries: he embraces brows of all dimensions because he's a natural dramatist." There was, also, inherent in his writing, a sense of detection: like Kipling's famous mongoose, his motto was "Run and find out," and he satisfied his readers not only by facts, tersely and vividly narrated, but by the synthesis which he was capable of developing to make sense of those facts.

Macdonald would have agreed with all these comments; the C.I.D. man had read Neville's books and enjoyed them, but he was aware of a quality underlying them which was less admirable than their prose—a self-assurance on the part of the author which amounted to a defect. Put in the plainest possible way, Neville was conceited, and it was this quality which had made Macdonald very guarded in his response to Neville's advances: the last thing the C.I.D. man desired was to find himself figuring in an unofficial investigation brilliantly described in a Neville bestseller.

Walsingham, for his part, was very much aware of what he called Macdonald's "caginess," and had been considerably irritated by it. The writer had gone out of his way to give Macdonald an opportunity to open up: while it was natural, perhaps, for a Superintendent of the C.I.D. to be cautious while talking to the Vanbrughs, pondered Walsingham, it had surely been unnecessary during their walk through the quiet streets. And it was this irritation which caused Walsingham to formulate an error of judgment.

"Holiday my hat," he said to himself. "He knows perfectly well that there's something damned odd in the offing and he's no intention of letting me in on it."

Walsingham walked back slowly to Trauttmansdorffgasse, and went up to the salon. Miss Vanbrugh had retired to bed, but Sir Walter was sitting over the wood fire, smoking a cigar. He glanced up as the younger man came into the room.

"I'm very troubled over the whole thing, Neville," he said. "My sister is still unwilling to bring those two maids to the notice of the police, and it did seem to me that Superintendent Macdonald was satisfied that accident accounted for that poor child's misfortune. He's an exceedingly nice chap—and I'd trust his judgment in a matter like this."

"A very nice chap," agreed Walsingham, forbearing to point out that Macdonald had urged the Vanbrughs to put all the facts before the Vienna police. "Have you had any further report about Miss Le Vendre?"

"The hospital thinks she is in no danger: there is no fracture, her general condition is good, and they think she may recover consciousness within twenty-four hours. But what a maddening *contre-temps*, Neville. She was exactly the person I wanted—intelligent, diligent, trustworthy, and a most delightful person to work with. Moreover, she really is familiar with the German language and script, and what I would call 'biddable.' I've suffered from a few erudite young men as my secretaries—they all knew better than I did."

"Yes. All very bad luck, sir," agreed Neville, "but if she makes a good recovery—as healthy young people do—is there any reason why she shouldn't resume her work with you?"

"The devil of it is—shall we ever know?" muttered Vanbrugh.

"Know what, sir?" asked Neville, and since there was no answer he went on: "Whether it was accident or assault?"

Sir Walter did not reply immediately, and then he said: "You know this city. It's not so simple as some people like to think. The old intrigues go on." He broke off abruptly. "I'm tired, Neville—and probably talking nonsense. I'll go to bed and think things out afresh in the morning. I'm sorry to be a bad host. There are some journals there you might like to look at, and if you want anything, ring for Josef. He's always around until midnight, and Anthony will be coming in later. He was dining with Sir Charles Bland."

"That's all right, sir," said Neville Walsingham. "Josef and I are old friends. He knows my uncivilised addiction to a pot of strong tea around midnight—so good night and sleep well."

Walsingham waited for some ten minutes after Sir Walter had gone, and then walked slowly through the music-room and paused to glance back at the salon, conscious of the beauty of the graceful rooms. He was deliberately memorising his impressions, knowing that some time he would use them as a background—star-studded arch, ormolu cabinets, the chessmen on the black table-top, the golden-shaded lights gleaming on cut glass, on silver and ivory. He went down the state staircase slowly and touched a bell when he reached the entrance hall: old Josef, solid, solemn and respectful, materialised like a silent apparition from the shadows of an archway.

"Sir Walter has gone to bed, Josef—he's tired. I'm going for a walk, it's a lovely evening now."

"*Bitteschön, Herr,*" murmured the old man. "You have only to ring."

"Thanks." Walsingham looked directly at the old man. "Clara or Greta—which of them told the truth, Josef?"

"Greta," he replied. "Clara should not have come here. I tell you this, Herr—but Frau Schmidt would be angry if she heard me saying it."

"All right. I won't quote you."

Walsingham spoke German easily, using the Austrian idiom, and the old servant smiled at him as he opened the front door and then went ahead to unbolt the complicated "postern" in the double doors which opened on to the street.

Walsingham was conscious of a sense of exhilaration as he strolled along the beautiful silent street, where the trees cast graceful shadows, thrown by the street lamps on to stone and stucco walls and elaboration of iron grille and moulded doorways. He loved foreign cities; the hectic never-ceasing movement and brilliance of Paris, the immense statuesque ancientry of Rome, the contrast of squalor and magnificence of Naples; yet for him Vienna had a charm all its own. It was a civilised city, Walsingham was apt to declare: but he knew also that Vienna of to-day still held the aftermath of its seventeen years' occupation. Seventeen years from the time the Nazis took control in 1938, ten years since the Quadripartite occupation: Germans, Russians, French, British and Americans, they had all been in "occupation." "And Vienna's not finished with them yet," thought Walsingham. "After all, under its gaiety and brilliance Vienna has always been a centre of intrigue: from the Romans to the Holy Roman Empire, Caesars and Hapsburgs, pro-Germans and anti-Germans, pro-Russian and anti-Russian, anyone with a gift for intrigue can make hay in Vienna."

He was rambling on, word-spinning, and he knew it, but the events of the evening had fired his imagination. These quiet dignified streets with their air of security and reticence, and the graceful Hietzing woods, had been the background to an "incident"—and Walsingham used that modern jargon-word in preference to simple "accident." He was in process of developing an idea, as he had so often done before; an idea based on correlating what he had observed, during and since his flight from London in the Viscount. "If he'd been willing to talk, I'd have talked too," thought Walsingham to himself, still resentful of Macdonald's guardedness. "Since he wouldn't talk, he's no reason to complain if I undercut him."

2

Walsingham's stroll was not as purposeless as an onlooker might have imagined: walking diagonally across the quiet streets of Hietzing, he was making for an inn which he remembered well—the Grünekeller—situated just beyond the main streets of Hietzing, in the direction of Hutteldorf. The Grünekeller stood just below the slopes which led up into the woods, and it had acquired a local fame because its owner, Frau Kahlen, had a fine singing voice. There was always music to be heard of an evening in the Grünekeller: a young zither-player made a habit of playing there, and the company in the inn (mellowed by the white wine which was a speciality) would join the zither-player in a chorus which always had quality. Towards the end of the evening, if the fancy took her, Frau Kahlen would stand up and sing herself: sometimes the traditional airs of the Styrian province where she had been born, sometimes Schubert, or Johann Strauss: and after a moment for consideration, the zither-player would improvise a soft accompaniment, never at fault in pitch or rhythm.

Walsingham was never quite sure if it was the quality of the music, the quality of the wine, or the fact that there were one or two outstanding old habituées at the Grünekeller which attracted an unusual clientele there, but he did know that you could count on finding a writer or two, some painters, some amateur politicians and a number of very vocal local characters, not excepting an occasional agitator, whose views were at variance with orthodoxy. Of one thing Walsingham was pretty certain. The story of the English girl's accident in the woods would be known to the habituées of the Grünekeller, and among the opinions expressed over the local wine there was a very fair chance that some interesting facts would emerge—even the truth itself.

The Grünekeller stood in its own garden, a little above the level of the road: lights were shining from its windows, and Walsingham was quick to observe that no cars were parked outside. This was a matter of satisfaction to him, because it implied that those within were local people, or at least Viennese: not foreigners or interested onlookers from the Embassies, who would certainly have come in cars. The sound of the zither, and of men's voices singing softly and tunefully, floated out across the leafy roadway, giving the whole scene a fairy story aspect.

When Walsingham got inside, he found the place was packed: the company sat around well-scrubbed tables, with their glasses or tankards, and a couple of plump red-faced maidservants pushed their way around, refilling glasses and collecting payment. At the far end, the kitchen door stood open, and the heat from the cooking-stoves could be felt right across the room, for supper had been served to those who asked for it. The whole scene was a complete contrast to the interior of an average English pub: more friendly, more domestic, more sedate, as though good music and good wine brought a measure of dignity and picturesqueness into the simple interior.

Walsingham stood against the wall, signalled for a drink,

and studied the faces around the tables, to see if he could recognise anybody he knew. At the end of the table nearest to him he saw a stout dark fellow whom he recognised as a music critic—a man he had met on earlier visits to Vienna— and when the chorus came to an end, he saw a hand raised in greeting.

"Come—Willi is going home, there is a place for you here," said the stout man.

"Boris Schulze," thought Walsingham to himself, remembering the other's name as he pushed his way between the tables and took Willi's vacated chair. Boris greeted the Englishman cheerfully, in a deep rumbling bass.

"And what are you doing in Vienna, my friend?" he asked. "Austria is no longer a problem country: we stand on our own feet, we are a second Switzerland, yes? Do you seek a story in a neutral state?"

"You're the focal point of the musical world again, Boris," said Walsingham cheerfully. "If I can get in touch with old friends, I may yet get a ticket for the reopening of the Opera House."

"Ach—you are an optimist. Half Europe hopes to be at the Opera House. That is not good enough. And as for old friends—the old friend who is your host has been in trouble to-day, I hear."

"And how did you learn that?" asked Walsingham, noting that Boris Schulze knew where he (Walsingham) was staying.

"All the world knows it," rejoined Boris. "A matter of a thunderstorm, I hear. Herr Vogel here knows one of the ambulance men: he knows everybody, does Vogel: he knows the Herr Doktor Natzler. I wouldn't put it beyond him to know the Herr Rittmeister, eh, Vogel?"

A short grey-haired man across the table turned and smiled obsequiously at Schulze, with a little bow: in contrast to most of the rubicund faces around the tables, Vogel's was pallid—damply, unpleasantly pallid. He was curiously colourless, with pale eyes and a long nose which twitched, so that Walsingham was reminded of an albino rat.

"As a man of law, I know the police of our district," he said mildly, "but I have no information I can give to your English friend; I only know that the young English lady was stunned by the thunder and taken to hospital in an ambulance." He turned more directly to Walsingham. "It happens that I drove an ambulance during the war," he said, "and I still know the ambulance unit—I am on the reserve, as you say. If you, sir, are a writer—a journalist, perhaps?—I think there is nothing here to make a story of. Though it was a violent storm. I thought my own house was struck by that first flash, the vibration was so great. You were, perhaps, out in this storm?"

Walsingham became aware of a curious quality in the obsequious voice: curiosity? suggestiveness? something with an undercurrent of unpleasantness. "Had you been at home, in the house, you would doubtless have gone to search for the young lady when she did not return," concluded Vogel.

"I drove up to Leopoldsberg after lunch," said Walsingham, "and I saw the storm break over Vienna—it was quite a spectacle." He returned Vogel's deliberate stare. "As Schulze says, you are well informed, Herr Vogel."

"There is very little information about the matter," rejoined Vogel. "I met Fräulein Brückner as I walked to this inn: it was at her house that Dr. Karl Natzler telephoned for the ambulance and the police, so she heard such details as there were—a most unfortunate accident." He pushed back his chair. "It is time I went home," he said. "I had expected to meet my young guest here—Herr Stratton: but he must have been delayed. He had business in Vienna to-day. I bid you good night, gentlemen."

Vogel got up and pushed his way to the door, and Walsingham became aware that the foregoing conversation had aroused considerable interest among the men who sat at their table. Schulze was smiling to himself and he grinned at Walsingham.

"Vogel is like that: he likes to make mysteries," he said, "while always explaining that there is no mystery at all. I also must be going. Will you stroll back with me, my friend? I go to catch the late train to town."

Walsingham finished his beer and got up, and the zither-player swept his fingers over the strings again, so that the hum of conversation was blurred by the music.

When they were outside, strolling down the shadowy road, Schulze said:

"It is an odd story, my friend. It is surprising how news travels. Did you notice the big fair young fellow at the end of the room? His name is Flüchs. He is a journalist—a reporter. He has collected enough facts to make an interesting story, though I doubt if his paper will ever publish it."

"Look here—I'm puzzled over all this," said Walsingham. "What business is it of Herr Vogel's where I am staying or what I've been doing?"

"Vogel makes everything his business," replied Schulze. "He is what you call a busybody. And don't try to appear too simple, my friend. A story like the accident to Sir Walter

Vanbrugh's secretary is a gift from heaven to those who like mysteries. Now tell me, isn't it true that you came to the Grünekeller this evening because you knew that they would be talking there of this accident?"

"Well, yes. I know it's a place where all the local news is debated," admitted Walsingham.

"And you are right," agreed Schulze, "and if you want to know the facts that were debated, let us wait a moment until Hans Flüchs catches us up. He will be following us—I know he will. You may be able to give him a warning about not being too clever. Myself, I think he is being too 'smart,' as you say in English."

Schulze stood still for a moment and lit a cigarette with deliberation, and Walsingham heard footsteps behind them. Schulze called:

"Hans—is that you? Come and join us. Mr. Walsingham, who is my friend and also a writer, would be interested to hear all those facts you have so industriously collected. Indeed, he may save you from putting a foot wrong. It is still possible for an industrious reporter to make mistakes in Vienna—even though Austria is now a neutral country."

"I do not wish to make any mistakes, nor to offend in any way," said Flüchs. He was a big fellow and he clicked his heels and bowed to Walsingham solemnly, his fair hair shining in the light which streamed out of the inn windows.

"Very correct," chuckled Boris Schulze. "Let us walk on. I will tell Herr Walsingham how all this started, and you shall tell me if I am wrong." They strolled on slowly and Schulze continued:

"Hans here is a reporter, as I said. If there is nothing to

prevent him, he likes to go to Schwechat airport to see who arrives on the B.E.A. plane. Sometimes there is news to be had that way: or, as one might say, the forerunner of news—the comings of important persons, whether in diplomacy or trade—or even the arts."

"That is a journalistic practice," said Hans Flüchs solemnly. "It is quite correct."

"Quite correct," said Schulze. "And last Monday several interesting persons arrived by the B.E.A. plane. Hans will tell us about them."

"There was Sir Charles Bland of the International Chemical Corporation," said Hans Flüchs. "There was Sir Walter Vanbrugh's new English secretary, met by Sir Walter himself. There was a Mr. Stratton, a writer, met by Herr Vogel. There was a high-ranking English police officer of the London C.I.D., met by Dr. Franz Natzler—"

"Here, steady on," put in Walsingham. "Where did you get that idea from?"

"Herr Vogel was told by Herr Webster, who was also on the B.E.A. plane," said Flüchs. "He was able to do him a small service, to help him to get a picture. Herr Webster is a cameraman: he knows the Herr Superintendent of Scotland Yard by sight; and the Herr Superintendent was met at the airport by Dr. Natzler. That I know. Also Herr Stratton, of whom Herr Vogel spoke, was met by Herr Vogel. It is all a very interesting story."

"What is an interesting story?" demanded Walsingham, and Flüchs went on in his careful precise voice:

"That all these people should have arrived in Vienna together, *mein Herr*. There was the young lady, the secretary, staying with Sir Walter Vanbrugh, she who had the unhappy accident: there is the C.I.D. officer, staying with Dr. Natzler, who helps to find the young lady. There is Herr Webster, who knows the C.I.D. officer by sight: there is Sir Charles Bland, who this evening is dining with Herr Anthony Vanbrugh: and there is yourself, Herr Walsingham, who left London on the same B.E.A. plane as the young lady and the C.I.D. officer, and you are staying with Sir Walter Vanbrugh in Hietzing."

"I told you Flüchs was industrious," chuckled Schulze. "See how he has worked to collect all his facts! Hans had German grandparents: the Germans are an industrious race."

"He certainly took a lot of trouble to check up on the B.E.A. passengers," said Walsingham, "but why did he bother about it? What made him think that the passengers on that plane were of such interest?—or was it second sight? Did you prophesy to yourself that there was going to be a story for you, Herr Flüchs?"

"Like any other newspaperman, I always look out for a story," said Hans Flüchs. "There are many stories in Vienna— even though we are now a second Switzerland, as Herr Schulze reminds us."

"Doubtless," said Walsingham dryly, "but I think Schulze was right when he warned you against being too clever. I think you are making a mistake in trying to connect the young lady's accident in the thunderstorm with your researches into the passengers on the B.E.A. plane: and I would give you a piece of advice. It is well for journalists to observe what might be called 'international courtesy.' If visitors come to Vienna on holiday, be they writers or detectives or business magnates, it is better to respect their desire for privacy on their holidays than to publicise them over hastily."

"I understand your meaning, Herr Walsingham," said Flüchs stiffly. "I told you I wished to give no offence: I wish to be very correct. But since you give me advice, I am encouraged to ask one question. Is it not true, Herr Walsingham, that you yourself came to Vienna to investigate a story—a story, one might say, of the writing world, since you are a famous writer?"

"No, it is not true," said Walsingham crisply. "I came to Vienna because I love Vienna, and because I wished to stay here again now that Austria has regained her freedom."

"There you are," said Boris Schulze. "You have been warned, Hans: do not be too clever. Do not be too industrious. Do not, in short, be too Germanic. And this is where I go to catch my train." He turned to Walsingham. "I have been a good friend to you: I have given you a 'close-up.' You now know all that was being said in the Grünekeller. So if, on another occasion, I ask you to get me music and books from London, I feel I shall have earned them."

"Right. Ring me up to-morrow and we'll have a meal together," said Walsingham.

Schulze walked off towards the railway station, and Walsingham turned to Flüchs. "Are you putting in a story for your paper to-night?" he asked.

"No. I have reported the facts of the young lady's accident. For the moment that is enough," said Flüchs. "I may, perhaps, approach those in authority before I go further. I wish you good night, Herr Walsingham."

Walsingham strolled back slowly towards Trauttmans-dorffgasse, sorting things out in his mind. Was there anything in the facts collected by the industrious Flüchs which could not have been collected by a journalist in search of copy, by the usual journalistic channels?

"What's the betting that Hans Flüchs made friends with pretty lazy Clara?" pondered Walsingham, "or even with Miss Le Vendre herself," he added as an afterthought, "and whether any of it has got anything to do with the matter in hand is anybody's guess."

VIII

1

ANTHONY VANBRUGH, SIR WALTER'S NEPHEW, WAS A MAN of fifty. Born into a family of diplomats, he had been in the Foreign Office until 1939. Thereafter, duly commissioned, he had spent the years between 1940 and 1950 in those branches of the Services covered by the generic title "Intelligence," including Field Security in Germany. Later he was drafted into Public Relations of a semi-diplomatic variety, and in 1955 he was attached to the British Mission in Vienna, though the exact nature of his work was known to few. It certainly involved regular appearances at those lunches, dinners, cocktail parties and even tea parties which are a feature of life for Foreign Office attachés stationed in European capitals. When his uncle took the big house in Trauttmansdorffgasse, Anthony Vanbrugh gave up his bachelor flat in the Ringstrasse and enjoyed the more spacious quarters of his uncle's house. He was a mannered, urbane fellow, settling a little too easily into middle-aged comfort, possessed of a large amount of miscellaneous information and an authoritative manner.

Anthony Vanbrugh's dinner to Sir Charles Bland had been one of those "semi-duty" occasions: he had enjoyed a good dinner and good wine, and if Sir Charles Bland had found his host's conversation (and information) less enlightening than he had hoped, Sir Charles was too much of a born diplomat himself to betray the fact.

Anthony Vanbrugh drove himself back from Vienna to Hietzing just before midnight on the evening when Walsingham had visited the Grünekeller. He drove by the route which took him past Schönbrunn Barracks, and just before he turned down the steep hill of the Wattmanngasse he had to brake violently because a van, or converted jeep, cut across his bows in no diplomatic fashion. Mr. Vanbrugh swore: he counted himself a pretty good driver and was easily infuriated by bad driving manners on the part of others. He saw the van (or jeep) go bucketing down the hill under the trees, and wished the driver no good. His wishes looked like being substantiated, because the vehicle in front bounced in a startling lurch, and then swung across the road in a manner which suggested it was out of control. "The damn' fool's drunk," thought Mr. Vanbrugh, taking the hill circumspectly. The thunderstorm of a few hours ago had brought down a lot of leaves, and these were still sodden enough to make the hill skiddy. Vanbrugh had his car well in control, but his attention was distracted by the tail lights of the van careering down the hill in front of him and it wasn't until he was nearly on to it that he saw the body lying in the road. His brakes squealed as he jammed his foot down but the wheels slipped on the wet leaves and then the car skidded sideways a bit, the wheels touching the body.

"Hell," thought Vanbrugh. "That blighter in the van ran this chap down and now I'm left with it, and no witnesses."

He turned on his headlights (he had been driving with spotlights), got out and went to examine the casualty. It was a man's body which lay face down on the road: he was dressed in a good raincoat, lightish in colour, and the wheel-marks of the jeep on the fine gaberdine left no doubt at all that the vehicle had literally run over him. Something about the raincoat and the good brown shoes which stuck out at a fantastic angle, made Vanbrugh think "He's British… that's an English raincoat…"

Then he realised that the skirt of the raincoat was under the front wheels of his own car: the wheel had not gone over the body, but Vanbrugh could not turn the man over or ascertain his injuries until he had backed his car. He touched one arm tentatively, said to himself, "Hope to God he's not dead…he must have been crashed face down… Hell, what a mess. Nobody to help…what do I do now?"

He did what seemed most sensible in the circumstances: got into his car, revved up the engine and succeeded in backing it clear of the body, though the wheels were difficult to control on the skiddy road and he found himself with the car slewed across the road.

"If anything else comes down the hill there'll be another smash," he thought. "I'd better straighten up."

It was as he got his car straightened by the kerb and turned the engine off that he heard footsteps and realised, thankfully enough, that somebody was approaching. "What do I do?

Send them for the police and a doctor?" he thought, as he got out and went forward to the body again, but paused as he realised the pedestrian was running forward towards him—a young man and a powerful-looking one.

"There's been an accident and I need help," called Vanbrugh. "We'd better lift him out of the road."

The newcomer stared, his blue eyes goggling in the reflected glare of the headlights. "*Gott in Himmel*...you've killed him..."

"I didn't kill him: it was the van in front that killed him," snapped Vanbrugh. "Now carefully—I'll take his shoulders—"

"We should not move him. The police will say—" began the other, but Vanbrugh cut in:

"I'm not going to leave his body lying there until the police come. Another car may come down the hill and it's difficult to pull up. Do as you're told."

He spoke with the curt authority of one who has been accustomed to giving orders, and the other obeyed, muttering to himself the while. They lifted the limp heavy body on to the pavement and laid the man on his back. Vanbrugh said:

"Good God... It's Walsingham... Of all the shocking things..."

He bent over the injured man, and the sturdy young Austrian said, "I will go at once for the police and call a doctor."

"Wait a minute," said Vanbrugh. "I know this gentleman: he is a guest in my uncle's house in Trauttmansdorffgasse— Sir Walter Vanbrugh's house. I'm going to lift him into my car and take him home. I'm not going to leave him lying here until the police arrive."

"You should not move him: the police will wish to see him," began the other.

"That's for me to decide," snapped Vanbrugh. "The car's pretty wide: we can get him almost flat if we lay him in the back. Now then—do as you're told. I'm taking responsibility for this... I'll move the car level with him and we'll lift him into the back. It's only a couple of minutes from the house and I can telephone from there—it'll be the quickest way of getting a doctor. He may die if we leave him lying here."

"I think he is already dead," replied the other.

2

"Don't be a damned fool," said Anthony Vanbrugh irritably.

It was not a wise remark to make to any police officer, anywhere: it was a particularly foolish one for a foreigner to make to a Viennese police officer, for the Viennese are still sensitive about being spoken to as though they were inferior beings.

"Gently, Anthony, gently," protested Sir Walter. "Get a hold on yourself."

"I've told the fellow exactly what happened, and he's trying to prove I ran Walsingham down," said Anthony indignantly.

"It is very difficult," said the police officer, and Sir Walter had enough common sense to see that difficulties existed.

By the time the doctor and the police had arrived in Trauttmansdorffgasse, Walsingham was dead. His body showed multiple injuries, but the obvious cause of death was a broken skull.

"I tell you that when that van hit him, it was travelling at over fifty miles an hour: it crashed him down and bumped over his body," declared Anthony Vanbrugh. But when the police officer asked his precise questions, Anthony found it difficult to give precise answers.

"Did you see deceased cross the road?" asked the policeman, "and if so, was he crossing towards Trauttmansdorffgasse or walking away from it?"

Actually, Anthony Vanbrugh had not seen Walsingham cross the road at all: he had seen the van (or adapted jeep) bounce over an obstacle and swerve violently, and had assumed the rest. Like many people who have not been accustomed to being interrogated, he was a very bad witness; he had formed his own conclusions and became irritated by the impartiality of a police officer who would not accept another man's conclusions. Neither could he give any useful description of the vehicle which had done the damage: it might have been a van with a canvas hood: it might have been an old jeep, adapted as a van. He could not give its number. "I tell you it cut across me travelling much too fast," he said. "I had my work cut out to avoid a smash. I saw it go bucketing down the hill and I thought it would capsize before it reached the bottom. The driver must have been drunk."

3

The pedestrian who (unwillingly) had helped Anthony Vanbrugh to move Walsingham's body was Hans Flüchs, the journalist. He, at least, was a very good witness. He told how he had seen Walsingham at the Grünekeller earlier in the evening and parted with him and Boris Schulze in the Hietzinger Hauptstrasse at eleven o'clock. Flüchs had then walked up to see a friend in the Rosengasse, to borrow a book, and he was walking back to his flat in Penzingergasse when he had first seen Anthony Vanbrugh's car.

"I saw it was a big American car," he said. "The headlights had just been turned on—I saw the lights come on. The car was half across the road, as though it had skidded. The driver roared his engine and backed a little. I said to myself 'There has been an accident' and I began to run."

"What made you think there had been an accident?" asked the careful policeman.

"It was the way the car was placed when I first saw it," replied Hans. "No driver would get his car in such a position unless something strange had occurred. Then, as I ran, the driver reversed a few yards back up the hill and I saw the body lying in the road. I thought 'He has killed a man.' Indeed, I still think so," he added. "I saw no other vehicle, I heard no other vehicle: I saw the big car back away from the body and the body was partly under the car before it backed. I said to myself 'He is going to drive on and leave this man he has killed'— that was why I ran, to let the driver see there was a witness." After which, Hans Flüchs explained that it was owing to Mr. Anthony Vanbrugh's insistence that the body had been moved. "I told him that nothing should be moved," he said. "I know the police rules, Herr Inspector. I knew it was not in order. I said I would go and fetch the police, but Herr Vanbrugh would not have it. 'He may die if we leave him lying here,' he said, though I told him the man was dead already. It was not easy to argue with Herr Vanbrugh, and I thought 'I will go in the car with him that I may give my evidence when the police come. If I do not go with him, who knows what may happen—and it might be his word against mine if our evidence is not the same.'"

The police inspector grunted. He was incensed with Anthony Vanbrugh, who had called him a damned fool: he was incensed that police regulations had been set at nought and he had got an idea into his head that these English "High Ups" were taking the law into their own hands. He fixed Hans Flüchs with a stern eye.

"You have given your evidence, the facts of the situation," he said. "You can now tell me, in confidence, the impressions you formed."

Flüchs was truthful and honest, and it was not his fault if the impressions he had formed were misleading. "I heard no other vehicle: I saw no other vehicle," he repeated. "To me, it looked as though the big car had just run the man down, and that the driver was backing away from the body so that he could get past, only when he saw me he changed his mind."

4

Hans Flüchs was allowed to go home. Inquiries were set on foot to find out if anybody had seen a van with a canvas cover (or a jeep) approach or leave the Wattmanngasse. Anthony Vanbrugh accompanied the police back to the scene of the accident to show them where he had first braked when he saw the van and where he had braked when he saw the body—and then it began to rain again: not thunder rain, but steady determined rain which washed away brake-marks and skid-marks and fallen leaves. Anthony was now in a very bad temper: he was sorry enough about Walsingham's death, but he was furious that his own statements were subject to question.

"I've told you what happened," he said. "It's your business to find that van driver—and if the driver wasn't drunk I shall be surprised. You've got all the proof you need, the marks of the van wheels on Walsingham's raincoat."

"There are also the marks of your own wheels," replied the inspector—and this was true. By the time the gaberdine raincoat was spread out, the marks of Vanbrugh's tyres showed very distinctly, together with the mud and sodden leaves left by the original impact.

By the time the police left, Anthony Vanbrugh was in a state of unreasonable fury. He went up the state staircase only too anxious to go to bed and forget his troubles, but he found his uncle waiting up for him, sitting under one of the shaded lights beside the chessmen in the salon.

"I am sorry, Uncle. It's a wretched business," said the nephew. "It was sheer manslaughter, nothing else. I saw what happened and that damned inspector can't recognise the truth when he hears it. I think I'll have a drink. I need it."

He went and poured himself a good tot of whisky and then added, "We shall have to let Walsingham's people know—next-of-kin, whoever it is." He paused, and then asked, "Is he married?"

"I don't know. I know very little about him, except as a writer," said Sir Walter unhappily.

"But you asked him to stay here," said Anthony.

"Yes. I met him in London when I was there in the spring," said Sir Walter. "Northington gave me lunch at his club and Neville Walsingham was also a guest. I had been discussing my own book with Northington, particularly those chapters dealing with the Anschluss period, and Northington said that Walsingham was remarkably well informed about certain facts, and that, as a writer, he might be able to give me some useful advice. At the end of luncheon, I invited Walsingham to dine with me. I found him intelligent and perceptive, and he was most generous in offering help and advice about my own memoirs—and not all distinguished professional writers are so generous. Eventually I invited him to stay here if he were passing through Vienna—and I was very happy to have him. He was able to give me a lot of help—as a writer, that is."

The old man's voice was very weary, but he went on: "Neville always wrote to me from his publishers—Bennet & Walbrook. I don't even know if he has a fixed address in London. I will telephone to Bennet & Walbrook as early as seems reasonable in the morning."

Anthony Vanbrugh put his glass down.

"Speaking frankly, it looks a fair-sized mess," he said, and then added, "I don't want to distress you, Uncle, but we might as well think out all the implications. Walsingham was, as you say, very well informed about a period which most Austrians are anxious to forget. For all we know, he may have come to Vienna to rout out a few more facts. Did he give you any reason for this visit?"

"He came to revisit Vienna, a city for which he had a great liking," replied Sir Walter coldly, "and I had invited him to stay with me."

"Don't think I'm being offensive," said Anthony, "but I can't help remembering that that police inspector was quite anxious to involve me in this story—as though it would have suited him very well if he could prove that I had knocked Walsingham down."

"Rubbish!" said Sir Walter, and there was an indignant light in his weary eyes. "The thing is distressing enough as it is, Anthony, without you making unjustified implications. It was the inspector's duty to get all the available evidence, and while I have every sympathy with the course you took, the fact that the body was moved made it more difficult for the police. And there is the additional fact that that poor child was injured in the thunderstorm. I am not suggesting for a moment that there is any connection between these unhappy incidents, but perhaps it is not unnatural for an Austrian police inspector to take a different view—to assume too easily that something sinister has been occurring in a foreigner's household."

"Yes. The whole thing's a wretched business for you, Uncle—but that doesn't justify the inspector's manner to me," replied the other. "In any case, there's something about these two accidents I don't like."

"Do you suppose I like it?" said Sir Walter wearily, "but the one thing I beg is that you will not start making wild assumptions. You have said that a van passed you at excessive speed: you saw the van going down the hill and you saw it swerve and bump over an obstacle—in other words you saw it run over Walsingham. You say that owing to the wet leaves it was difficult to brake on the hill: the answer to all that seems plain— the van driver couldn't check his vehicle in time to avoid an accident. But I refuse to admit that because we have had two accidents in one day to inmates of this house that there is of necessity any connection between those accidents."

Anthony Vanbrugh poured himself another drink and took his time over it. Then he said, "Look here, I'm sorry, Uncle. If I've been talking unguardedly, it was because I was livid over the inspector's attitude. He seemed to me to be unnecessarily aggressive. But leave that for the moment. What has been actually happening we're not in a position to know at the moment, but credit me with enough common sense not to make sensational suggestions to the police. I've said whatever came into my mind to you. I shan't say it to anybody else."

"All right, all right," said the old man. "These things have got to be investigated, we both know that—and to my mind the problem will have to be dealt with on a higher level than the local police. You heard me mention that there's a Scotland Yard Superintendent staying with Dr. Natzler—Macdonald. He was round here this evening, because it was he and young Natzler who found Elizabeth Le Vendre up in the woods. Macdonald made it very clear that he was in Vienna in his private capacity, on holiday. But I don't think he will maintain his refusal to act after this second...accident. Two British subjects are involved. I think the formalities can be arranged— it's not an unknown thing for English police to co-operate in a foreign capital. And I can think of nobody I would be more glad to have in this investigation than Macdonald."

"Well, that's the best piece of news that's emerged yet," said Anthony. "I only wish you'd got hold of him at once: he could have kept that local inspector on the rails. What about ringing Macdonald up?"

"You know as well as I know that we can't do things like that," said Sir Walter. "This isn't a case of asking a London

C.I.D. man to act for us, in a friendly capacity. The thing's got to go through the proper channels, so that the investigation will be an official one, with full recognition from the Police Commissioners in both capitals. And get this quite clear, Anthony: you won't get any preferential treatment from a man like Macdonald. He will be entirely impartial—and rightly so."

"I'm not asking for preferential treatment," grunted Anthony, "all I want is fair play."

Sir Walter raised his fine eyebrows but forbore to comment on this one: he had never had a very high opinion of his nephew's intelligence despite Anthony's successful career in "Intelligence."

After Anthony Vanbrugh had gone to bed, Sir Walter sat down at the telephone. There are some advantages in putting through long-distance telephone calls in the small hours— provided the person or department you are calling can be relied on to answer. Sir Walter Vanbrugh knew that he would be given a clear line if he asked for it and at that hour speaking to London from Vienna was as easy as speaking from Vienna to Hietzing. It was only a few minutes before he got his number—London, Abbey XIXI.

"Is that you, James? Walter Vanbrugh here. I wouldn't have called you at this hour without adequate reason, but there's trouble this end which needs looking into. I'll tell you the facts as briefly as I can."

It was about three minutes later that James grunted, "I've got all that: very troublesome for you. What can I do about it?"

"Put the facts before the Commissioner, James. You know him, I don't. It happens that there's one of his Superintendents here, staying in Vienna, on holiday. I hate to interfere with a man's holiday, but his leave can be extended later..."

While Robert Macdonald slept the sleep of the just on the good Viennese bed in Altzaugasse, the telephone service in London and Vienna disposed of his well-earned holiday. As the authorities said, "His leave can be extended later..."

Macdonald was not a victim of telepathy. He slept on, untroubled. It was not until eight o'clock in the morning that the Commissioner's Office in London called him—and then it was Ilse Natzler who uttered most of the complaints.

IX

1

"Superintendent Macdonald? Albrecht Nauheim; Chief Inspector, Vienna City Police. I feel very ashamed to trouble you while you're on leave, sir."

Standing in Franz Natzler's small study, Macdonald looked at Chief Inspector Nauheim with some surprise: he did not look English: his dark eyes were too lively, his skin too olive toned, his lips too mobile, his build too lissome—but his voice and accent might have come from a young inspector of the Metropolitan Police.

"No, sir. I'm not English, I'm Austrian," said Nauheim, responding to the unspoken thought, "but I was brought up by an English aunt and she taught me her language from the cradle, so to speak. Our Commissioner thought I might be of use to you as an interpreter."

Macdonald laughed. "You certainly will. I've hardly got enough German to be ashamed of. Very decent of you to come out here to see me—I was just going to drive in to your H.Q."

"Well, sir, the problem's centred here in Hietzing, at the outset, anyway. Can I give you the latest facts? I gather you were only involved in the first part of the story."

Nauheim gave a brief account of Walsingham's death, as described by Anthony Vanbrugh, and an equally terse résumé of the evidence given by Hans Flüchs. As Macdonald listened, he was able to sum up this English-speaking Chief Inspector of the Vienna police: Nauheim was certainly young—probably under thirty—but his ability was plain to Macdonald. He was pretty sure that Nauheim had been sent as liaison officer in this case not only because he spoke English like his own language but because he was an outstandingly able young officer. At the close of Nauheim's narrative Macdonald said:

"I should be interested to know your own opinion of those two statements—off the record."

Nauheim flashed him a smile—and became at once Viennese: his face was more mobile, his changes of expression more sudden than those of an Englishman.

"Well, sir, it isn't an easy question to answer—and I think you'll understand what I mean when I say my opinion is swinging like the pointer on a balance before the weights are equalised. At first I accepted that Mr. Vanbrugh spoke the exact truth as far as he saw it—which wasn't very far, because he's unobservant and tends to think he saw what he expected to see. I take it as axiomatic that an Englishman of his upbringing and status does generally speak the truth—he's never had to do otherwise. It's not only principle—it's profit. Telling the truth pays bigger dividends in England than in some places I know."

It was Macdonald's turn to chuckle. "All right. I know what you mean—or I understand what you mean."

"Perhaps I can explain that more fully later," said Nauheim. "All my experience of Englishmen in authority tended to make me think 'He's a bad witness but he's giving us the facts as he thinks he saw them.' And then I said to myself, 'This man Walsingham was probably murdered'—and in a murder case a detective can't afford the luxury of assuming that any witness is speaking the truth, even an Englishman with a background like Vanbrugh's."

"I quite agree," said Macdonald, and saw a flicker of relief on Nauheim's expressive face. "Look here," went on Macdonald. "If you and I are going to co-operate, let's get this clear. I hold that no persons, no matter what their birth or status, can claim privilege in a criminal investigation: if I add nationality, I am not going to assume that because a man is British he will therefore tell the truth—and vice versa, but I think I might add this. I should expect Anthony Vanbrugh to tell the truth: if it's proved that he doesn't, the implications would be pretty serious."

"Thank you for that," said Nauheim. "Now, about Flüchs. He's a good witness, and he knows the difference between a fact and an opinion. He gave an exact description of what he saw and then added, 'I thought the big car had knocked the man down and the driver meant to drive on and leave the body, until he saw there was a witness.' And in my opinion, Flüchs was telling the truth—also as far as he saw it."

"Now let's get back to your own statement, 'I think Walsingham was probably murdered,'" said Macdonald. "Why do you think so?"

"When he was asked the question point-blank, Mr. Vanbrugh could not say that he saw a pedestrian crossing the road," said Nauheim. "What he actually did see was a van bumping over an obstacle and then skidding across the road. My own belief is that Walsingham was lying in the road before the van approached and that he was not crossing the road. The marks on his coat suggest that the van ran over him rather than knocked him down—but you will be using your own judgment about that."

"You are satisfied that another vehicle was involved?"

"Yes: I think he was hit by another vehicle at some stage. If the body hadn't been moved it would have been much easier to have seen what happened: when Vanbrugh and Flüchs lifted the body on to the path, they laid him on his back in the puddles and the coat got soaked. It is now very difficult to say from the traces exactly what happened—and when it happened. It was Mr. Vanbrugh who insisted on moving the body, though he could have ascertained for himself the man was dead."

"It's hard to blame him for moving the body," said Macdonald. "It goes against the grain to leave a chap lying in the road—but the result certainly confused the evidence. What are the chances of getting a line on the other vehicle?"

Nauheim shrugged his shoulders. "We are trying, but the chances are not good. A van or a converted jeep—no number, nothing to distinguish it by."

Macdonald nodded: he realised without being told that Anthony Vanbrugh had not endeared himself to the local police. "Before we go any further, would you like to sum up your impressions?" he asked.

Nauheim replied, "I'd like to state what seems to me to be the outstanding facts, sir. There were two 'accidents' in one day: both occurred in Hietzing, a neighbourhood generally free from crimes of violence. Both victims were English, both were staying in Sir Walter Vanbrugh's house. Neither victim was robbed: Mr. Walsingham's purse, passport and note-case were still in his pockets. Of the two victims, one was secretary to Sir Walter, who is known to be working on his memoirs; one was a well-known writer, who may have been giving advice to Sir Walter on the same subject. When Mr. Walsingham was at the Grünekeller he was trying to get any comments he could on the first accident. One feels that the two accidents must be connected in some way—and that the problem involves the English as much as the Austrians."

"I think that's very moderately put," said Macdonald. "I might add, for your information, that the victims of both accidents left London on the same B.E.A. plane last Monday, the plane on which I travelled myself, though Walsingham left the plane at Zürich and came on to Vienna later."

Nauheim looked at Macdonald thoughtfully: "You yourself would make a very good and interesting suspect, sir," and Macdonald replied:

"You're perfectly right, I should. I talked to Miss Le Vendre at Zürich, I followed up the acquaintance by talking to her in the Schönbrunn gardens, and I went out with Karl Natzler and found her unconscious in a place in the woods which I had described to her myself. I'm just the sort of person you're looking for—the obvious suspect."

"And you concealed from the Herr Rittmeister Brunnerhausen that you were an officer of the London

C.I.D.," grinned Nauheim. "Brunnerhausen is very much hurt."

"Sorry about that: I'll see him and apologise," said Macdonald. "If you had been in London on holiday you would probably have done just what I did. However, now we're working together we'd better determine the best way we can correlate activities. Now you are obviously better equipped to deal with the local inquiries."

Nauheim nodded. "The van—or jeep—mentioned by Mr. Vanbrugh: the activities of Mr. Walsingham between eleven o'clock (when Flüchs and Schulze left him) and midnight: the activities of Flüchs and Schulze in the same period: persons in the Hietzing Woods when the storm was coming up: the identity of the cameraman who evaded Brunnerhausen when he was talking to you."

"Ah, he hasn't been traced then," observed Macdonald. "My own guess is that that cameraman is named Webster, and that he also came to Vienna on the B.E.A. plane on Monday."

"What did he come for?" asked Nauheim promptly.

"What did any of them come for?" asked Macdonald. "I suggest that I make it my business to follow up my fellow-countrymen and to find out exactly what brought them to Vienna and what they have been doing since they arrived: that holds for other passengers in the plane in addition to those already brought to our notice." He paused for a moment and then asked, "Have you seen Sir Walter Vanbrugh and his sister yet?"

"No, sir. I thought it too early to disturb them, especially after the troubles of last night. Also I think it probable that they will talk to you more freely than they would to me."

"I'll make them my first job," said Macdonald. "If I'd been gifted with second sight I should have tackled this problem last night. This is one of the occasions when a laudable desire not to interfere has contradicted its own intentions. Walsingham wanted to talk to me last night. If I'd encouraged him to do so, he would probably be alive now."

"You think he was killed because he knew too much?"

"More likely because he tried to find out what he didn't know," replied Macdonald. "Now to get the preliminaries settled: will you deal with the airport authorities at Schwechat: ascertain the names of all arrivals on the B.E.A. plane on Monday and their present domiciles as far as is known, as well as checking later arrivals? I will check with London airport. And I think it would be a good thing if you saw Dr. Natzler and his son while you are here. They have both got some information which may be germane to the case. I will see Sir Walter and his sister and also get in touch with Sir Charles Bland. He was going back to London by the midday plane to-day, but he may be willing to stay on if we ask him to do so."

"Very good, sir." Nauheim hesitated a moment and then said, "This case is going to have repercussions—to cause a lot of trouble among important persons, mainly because I told you that, in my judgment, Mr. Walsingham was probably murdered."

"And you may have been mistaken," said Macdonald. "There is a possibility that Mr. Anthony Vanbrugh was right, and Walsingham was killed by a drunken driver who lost control of his vehicle on the Wattmanngasse, and that Miss Le Vendre fell backwards down the steps of the gun emplacement during the thunderstorm. I admit those possibilities.

Last night I let the accident theory have the benefit of the doubt and I blame myself for doing so. It's not going to happen again. So whether we are right or wrong, we are going to cause a lot of trouble to a lot of important people: make a nuisance of ourselves, in short."

Albrecht Nauheim chuckled and Macdonald added, "I don't often make forecasts, but I rather hope that somebody may think it worth their while to put paid to me: in which case things may be expedited considerably. Go and talk to Dr. Natzler: I think you'll find him illuminating."

2

Macdonald's first action was to telephone to Sir Charles Bland. He gave a brief report on the events of the past eighteen hours and then went on:

"I should like to confer with you, sir. Would it be possible for you to put off your return to London? I would have come to see you immediately, but other matters must come first."

"That's for you to decide," said Bland. "In the light of what has occurred I will stay on in Vienna while you need me."

"Thank you, sir. And don't take it amiss if I suggest that you stay indoors. Somebody has already given hostages to fortune, if I may put it that way."

"I see. I was going to suggest that I come out to Hietzing to see the Vanbrughs—and yourself."

"Don't do that, sir. We don't want any more traffic accidents," replied Macdonald dryly.

Macdonald's next call was to one of his own colleagues Chief Inspector Peter Reeves, in London. Having given him certain instructions, Macdonald added, "It's an ill wind that blows nobody any good, Pete. You've never seen Vienna: this may be your chance. Report to me this evening—Vienna 72577—around eight o'clock. If I'm not in then, I'll ring you at home later."

After that, having reported his intentions to Vienna headquarters and received an assurance that a police interpreter would await him in Hietzing, Macdonald set out for Trauttmansdorffgasse.

Rather to his relief, he was not led again up the state staircase: old Josef led him into a study on the ground floor, where Sir Walter sat at a desk against a background of books. The old man's face looked bleached and weary and Macdonald said at once:

"I'm very sorry you are having all this distress, sir. If I hadn't stood on ceremony last night, I might have saved you some of it—but it's easy to be wise after the event."

"I'm glad to have you here, Superintendent. As you probably know, I rang through to London and asked the Commissioner for your co-operation. I don't want to show lack of confidence in the Austrian police, but I do feel that their attitude towards my nephew is preposterous. If they do not go so far as to accuse him of running Neville Walsingham down, it is plain that they consider it as a possibility."

"All impartial and competent policemen, of all nationalities, have to envisage every possibility," said Macdonald quietly. "In this matter the police have to envisage three possibilities: the first is that Walsingham was knocked down and killed by the van your nephew saw: the second is that he was killed by Mr. Vanbrugh's car: the third is that he was killed by neither of those vehicles, but was killed a few minutes earlier and his body left lying in the road in the hope that a car *would* run over him."

"But *why*?" cried Sir Walter, "why on earth make such a far-fetched assumption?"

"It isn't an assumption, sir. It is a possibility, and the evidence for it is being carefully considered. And because the possibility exists, it is my duty to ask you to tell me the reason for Mr. Walsingham's presence in Vienna."

Sir Walter Vanbrugh sat and considered for a moment; then he said, "I could give you a very simple answer to that question, Superintendent. Walsingham came to Vienna to stay with me as my guest, because I had invited him to stay here, at any time convenient to him. He had been helpful to me in London, giving me advice about my book—the sort of advice that an experienced writer can give to an inexperienced one—and I was anxious to repay his generosity."

Macdonald waited for a moment before he replied. Then he said, "You used the word 'could,' sir."

"Yes. I used it advisedly. The answer I have given you is true as far as it goes. Walsingham wrote to me some ten days ago, saying he would like to revisit Vienna—he had known it for years—and asking if it would be a convenient time to take advantage of my invitation. I wired back at once, saying we should be happy to have him here. But as to *why* he came, I can only tell you that I do not know."

"Do you think he had any ulterior motive, sir—apart from enjoying a holiday?"

"I should say that it is very probable. To my mind, Walsingham is not the type of man to travel thus far, and to stay with elderly people who can offer him little in the way of amusement, unless he has some underlying reason. But what the reason was he did not divulge. He had only been in this house since the day before yesterday, you must remember."

"When Mr. Walsingham walked home with Karl Natzler and myself, he suggested that he might be able to offer me some information if I would reciprocate—or words to that effect," said Macdonald, and Sir Walter nodded.

"Yes. I can well believe he might have expressed himself thus: and I can also well believe that he came to stay here in Vienna because he thought I could give him some information which he needed. But as to what he wanted to know, I have no idea. Neither am I prepared to believe that it was his desire for information which led to his death: the idea seems to me out of all proportion."

"Well, let us leave that for the moment, sir, and return to Miss Le Vendre's accident. What was the nature of the work she had begun for you?"

Sir Walter gave a sudden movement of impatience. "I cannot believe that a man of your intelligence would imagine that a young girl, newly arrived in my household, would be entrusted with information coming under the head of 'Top Secret,'" he said. "Such an idea pertains to the romantic novel. There was nothing in the work she was doing that was of the remotest interest to anybody beyond my own family. She was typing my original notes on family origins, on my childhood and upbringing. In addition she was translating and transcribing personal letters written in German by members of my own family who were brought up in Germany. The only papers she had access to were personal papers—the sort of collection which any writer of a biography works through in order to sift out a few picturesque recollections of a by-gone era. To assume that her work here could have in any way instigated violence is absurd."

"Did she have any conversation with Mr. Walsingham?"

"She met him at dinner the night before last. The conversation turned mainly on travels in Europe—all of a quite trivial nature, though the child talked charmingly enough of her wanderings in Germany, in the Black Forest and the Rhineland, and Walsingham reciprocated with anecdotes of his own youth—he was a student at Heidelberg University in the mid-twenties. He was out to luncheon yesterday, so they did not meet again."

"Do you know where he went yesterday?"

"He took the small car and drove into Vienna: I gathered he went to see the publisher who has translation rights in Walsingham's last book. After lunch he drove up to Leopoldsberg—as all visitors do."

"Well, sir, I won't trouble you with any further questions now," said Macdonald. "I should like to look through Mr. Walsingham's baggage, and to see Mr. Anthony Vanbrugh when he comes down. And I think you will agree that the story told by the two maids—Clara and Greta—must be given to the local police. That is their business, not mine. In any case, I should be of no value as an interrogator: my German is quite inadequate."

"Yes, yes: I realise I made a mistake in deferring to my sister's wishes over that," said Sir Walter sadly, "but I should like to stress one point. My nephew, Anthony, was very misguided in his attitude to the local police: he put their backs up. But they—the police—will be even more misguided if they assume he was not telling the exact truth."

"Perhaps the trouble there is that Mr. Vanbrugh is not accustomed to giving evidence or to being interrogated," said Macdonald. "He is more used to interrogating others and the two experiences aren't identical. One of the advantages of a policeman's training is that he has to give evidence, and, if necessary, stand up to cross-examination on it. There is one question I might usefully ask here: was Mr. Anthony Vanbrugh previously acquainted with Mr. Walsingham?"

"No. They had not met until Walsingham came to this house. Neither did they show any interest in each other—their interests are quite dissimilar. Oh, I know what you're going to say," added Sir Walter. "Neville Walsingham's researches into European problems might well have come to the notice of Anthony's department, but Anthony is not interested in a writer's world. The two were naturally bored with each other." He pushed his chair back, adding: "You have asked to see Walsingham's baggage. I will take you up to his room. The local police have already examined it, but found nothing to interest them, I gather. The key of his room has been left here with me."

3

Neville Walsingham had only brought one suit-case with him—one of the light-weight cases manufactured for air travel. It was empty, and his belongings were neatly put away in wardrobe and chest. There was an evening suit (dinner-jacket), a dark lounge suit, underwear, shoes, ties, pyjamas and washing kit. A zipped-up writing-case held writing-paper and an unused note-book: a wallet held Travellers' cheques, an English cheque-book and English currency notes. It was a new wallet, practically unworn, and Macdonald guessed that the dead man had carried another wallet in his pocket. The only books (apart from a selection on the bedside table which obviously belonged to the Vanbrughs) were two Penguins— detective novels—and a copy of Cocteau's *La Machine Infernale*. Macdonald knew that passport and money had been found in Walsingham's pockets, but Nauheim had not mentioned any diary or note-book. "If those weren't on him, it's pretty sure proof that somebody had been at his pockets," thought Macdonald. "No man travels without something in the nature of a note-book or diary or address book. And very few men refrain from stuffing old letters in their pockets. Well, I'd better have a word with Anthony Vanbrugh and then go and consider Walsingham's remains. It's a case of 'Back to the Army again, Sergeant, back to the Army again.'"

X

1

Mr. Ernest Henry Webster, described on his passport as a professional photographer, had not the good fortune to stay in the gracious quarter of Hietzing, near to the
Schönbrunn Palace and the wooded hills, when he came to
Vienna. Not that this troubled him: Mr. Webster was not, as
he himself put it, "choosey." He considered that he was very
fortunate to be given hospitality in Vienna at all, hotels cost-
ing what they do. "If it hadn't been for Auntie, I shouldn't
have risked coming," he said. Ernest Henry Webster was a
gregarious soul: he liked talking and he talked to anybody he
could find who spoke English—and a surprising number of
Viennese had picked up some English during the Occupation.

"Auntie's an old inhabitant," said Mr. Webster. "Came to
Vienna in 1905—and that's a long time ago, that is, even to a
middle-aged chap like me."

"Auntie," known as Fräulein Braun, was known to a

number of charitably minded English persons in Vienna: she
was a survival of a once well-known type—the private governess. She had come to Vienna in 1905, at the age of twenty,
as English governess to a prosperous family of Viennese
bankers, and she had stayed in Austria ever since. During the
troubled days of the First World War she had accompanied
her original employer to a country refuge in Carinthia, where
she had spent the next ten years, teaching English to another
generation of young Rothmeisters and helping to run a house
where poverty had superseded wealth. Undoubtedly Auntie
(her real name was Elsie Brown) had shown the qualities of
devotion and faithfulness which did distinguish the English
governess of long ago, and she had returned to Vienna with her
original mistress in 1930 and had cared for Frau Rothmeister
until the latter's death in 1940. "Fräulein Braun," a poor and
prematurely aged spinster, had been ignored under the Nazi
régime—there were many ageing Englishwomen of her type
in Vienna, too humble to attract retaliation for their nationality. She was left a small bequest by the Rothmeister family,
who installed her in a two-roomed flat not far from the West
Bahnhof. During the rest of the Second World War she had
let one of her precious rooms (house room was at a premium
in Vienna) to an Austrian bank clerk and his wife who "collab-
orated." When the war came to an end and the Occupation
began, she had once again let her room. It was not until 1955
that she had found herself in possession of two rooms again.
Then, having established contact with her English relatives
again, she had invited her unknown nephew—Ernest Henry
(son of her married sister), to visit her in Vienna. Fräulein
Braun was very poor: she had survived because she had a

room to let, and since the Occupation the charitable English and American families resident in Vienna had helped to keep her in food and firing. Small blame to her if she thought her English nephew might do something to assist her—and so Ernest Henry Webster came to Vienna "to look up Auntie," occupied her spare room, and not ungenerously spent his Travellers' Allowance in buying her some much needed comforts. In a poor house in a poor street, Webster attracted very little attention: it was a crowded neighbourhood and the Viennese had become accustomed to the English—and French and Americans—in their midst. If he had wished, Ernest Henry Webster could have stayed on there unnoticed, for he had a trick of taking colour from his environment and becoming one of a crowd in a crowded quarter, and he could pass the time of day and say a few phrases in very passable German.

2

On the Friday morning after Walsingham's death, Mr. Webster set out for Schönbrunn Palace. He was a very skilful photographer, and he had in mind a possible sale for a series of unusual photographs of Vienna. Whatever artistry he was capable of expressed itself in the ability to "see a picture" through the medium of his viewfinder. He had already spent several days in the heart of the city, getting pictures of people as well as streets and buildings: the old market women, the children who played in the parks, the professors who came and went in the University. Now he had decided to concentrate on Schönbrunn, the gardens, the fountain, the

Tiergarten and the Gloriette. The arches of the Gloriette, mirrored in the still waters of the pool, attracted him particularly. "They ought to use it for a film," he thought, "ballet, maybe… there's something about it…"

He took a tram out to Hietzing and strolled across to the Schönbrunn entrance. It was a beautiful day after a night of rain, and Mr. Webster walked slowly round, studying the vistas between the avenues of clipped trees and keeping an eye open for interesting types. After a while he climbed slowly up the paths which led to the Gloriette, noting the play of sunlight and shadow on the open arches and under the colonnade, and the great imperial eagle which crowned the central pediment. He took a number of shots, concentrating on his work, before he strolled to the path by the pool and looked back to the palace, away down below. A young man was sitting on a bench just below the Gloriette, reading in the sunshine, and Mr. Webster, conscious of a picture, turned his camera towards the solitary figure.

"A student," hazarded the cameraman, and from habit his mind formulated a caption for the shot. "Young Austria… studying history in the grounds of the Hapsburg Palace."

Then, as the young man turned to look at him, Mr. Webster hurriedly beamed and hurried forward towards the bench.

"What a bit of luck!" cried the cameraman cheerfully. "I mistook you for an Austrian, but of course you're English. Now I never like to take liberties, although I'm a cameraman with my living to earn—and folks sometimes forget that— and it's not always easy. Would you mind if I used you as a model, so to speak? 'Student of history in the shadow of the

Hapsburgs' Folly'—if you take me. A good picture needs a striking caption, and I'd say that's a good one, though I says it as shouldn't."

"Matter of opinion," replied the other, "and why were you so sure I'm an Englishman, anyway?"

Webster chuckled. "Matter of observation," he replied. "As it happened, you came to Vienna on the same plane as I did— last Monday. You've got an English passport—I saw it. Not that you wouldn't pass for an Austrian: quite a continental look about you. And you talk the language—like any native." Mr. Webster smiled happily, sat down and produced a cigarette, quite indifferent to the fact that his companion on the bench looked anything but encouraging.

"It's a funny thing," went on the cameraman. "I've often noticed when I'm on holiday in foreign parts—and I get around quite a bit—that if you observe fellow-travellers— (no offence meant, just a descriptive phrase)—on the train or coach or what have you, you often happen across them again when you get to your destination. Just chance, of course. All a matter of being observant."

"There might be other ways of putting it," rejoined the dark fellow.

"Nosey Parker? That sort of thing?" queried Mr. Webster affably. "I'm a good-natured sort of bloke myself, and not thin-skinned either. No cameraman can afford to be thin-skinned. Now there's one thing I should like to have your opinion on. What did you think of that film we both saw last night?"

The other still did not reply and Mr. Webster chuckled.

"Bless you, I sat behind you best part of three hours in that picture house—the Apollo, in the Gumpendorfer Strasse: or if I didn't, I'll eat my hat. I'll swear it was you, besides…" He broke off, a look of doubt crossing his face for a moment. "If I'm wrong, tell me so," he added. "I'll always admit it if I've made a mistake—but you've got a striking face, if I may say so."

"I didn't say you'd made a mistake," rejoined the other. "I was at the Apollo, and I did sit through the Streicher film—a damned good film, too—but I didn't see you there."

"You wouldn't have, would you: I was sitting behind you," replied Webster. "Fact was, I nearly spoke to you as we went out. Just because I knew you were English. I get a bit lonesome in foreign cities: I'm not so good at the lingo as you are, though Auntie does her best to improve me. Auntie's lived in Vienna since nineteen-o-five. What was the name of that joint you went to after the picture? I went there, too. I like these light ales… What was the place called? Liesinger something?"

"Liesingerkeller," replied the other. "If you've been following me around, I'd like to know why."

"No offence meant," replied Mr. Webster. "As I said, I sat behind you in the cinema and after the picture I thought I'd stroll around: very gay the city looks at night—animated as you might put it. Maybe I did say to myself 'He's English: if I could cotton on to him, perhaps we could have a drink together.' Comes of that lonely feeling you get in foreign parts—or I get it, anyway."

The younger man suddenly laughed. "You're a rum cove," he said.

"Name of Webster," rejoined the cameraman. "Mr. Stratton, isn't it? I saw your name on your suit-case while we were in the Customs at Schwechat. Well, there it is. I sat and drank light ale in the Liesingerkeller two tables away from you. You speak the lingo," he added sadly. "I don't. That adds up to the fact that you got off. I didn't. Makes a fellow sort of shy when he can't get beyond '*Wiegeht es Ihnen?*' or whatever it is. Then anno domini has something to do with it. No one'd ever suggest I'm the answer to a maiden's prayer." Mr. Webster broke off for a moment and then asked, "Staying here long?"

"Just a few days," responded the other. "Are you taking pictures for one of the English papers? Vienna's quite in the news these days."

"You're right, it is," rejoined Mr. Webster. "I haven't any contract—mine's free-lance stuff, but I've a chance of selling a series to a publishing bloke—European cities, you know the sort of thing. Quite a good sale for that type of book now tourism is on the increase—and it's not easy to get books about Vienna in London." He paused and then went on: "Well, that explains me—just a chap with his living to earn. Of course I wouldn't have risked coming so far if it hadn't been that Auntie could put me up. Simple but homely—she's a wonderful old lady. Keeps up with the news, too. I always try to take back a few newsy items: she likes to know what's going on. And that reminds me—isn't there a story in these parts? Accident to a young English girl up in the woods, during that thunderstorm?"

"I believe so," rejoined Stratton, "though I can't see there's anything to make a fuss about. She wasn't killed. If you want to know about it, it's reported in the local paper."

"I've no doubt it is: the trouble is that I'm no good at the language," said Mr. Webster plaintively. "I'd like to know about it—I've a reason for being interested."

"Why?" demanded Stratton. "Is she a friend of yours?"

His voice was curt and scornful, and he took up his book as though his patience were exhausted, but Mr. Webster talked on as affably as ever.

"A friend? No, I couldn't put it quite like that, although I've seen her. You saw her, too. Come to think of it, you sat next to her in the plane when we left London. You can't have forgotten her—pretty as a picture she was."

"Good lord, I don't notice whom I sit next to while I'm travelling," retorted Stratton scornfully.

"Well, I do. And there were some very interesting passengers: very interesting indeed," said Webster. "I happened to notice this young lady particularly. For one thing, she was met at Schwechat—on the runway, too. Sir Walter Vanbrugh met her. One thing about my job, you do get to know the faces of all the celebrities, and Sir Walter always made a fine picture—that white hair and fine-cut profile. I remember getting a very good picture of him at the Foreign Ministers' Conference way back in '49. I only mention that to explain why I recognised him at Schwechat."

"Good lord, everybody knows Vanbrugh by sight," retorted Stratton. "He's been at every Foreign Ministers' Conference this century: might have been better for international relations if he'd stayed away."

"Not for me to say," rejoined Webster. "I've only studied their faces, not their policies. Now you're probably a student—an intellectual. I noticed your face at once—very fine head you've got if I may say so. That's why I wanted you in this picture I spoke about—'Student of history' and so forth. But to get back to this story, the young girl who was hurt in the storm—"

"Oh, for God's sake!" groaned Stratton, "if you've got to go on talking, can't you find someone else to talk to? Must it be me?"

"Just wait half a jiff," said Mr. Webster. "I'm slow in getting to the point—comes of not having a good education—but there's a fact or two I found very interesting. Now when we were at Zürich on Monday, you got a drink at the bar there: I was beside you as it happened—didn't you notice that nice young lady? Are you going to tell me you're so highbrow you don't see a pretty girl when you're near one? Don't seem natural to me. Now as it happened I noticed her palling up with another Englishman: a tall dark fellow, chap about fifty, with a good profile. I couldn't help being interested because it happened I knew him by sight—quite famous in his own line, he is. They had some coffee together, you may remember, sitting by the window in the main hall."

"Well, why not, for the love of Mike?" groaned Stratton. "He looked respectable enough. Why shouldn't she have had coffee with him—and what's it to do with you or me or anybody else?"

"Nothing," agreed Mr. Webster hastily. "Don't think I'm making any insinuations, nothing of that kind. It just happened I knew who this chap is—the one who got coffee for her. His name's Macdonald: Robert Macdonald. Senior Superintendent, C.I.D., Scotland Yard. That's who he was."

"C.I.D.? Good God! What was he after?" rejoined Stratton.

Webster chuckled. "Ha ha—you're like all the rest: mention a Yard man and you take notice. Not that I wasn't interested myself—I was. And I had my own private guess as to what he was after—but when I spoke to him at Schwechat he said he was on holiday. Stuck to it, too."

"Do you know him then?" asked Stratton.

"Don't you go getting ideas into your head, young fella-me-lad," said Webster. "I've never had the Yard on my tail—rather the other way about. I've tailed some of these big noises, like Macdonald—to get a picture. That's all, but I've a good memory for faces, and it'd be asking too much of a chap like me not to let the Super know I'd recognised him. I like my little joke."

Stratton sat and studied the garrulous little man. "Quite a chap, aren't you?" he said. "Well, having gone so far, you might as well tell me what your private guess was: what brought a C.I.D. man to Vienna?"

Webster gave his companion a dig in the ribs: a jovial vulgar gesture. "Sitting up and taking notice at last," he chuckled. "Out to pick Uncle Ernest's brains after all. If you don't do a spot of journalism, I'm a Dutchman. You're a highbrow, I recognise that—but you've got your living to earn like the rest of us, eh? Well, I'll oblige with my own ideas if you'll oblige me for a moment." He pulled a newspaper out of his pocket and unfolded it carefully. "Bought it as I came along," he said, "but it's pain and grief to me to read German. I know some of the words but they're all in the wrong order. Now if you'll just translate this bit about the accident to that young girl."

"All right, bung it over—not that there's anything more than you know already," said Stratton.

He translated the short paragraph and passed the paper back. "Why you're making so much fuss about it beats me," he said.

"I'm interested. There's more here than meets the eye,"

said Webster. "I thought I'd got that bit right, but I couldn't be sure. It was a Dr. Natzler who found her: that's right, isn't it?"

"Yes: he's the son of a well-known doctor in Hietzing—Dr. Franz Natzler. Everybody round here knows him: the son's name is Karl."

"And he was accompanied by an English guest who is staying with them," persisted Webster, "and I know who the guest is. You see, I saw Macdonald having lunch at Sacher's two days ago—I looked in there, knowing it's a famous place, and I asked a waiter the name of the gentleman with Macdonald—all these waiters talk English—and I was told it was the Herr Doktor Natzler. And if you put all that into short words of three letters," concluded Mr. Webster triumphantly, "it's as good as saying that it was Superintendent Macdonald who found the young lady after her accident. And that's what you might call a different bag of tricks altogether."

3

"Do you generally trail round after your 'fellow travellers,' snooping?" demanded Charles Stratton, "because that's what it seems to me you've been doing."

"Call it snooping if you like," rejoined Webster placidly. "Takes a lot to hurt my feelings. I've told you I'm a free-lance cameraman with my living to earn, and you don't earn a living my way by being shy. If so be I spot a personality I know and they're with someone I don't know, well, I take steps to find out. I admit I hoped the old chap having lunch with Macdonald would be one of the police 'high-ups' in Vienna, but I'm not sure it hasn't turned out better as it is. If there's not a story in this I don't know my onions."

"Well, as you say, you've got your living to earn," rejoined Stratton, "and it takes all sorts to make a world. I've done your bit of translating for you: now you can reciprocate. What did you think a C.I.D. man came to Vienna for?"

"To watch one of the passengers on that plane," replied Webster promptly. He sat back, his thumbs in his armholes, his coat thrown back, a cocky cheerful vulgar little man, completely at his ease. "You've got education," he went on. "No doubt about that. Likely you're a scholar—Oxford and Cambridge and that: and I reckon you make a living the high-brow way, perhaps with a little journalism thrown in to help with the b. and b. Ever since I was a nipper I've earned my living by noticing things and noticing people. Particularly people. I get the butter on my bread by remembering people's faces. And as it happened there were some faces I knew on that plane. Of course," he added, "the minute I saw Superintendent Macdonald was aboard I looked round to see if I could spot anyone else. That was only common sense. Cause and effect, if you take me."

Stratton laughed, but Mr. Webster had his attention now: there was something oddly impressive about the fat little man and his air of being completely master of the situation.

"Go on," said Stratton. "Sorry if I underrated you. You're being damned interesting."

Webster chuckled again, a wheezy cheerful sound. "Thinking of writing me up?" he queried. "Types I have met. A publicity hound with his nose to the trail. Some of you clever chaps can be funny and no mistake when you try.

Don't think I mind. I take your pictures—you're welcome to mine. Now you never thought of giving the other passengers the once-over: got your nose in a poetry book. All very high-minded. Not that I'm being rude about poets, or poetry either, mind you—"

"Oh, spare me your reflections on poetry," groaned Stratton. "Why not come to the point—if there is one."

"There's a point all right," said Webster. "As I told you, I had a good look round at the other passengers: got up and walked down the gangway to the Gent's and took my time over it—and sure enough there was another face I knew. You can say I make my living by a memory for faces," he added.

"And so what?" asked Stratton.

"Right forward, nearest the flight deck or whatever you call it—a place I don't fancy in any plane, liking to be near the exit myself—there was a young chap whose face I knew. Do you remember, about six months ago, it was, a Foreign Office clerk was charged under the Official Secrets Act: name of Rimmel. Got five years. This chap in the Viscount with us was his brother. I should know: I spent hours round their place. You never know, you know. Those shots may be worth the time I spent on them."

"Aren't you just jumping to conclusions, or making up a story to please yourself?" asked Stratton scornfully. "D'you really believe a Superintendent from Scotland Yard travels round with a bloke whose brother's been quadded for selling Government papers? Because I don't."

"Please yourself," rejoined Webster. "You can say I'm making things up if you like—but if you'd had the gump to notice as much as I did, you might have had a story to write up—and some stories are worth big money. I tell you it happened under your very nose—and you never noticed."

"I don't know what the hell you're talking about," said Stratton.

"No, I know you don't," said Webster. "You sat there, in the main hall at Zürich airport, reading a poetry book: and you weren't a coupla' yards from the C.I.D. Super and the young girl, and you never noticed them. And you didn't see this chap Rimmel. I reckon he didn't see you either. He was listening-in to the C.I.D. chap talking to the young lady: listening till his ears flapped." He broke off. "And you still can't make any sense of a story, even when you're told it in short words of three letters," he groaned.

"Oh, my God!" groaned Stratton. "It may be a story—but it's not my sort of story. Just doesn't interest me. And anyway, how do I know you're not talking through your hat?"

"Making it all up, eh?" rejoined Webster. "Well—you watch out. You'll find Superintendent Macdonald's name will be in the papers soon: and as for that young girl—well, she's in the papers already. Had this accident, poor young thing."

"But why tell me about it?" groaned Stratton.

"I'll tell you for why," rejoined Webster. "First: you're English—which means I can talk to you: second, you talk German—which means you can tell me what's being said and written about all this: third, you've got brains and you've got education. Now I've got a memory for faces and a nose for a story, and my bet is you and I together could make a good thing out of this. If you'll co-operate, that is."

"Co-operate how?"

"Well, if a story breaks, you can do the writing—English

or German or both—and I provide the pictures and some of the trimmings," replied Webster. "I tell you there's something in it—and I'm not often mistaken when it comes to smelling a story. I'm offering you the chance to pay for your holiday: 'holidays with pay'—that's the slogan for the blokes who call themselves the world's workers. I pay for my holidays by using my wits and I tell you it's not often I haven't gone home with more cash in my pocket than I had when I left. What about it?"

"Well, I don't mind writing up a story when there's a story to write," rejoined Stratton, "always provided it's not asking for trouble. If there's anything in what you've said—and I tell you I don't believe it without proof—we might both get into trouble by trying to be too smart."

"Quite right, quite right: careful does it," agreed Webster. "Now say if we leave it like this: I'll go in for a drink at that dive where I saw you last night—Liesingerkeller. Seven o'clock any evening this week. If you like to join me there, I'll tell you if there's anything in it for us. If not—well, you're losing an opportunity. Can't put it fairer than that."

With a cheerful nod Mr. Webster touched his hat in salute and strolled off down the steep path, leaving Charles Stratton staring after him.

"Bats or not bats?" he asked himself—and though he went back to his book, he found it oddly difficult to concentrate on the printed page.

XI

1

WHEN MACDONALD LEFT THE VANBRUGHS' HOUSE, bowed out solemnly by old Josef, who closed the double doors behind the visitor with a resounding clang, there was a group of people standing on the opposite side of the road. Their presence was inevitable and Macdonald knew it. Vienna was the same as London or any other city: where there was an "accident" or an "incident," sightseers would gather; pressmen, gossips, passers-by. The story of Neville Walsingham's death was becoming known in Hietzing, and from Hietzing it had spread into the city and brought the pressmen out.

Just as he was getting into the car Macdonald caught sight of a figure he recognised—Mr. Webster. The stout camera-man was making no attempt to take photographs, though his camera was slung around his neck, but he smiled cheerfully at Macdonald and saluted him with a raised hand. Macdonald beckoned to him.

"Good morning, Mr. Webster. What are you doing here?"

"Good morning, sir. I don't want to intrude, but I heard about the accident to that young lady and very sorry I was to hear it. I couldn't help admiring her when I saw her in the plane—as pretty a young thing as I ever set eyes on. I hoped there might be some news of her, but I didn't expect to see all these chaps here. I hope it doesn't mean bad news."

"I'm driving along to the High Street: if you want a word with me, get in."

Webster beamed. "That's uncommonly kind of you, sir. I'd be very much honoured."

He bundled into the back of the car and chuckled as he saw cameras raised on the pavement. "That's a new experience for me," he said, "but I do hope it doesn't mean the worst. I'm no good at the lingo, but it did seem to me these chaps thought they was on to something in the way of news."

"I've no doubt they do think so, but it's not the accident to the English girl they're worrying about," rejoined Macdonald. "The hospital authorities are quite satisfied with the way she's getting on. There's been another accident, Mr. Webster, but it hasn't got into the papers yet. Hadn't you heard anything about it?"

"No, sir, I haven't. As I said, I'm no linguist: I can pass the time of day in German and say please and thank you, but I'm sunk when it comes to conversation. I'm sorry there's more trouble, sir." He paused and then added, "Spoilt your holiday, so to speak, sir."

"Yes, I'm afraid it has," replied Macdonald. "I don't want to spoil yours, too, but I'd be glad of a word with you. Have you any objection to coming into the local police station and answering a few questions?"

"Bless you, no, sir. Why should I have? Only too glad to help if there's any way I can. You should know, sir. If I'd been up to any funny stuff I shouldn't have gone out of my way to get into yours, if you take me."

"That's what I thought," replied Macdonald. "Here we are, come along in."

A few moments later, seated in a bare little office which might have been in any police station in the English provinces, Macdonald said:

"D'you mind telling me just why you came to Vienna, Mr. Webster?"

"Only too glad, sir: I've no doubt you've your reasons for asking. It's like this: first, I came to take pictures as I told you, but I also came because of Auntie—my mother's sister, Elsie Brown her name is, only they all call her Fräulein Ilse Braun here. Been in Vienna since nineteen-o-five, if you'll believe it. A governess, she was, in a very good family, too. Name of Rothmeister. Now I needn't go telling you all Auntie's history. If so be you're interested you can find out all about her from the British Embassy ladies. Very good they've been to her, very good indeed. She's as poor as a church mouse, Auntie is, but she's got a couple of nice little rooms, not far from the railway station—West Bahnhof." Mr. Webster scratched his head and added apologetically, "Afraid I run on—not much good at telling a story, never have been, but to cut the cackle, it was like this. Auntie wrote to me in London—always kept in touch with the old folks at home, she has—and she asked one of us to come and pay her a visit before she got too old.

It was that bit about her having a room settled it. Hotels cost the devil, wherever you go. And as it happened, I had a chance of selling some good pictures of Vienna—Tucker & Tucker are producing a series of picture-books on European capitals—so I thought I'd risk it. Not that I could remember Auntie myself—I was only a small nipper fifty years ago—but my mum often talked about her, and I thought it'd be nice to look the old lady up, and maybe help her along a bit, as far as the Government'll let you, anyway."

"And you decided you'd fly to Vienna, Mr. Webster?"

"Yes, sir. It was an extravagance, I know. I could have done it cheaper if I'd travelled by rail, third class. But I had a fancy for a nice air trip, and them Viscounts—well, I'd always wanted to sample them, and they are a proper treat. If I never have another such trip, well, I enjoyed that one. Makes travel a pleasure and no mistake. And then there's this to it: you pay B.E.A. in sterling—no extras, like meals on the train, which run away with your currency allowance, and that meant I could do a bit more for Auntie: new blankets and suchlike, and a few comforts she can't afford for herself." Again he broke off, and then added diffidently, "If ever you could find the time to pop in and see her, sir, it'd please her a lot. Loves to hear an English voice, Auntie does. West Bahnhofgasse 295, that's her address."

"And what's your own address, Mr. Webster, when you're at home?"

"75, Nightingale Buildings, Clerkenwell, sir. Not what you'd call classy, but I've lived there for years—right through the blitz and buzz bombs and all the rest."

Macdonald often enjoyed listening to the odd characters

he interviewed in the course of the day's work, and he enjoyed Mr. Webster very much: he sounded so absolutely genuine. The story of "Auntie" was told with such simple gusto, including the bits about the Embassy ladies and the appeal to go and visit the old governess in her rooms by the West Bahnhof: and there was the (verifiable) touch about Tucker & Tucker's projected book—all as genuine as sterling.

"And I've got some good pictures, sir, out of the way good," went on Mr. Webster. "There's something about this city: it's got drama—great buildings and that, and some lovely detail—by jiminy, they don't half let 'emselves go over decoration—rococo or whatever they call it. Got our St. Paul's beaten hollow when it comes to gilding and twiddly bits: it's gay all through. Not jazz stuff: nothing vulgar. Seems right the waltz should be Viennese: that's what Vienna's like, a lovely old-fashioned waltz. Nothing to touch it."

He stopped for a moment and added, almost shame-facedly, "I always was a one for talking, and staying in foreign parts makes me want to let off steam when I meet a fellow-countryman. Now you said there'd been another bit of trouble, sir?"

"Yes. There's been an accident to another of the passengers who was in the Viscount with us last Monday, Mr. Webster. Now it seems to me that you're an observant person. You noticed I was on the plane, for instance: and you noticed Miss Le Vendre, who had an accident during the thunderstorm. I'm wondering if you noticed anybody else."

"Well, sir, I did. I had a good look round: and the reason I had a look was because you were aboard, sir. Somehow I never thought of you being on holiday; silly, perhaps, but there it was. I just said to myself, 'Anything here for me?' Comes of looking out for notabilities. You can make good money from pictures as well as from a write-up."

Macdonald nodded. "True enough: and did you find anybody to interest you?"

"There was that chap Rimmel, sir: brother to the fellow who got a stretch for stealing papers from the F.O. But you know all about him."

"I don't know anything about a Rimmel on that plane. What made you think he was a passenger?"

"Using my eyes, sir. I hung around Rimmel's house in Watford when the case was on—all in the way of business—and I saw this chap come out of the house and one of the neighbours told me he was J. N. Rimmel's brother. I don't often forget a face, and when I saw him on the plane, well, I thought that accounted for you being there."

"You got that wrong," said Macdonald, "but where was this man sitting, and what was he like?"

"Thin weedy fellow, mousey-coloured, very unnoticeable. He sat right forward, next to a gentleman in a light Burberry and a good tweed suit—I summed that one up as a personality, something striking about him. Rimmel's a commonplace-looking chap—not the sort to make a picture. But he was interested in you, sir, even though you weren't interested in him."

"How do you know that?"

"Because he was watching you. At Zürich it was." Mr. Webster gave a little chuckle. "I've been called a Nosey Parker once to my face already to-day—but you're asking me, sir: you're saying, 'Webster, what did you notice?'—and I'm

going to tell you. You can stop me if what I'm saying's neither here nor there. Now at Zürich, I had a good look round
at all them pretty things they sell for souvenirs in the main
hall, and I had a drink and kept my eye on Rimmel. You'll
remember, sir, you went and had a look at the watches they've
got in the show-cases—very nice, too, but they cost a pretty
penny. Then—no offence meant—that young lady—Miss
Le Vendre, is it?—she spoke to you. Asked if you were going
to Vienna. That right, sir?"

"Quite right."

"I was just behind you as it happened. You two went to a
seat by the windows and you got a waiter to bring coffee. I
had another look at the watches, and I noticed Rimmel (I was
sure it was him, sir), he took a seat near to you and the young
lady. He was sitting behind you, and I'll lay any money he was
listening to what you said. You can always tell when a chap's
listening. And if you don't believe me, there was another passenger noticed Rimmel sitting there. A young fellow name
of Stratton—I've seen him around in Vienna once or twice
since I've been here, and I had a word with him, too, only
this morning it was. Young fellow in a camel coat, very posh.
A la-di-dah young fellow, I'd call him, but something about
him caught the eye, so to speak. Next to you in the Customs
at Schwechat, he was."

"You seem to have noticed a lot more than I did," said
Macdonald.

"Well, sir—I had my reasons: you being the reason. If I see
a Yard ace travelling almost beside me, I've got to take notice.
Business is business—and you're pretty famous in your own
line, if I may take the liberty of saying so." Mr. Webster sighed

a little. "Perhaps I'm putting my foot in it, but I told you at Schwechat I knew your dial—told you so straight. You see, sir, I've made my living by spotting the news and putting Who's Who into pictures, and when I saw a notability like you, well, I watched out."

"Very enterprising of you," said Macdonald. "Your methods seem to be successful, too. For instance, how did you learn Miss Le Vendre's name, and that she was staying with Sir Walter Vanbrugh?"

"I recognised him when he met her at Schwechat, sir: as young Stratton said (and he's not what I'd call an observant chap), Sir Walter's face is familiar to everybody who buys the picture papers. And then there's this." Webster pulled his *Hietzinger Zeitung* out of his pocket. "Local paper, sir. Not that I can read the lingo, but I got young Stratton to translate that bit about the accident: and then I put two and two together a bit: if my sum wasn't quite correct, I still thought it was an interesting set-out. Seemed to me you were in the picture somehow, sir."

"Why?" asked Macdonald.

Webster tilted an eyebrow at the curt monosyllable and then sighed. "Seems to me I'd better've kept quiet," he said. "You're thinking I know a bit more than I do. Well, all I know is along of what I've seen keeping my eyes open and asking who was who if I didn't know. On Wednesday I looked in at Sacher's, sir: very famous place it is. Auntie told me not to miss it. And when I saw you lunching there, I thought maybe your friend was a big pot in the Austrian police. I asked the waiter and he told me the name—Dr. Natzler." Webster pushed his newspaper across to Macdonald. "Natzler," he repeated: "he found the young lady up there in the woods: something about an English guest with him. Well—I ask you."

Macdonald chuckled. "What you'd call a logical deduction," he said. "Very intelligent, Mr. Webster. Now by way of clearing the decks, where were you yesterday (Thursday) evening, between five and seven o'clock?"

"Bless you, I'm glad you've asked that one," rejoined Webster heartily. "I hate going round in circles. If you think I've been up to any funny business, I'd rather get it straight. Between five and seven yesterday I was at home with Auntie. She's nervous of thunderstorms: nervous as a cat. She said to me earlier, 'Ernie, don't you stay out too long this afternoon. It's going to thunder. I know it.' So I went home early—four o'clock it was—and took the old lady some nice cakes and got her tea. Not that she ate anything; much too upset she was with the storm." Mr. Webster prodded Macdonald's arm. "You go and see the old lady, sir, like I said. She'll be that pleased to see you. Quite compos mentis, she is. She'll tell you I stayed with her till the storm was over, and then I went to the flicks after I'd tucked her up in bed."

2

Macdonald was called to the telephone at this juncture. He offered Mr. Webster a cigarette and said, "D'you mind waiting a few minutes?"

"Not me. I'll wait till you're ready, sir. If you think I want to do a bolt, you think again. This is jam to me, sir. I've often longed to get behind the scenes at the Yard, and I reckon this is the nearest I've ever been to it."

When Macdonald came back, he found Webster chatting to a young constable, teaching him the days of the week in English.

"*Montag*, Monday; *Dienstag*, Tuesday; *Mittwoch*, Wednesday; *Donnerstag*, Thursday; *Freitag*, Friday," chanted the cameraman. "Auntie taught me that. *Meine Tante*. Ah, here you are, sir. I've been improving the shining hour. Now where were we?"

"We were hearing about yesterday afternoon," said Macdonald, "but I should like to go back to Monday and the wait at Zürich. You said you saw this man Rimmel sitting behind Miss Le Vendre and myself while we were having coffee. How long was he there?"

"Matter of ten minutes, I'd say. He got up when they called the passengers for another plane—Prague, wasn't it? You were there, sir, you'll remember. They called two planes: one for Amsterdam, I think it was—the K.L.M. I saw it take off. Then there was another. Prague that was—if I heard aright. I was listening carefully, too. I didn't want to miss our bus. Like the young lady—she was all in a flap, wasn't she, afraid she'd get left behind."

"And did you see if Rimmel went out to the Prague air liner?"

"I saw him go through the door and into the lobby, sir. I'd've liked to follow him up, but one of them air hostesses asked to see my card—you know the card they give you when you leave the plane for the refuelling stop—and she sent me back. Said we wouldn't leave for another twenty minutes. A lot of trouble they take for you."

"They certainly do," rejoined Macdonald, and Webster went on:

"I thought I'd have a word with that young chap in the camel coat: something about him took my eye. He'd been sitting there in a corner—behind one of those newspaper stands he was—with his nose in a book as though nothing else in the world mattered. Don't seem natural to me for a young chap travelling around to keep his nose in a book all the time. I suppose he'd done it all so often he was blasé, as they say. But when I said my little piece—'Nice flying weather,' or what have you, he just stared at me and went back to his book."

"You mean he sat in the same place all the time we were at Zürich?"

"Apart from having a drink at the bar when we first went in, he just stayed put with his book," said Webster, "but if you want a line on Rimmel, the chap you should go for is the tall grey-haired gent who sat next to him in the plane: though now I come to think of it, that gent left the plane at Zürich, too. A bit odd, that. Don't you call him to mind, sir—very blue eyes, he'd got, and a small moustache. I remember looking out for him when we got going again after Zürich: had an idea he might be somebody who was somebody."

"You've given me a recognisable description of three of the passengers," said Macdonald, but Webster cut in:

"I've done better than that, sir. I'd describe you to anybody: then the young lady, fair, neat, stylish: slick little black suit and a tiny hat with a diamond pin and very nice pearls round her neck: that makes two. Then the dark nose-in-the-book fellow with big horn-rims and a smashing coat, that's three. The big grey-haired gent who left at Zürich, and Rimmel, that's five. And the white-haired old nobleman who came and chatted to you—looked like a duke any day, he did, I could list him for you. And the stout dame who looked like a dying duck in a thunderstorm and the young lady in a grey pin-stripe and a mink stole. Eight passengers that is—and I'd swear to any of them, wherever I saw them. It's the one thing I'm good at, remembering faces." Webster sat silent for a moment and then went on: "You said there'd been another accident, sir. I know it's not my business to ask questions, but fair's fair. I've done my best to help you as far as I could."

"A very good best, too," rejoined Macdonald. "You'll hear all about this other accident before long—the facts will be in the papers. A gentleman named Walsingham, who was staying with Sir Walter Vanbrugh, was killed in a traffic accident last night, on the Wattmanngasse."

Webster's eyes were naturally a bit protuberant: blue eyes in a rubicund face, and he fairly goggled at Macdonald. "Staying with Sir Walter…by heck, now I understand why those chaps were queueing up outside the house. Two accidents to residents in that house—doesn't look too good. And then look here, sir"—Webster was getting excited—"didn't you say this gentleman was a passenger on the plane we came in?"

"Yes, he was. He left the plane at Zürich and flew on to Vienna on Wednesday."

Macdonald produced a photograph from his pocket (it had been cut from the jacket of J. B. S. Neville's last book) and handed it to Webster. "Do you recognise it?" he asked.

"By jiminy," said the cameraman. "This is the gent who sat next to that Rimmel on the plane. That's the one. I'll swear it is." He gave a long whistle. "This is a story, sir, by heck it is. And to think I could have got a picture of the pair of them if only I'd known. Both on the same plane, both staying at the same address. Was he in the Diplomatic, sir?"

"No, he wasn't. He was a writer," replied Macdonald. "Now there's one last question I'd like you to answer, Mr. Webster. When you spoke to me at Schwechat you mentioned the old opera singer, Hedwige Waldtraut Körner, and you said there was a story which brought her into the news. What is the story?"

"That? Oh, that's neither here nor there, sir, not so far as all this is concerned. It's just one of those silly stories which get into the gossip columns. I brought the cutting for Auntie to see—in *World Pictures* it was. 'The Hapsburg Jewels' was the heading. It said the old emperor—Franz Josef—took a fancy to Waldtraut Körner in the long ago and gave her a famous necklace or tiara or what have you, and some chap raked the story up and said the old lady was going to wear the sparklers when she's present at the reopening of the Opera House here. You ask any newspaperman in Vienna—they've all got one version or another of the same story, or so Auntie tells me. Romance stuff, I call it—just what some of the picture papers like, a bit of old-fashioned scandal and some outsize diamonds: that's a recipe which always goes down when there's no straight news." Webster stared at Macdonald for a moment and then chuckled. "Look here, sir, if I gave you a wrong impression, I'm sorry. The trouble with me is I talk first and think afterwards. I mentioned the Waldtraut Körner dame to you on the spur of the moment—famous diamonds plus C.I.D.—the sort of thing which comes into my head when I'm looking for a caption for a picture. Silly, I know—but I dare say I am silly. There's just the one thing I'm good at and that's remembering faces. I've made my living out of that and I'm proud of it."

"You've a right to be," rejoined Macdonald. "Well, thank you very much for answering all my questions, Mr. Webster. How long will you be staying in Vienna?"

"Perhaps it's not for me to say, sir," rejoined Webster, and for once there was irony in his hearty voice. "I'd like to stay till this story gets sorted out. If there's anything I can do to help, I'll do it: and maybe you'll let me in on the picture angle if there's anything doing in that line."

After Mr. Webster had gone, Macdonald called in his young interpreter—the English-speaking Austrian police-man who was detailed to assist the C.I.D. man, who had been in a position to hear Mr. Webster's conversation.

"You heard the story Mr. Webster told about Waldtraut Körner's Hapsburg diamonds, Schmidt. Had you heard of it before?"

"Yes, sir. As the gentleman said, it was a bit of gossip—scandal you call it?—which got into some of the papers when Waldtraut Körner came back to Vienna. Nobody believes it—no sensible person." The young man paused a moment and then added, "If she had any 'Hapsburg diamonds' she would have sold them long ago. Life was hard for her after the war."

"That seems common sense to me," agreed Macdonald.

"This Mr. Webster, he likes romances," said Schmidt. "Romance pays better than common sense in the picture papers."

"Quite true—but he gets some of his facts right," said Macdonald, "and it's true he remembers faces. He remembered mine—and told me so when he needn't have."

XII

1

IT WAS THAT ADMIRABLE WITNESS HANS FLÜCHS WHO had testified that Neville Walsingham had visited the Grünekeller the previous evening, and the Hietzing police had obtained a list of other persons present at the inn as far as could be ascertained. Glancing through the list (without much hope of enlightenment), Macdonald spotted the name of Herr Friedrich Vogel of 159 Neueweltgasse and the C.I.D. man's exclamation of "'Curiouser and curiouser,' said Alice," completely foxed his Austrian interpreter, who had never heard of Alice.

"Never mind," said Macdonald. "Can you tell me anything about Herr Vogel? Has he ever attracted the attention of the police?"

Vogel, it appeared, had never been charged with any offence against the law, but he was considered a slippery customer and was known to have been pro-Hitler when it was profitable to be so.

"It's odd," said Macdonald. "Mr. Webster, a passenger on the Viscount, waited on the pavement, out of sheer goodness of heart, and saved me having to hunt for him. Herr Vogel, acting as host to Mr. Stratton (another passenger on the Viscount), is almost equally accommodating, having attached himself to last night's party, and his residence is conveniently situated in Hietzing. I think we will visit Herr Vogel and his guest next."

As he was driven to Vogel's apartment, Macdonald remembered passing Vogel's Volkswagen, with young Stratton aboard, when he left Schwechat airport. "Vogel was pointed out to me," he pondered. "Was I also pointed out to him?"

Herr Vogel was at home. He lived in a small flat on the first floor of a rather depressed-looking house and he opened the door himself and gazed at his two visitors with evident curiosity but without surprise. The subsequent interview was conducted through the medium of the police interpreter, since Herr Vogel regretted that his knowledge of English was but rudimentary. In one way, Macdonald found the method satisfactory: his own German was beginning to come back to him, in the way a long unused language can revive when heard again, and he found he could follow most of Vogel's answers and had additional time to assess them while they were repeated in English. The interview started by an inquiry for Mr. Charles Stratton. Vogel regretted that Herr Stratton was out at the moment, but was expected to return for *Mittagessen*. Was there anything he (Vogel) could do to be of assistance? Macdonald then gave his own name and status, and they were invited into Herr Vogel's extremely tidy (and very stuffy) office.

"You will doubtless have heard of the accident to Mr. Walsingham on the Wattmanngasse?" asked Macdonald (who spoke throughout via his interpreter). Vogel had indeed heard of it—a tragic and deplorable happening.

"Then you know that two accidents occurred within a few hours of each other," went on Macdonald. "Both to English nationals who left London on the same aircraft last Monday. You will understand, therefore, that an inquiry is being made regarding other passengers who travelled on the same aircraft, so far as their whereabouts are known."

Vogel bowed. "That," he observed dryly, "was a natural precaution on the part of the police."

Macdonald then asked for the circumstances whereby Mr. Charles Stratton came to stay with Herr Vogel.

"Mr. Stratton, I take it, is a friend of yours?"

The answer was a long one, but Vogel expressed himself clearly and straightforwardly. "I was in London last year on business," he said. "I was making inquiries for a client concerning the death of my client's brother, the latter having gone to London as a refugee during the war. It was a matter of testamentary dispositions, deceased having been named as co-executor with my client. It was necessary to get documentary proof of death. During my stay in London, I made contact with a German-speaking lawyer to whom I applied for professional help—a Mr. Bowley of Chancery Lane. It was through Mr. Bowley I made contact with Mr. Stratton, professionally I might say. Mr. Stratton had relatives in Germany and he had lost sight of them during the war. He had reason to believe that one of these relatives had gone to Vienna, and Mr. Bowley suggested that I might assist in tracing this person. I have not succeeded in doing so, but I suggested to Mr. Stratton that he might care to come to Vienna to look into certain aspects of my inquiries." Here Herr Vogel paused: he had been talking slowly, in order to allow the interpreter time to translate each phrase into English. Finally he said, "I think I have said as much as I should, having regard to the confidence which exists between principal and client. If you wish for further information in this matter, you can ask Mr. Stratton himself."

"Certainly," agreed Macdonald. "I take it that you are a lawyer, Herr Vogel?"

"I am a qualified lawyer. Owing to my health I no longer practise, but I undertake certain commissions or inquiries for which my legal training qualifies me."

"Do you mean that you are a private detective?"

"Certainly not," replied Vogel. "The inquiries I undertake have no bearing on crime." A bell jangled as he finished speaking and he added, "Excuse me. I will go to the door: my housekeeper is deaf."

He got up with more alacrity than might have been expected from one of his build and lethargic appearance and returned in a moment or so. "Mr. Stratton has come in, Herr Superintendent. You would doubtless prefer to talk to him alone."

2

Macdonald had no difficulty in recognising the young man he had studied at Schwechat airport and whom he had glanced at cursorily in the Viscount. Charles Stratton was a tall long-limbed fellow with a well-shaped dark head: his hair was thick and straight and somewhat unruly, a lock tending to flop forward over his eyes. He was pale-complexioned and he wore noticeably big horn-rim spectacles: Macdonald guessed that he was short-sighted and noted again the supercilious expression which detracted from the pleasantness of a face which was good-looking enough to attract attention. Stratton gave him a steady stare.

"Good morning. Superintendent Macdonald? My name is Charles Stratton. I remember seeing you at Schwechat. So that garrulous little cameraman was right in his identification."

"I take it you mean Mr. Webster," rejoined Macdonald. "He spotted me all right. He seems to make a habit of spotting people."

"He may be good at remembering faces, but I think he talks a lot of hot air," rejoined Stratton. "Well, Superintendent, what brings you here?"

"I am on duty, acting on instructions from the Commissioner's Office in London to co-operate with the Vienna police," rejoined Macdonald. "As you probably know, there have been two accidents to English nationals in this district, both persons concerned having travelled on the same aircraft as ourselves. I am trying to locate other passengers on the same plane."

"I read about the girl's accident in this morning's paper," said Stratton, "and I heard about Walsingham's death a few minutes ago, in the bar of the Neuebaukeller. Was Walsingham a writer—J. B. S. Neville?"

"He was. Did you know him?"

"No. I never met him, but I've heard him talked about,"

said Stratton. "I write a bit myself and so get to hear some of the chirp and chat that goes round among the publishers and agents. What is it you really want to know, Superintendent?"

"First, to identify travellers in the Viscount: next, to ascertain their reasons for being in Vienna."

"I see. The assumption being that one of us indulged in assault and battery," replied Stratton. "It's not for me to argue the soundness of your reasoning. As to myself, my name you know. My address in London is 20^x Trinity Court, Gray's Inn Road. Occupation, tutor in modern languages at the Bloomsbury Coaching Association, also part-time novelist. Reason for being in Vienna, holiday plus research into family ramifications. Vogel probably told you that bit."

"He told me that he had been making inquiries on your behalf."

"Perfectly true. Do you want chapter and verse?"

"I should be interested to learn a little more. You speak excellent German, Mr. Stratton."

"I was born in Germany, though I was registered as a British subject. My father was in a shipping company and he went to Hamburg when trade was picking up in 1925 and I was born a year later. As a kid I lived in Hamburg, Rotterdam, Antwerp and Barcelona—hence the modern languages. As for the family research—if you want to know it and much good may it do you—here it is. My mother left my father in 1938 and went back to Germany to live with her half-brother—Wilhelm, or Bill as we called him. He is a German. I heard from my mother just before war broke out in 1939. Then nothing until 1946, when I had a card sent through the Red Cross to my grandparents in London. It was posted in the Russian sector of Berlin. Ever since then I've been trying to trace my mother and Bill. I've got on their tracks once or twice and I think they're alive—but I'm not even certain of that. I got a report from a chap in a D.P. camp that Bill had got a job in Austria and my mother was in Vienna. So when I happened across Vogel I asked him to make inquiries this end. Eventually he asked me to come over here because he thought he'd spotted them. He hadn't, of course. It was all quite futile—but I'm glad to have seen Vienna."

Stratton broke off, and Macdonald sensed a different person behind the supercilious mask: a being at once more sensitive and more troubled.

"I don't suppose you've ever had to apply your detective technique to the problem of 'Displaced Persons,'" said Stratton. "Some still rot in camps: some keep moving and survive somehow, often on faked or stolen papers: some develop a cover story which really does cover their origins. I know enough about it to be careful of making straightforward inquiries: the subjects of the inquiries might not thank you." Again he broke off, his deep voice uncertain, and then he added, "Well, you asked me. There it is: one of a million similar stories. Displaced Persons are still a blight right across Europe. And if you can connect up all that with a motive to bat the Vanbrughs' guests over the head, well, tell me the answer."

"What I am really trying to do, in the first stage of the inquiry, is to get information about the passengers on the aircraft," said Macdonald. "It may seem a futile proceeding to you. A lot of detection proves to be futile—like your inquiries about your mother and brother: but sometimes facts do emerge which give us a pointer. I hope they will do so in your own inquiry, and I should like to thank you for telling me the facts as you did."

A smile twisted Stratton's mobile lips. "I've got a modicum of horse sense," he retorted. "If a chap like you starts a police investigation in a place like Vienna, there's obviously something serious behind it. If I'd told you to go to hell, or the equivalent, you'd have got busy on me at the London end, and you'd soon have found out that I'd been chasing lost relations in Eastern Europe. I think it was more sensible to tell you myself."

"Much more sensible," agreed Macdonald, and Stratton went on:

"Then I'm staying with Vogel. I don't want to crab him, he's been very decent to me, and I think he's the right sort of bird for the job I want him to do. But for all I know, Vogel's stock isn't too high in his native city: and on the whole it may be better for you to know just why I'm his guest. Mutual convenience rather than mutual esteem. Now what about the Viscount? I hope you don't expect me to be full of information, like Webster. I never notice people I'm travelling with. I generally hate the lot of them."

"When did you first notice Mr. Webster?"

"At London Air Terminal. He tried to get chatty while we were getting on the bus. I hate chatty people when I'm travelling, so I took evasive action. Once on the plane I had my head in a book all the way to Zürich. I thought that girl next to me was going to be one of the talkative variety: anyway, she fussed. So I changed seats at Zürich and struck it lucky—I got a place to myself. Then Webster had another go at me during the wait at Zürich, but I didn't answer him."

"Are you always allergic to people while you're travelling?" asked Macdonald.

"I never talk to people in trains and planes if I can help it. Once they start talking to you they never leave off. Women are worse than men, generally speaking, but a man of Webster's type is the worst of all. He's pachydermatous, no snub penetrates his hide."

"You sound rather embittered," said Macdonald. "Now getting back to Zürich: did you notice any of the B.E.A. passengers during the wait there?"

Stratton groaned. "Lord, oh lord. That's the sort of question I loathe answering. I don't notice people: for one thing I'm hopelessly short-sighted, and for another I'm not interested in humanity in bulk. Who did I see at Zürich? I saw you, for one, and the girl all the fuss is about: you and she had coffee sitting near the windows I saw the tall white-haired bloke—a V.I.P. of some kind, judging from the way he was met on the tarmac. I saw Webster, because he came and spoke to me. That's about all. You see, I didn't join in the general milling about; I had a drink and then stayed put. I bought a couple of newspapers and glanced through them—and that's about all."

"Can you remember where Webster was when you first noticed him at Zürich?"

"Just behind you, near the window. I noticed him because he's such a preposterous-looking object. I think he was standing beside another bloke who was in the same group as ourselves when we were shepherded into the main hall—a greyish nondescript-looking bloke. I remember seeing him as we first got in the plane, but I can't describe him. Sorry, but that's the best I can do." He paused and stared at Macdonald with the intent gaze of the short-sighted. "Webster picked on me again this morning," he went on, "up by the Gloriette. He plumped himself down beside me and fairly started in babbling like a ten-year-old. I think he fancies himself as a detective."

"He's got certain qualities which fit him for the role," said Macdonald.

"A memory for faces—which I haven't," said Stratton. "But all this hot air about Rimmel's brother—I just don't believe any of it. He makes things up—at least, that's my opinion. Webster's a laughing stock to look at, but he's a romantic at heart. I believe he kidded himself I was a notability of sorts: anyway, he's been more or less chasing me round Vienna, and finished up by taking a photograph of me up at the Gloriette. 'Student of history in the shadow of the Hapsburgs' Folly'— that's typical Webster. Caption-minded."

"What do you mean exactly by his chasing you round Vienna?"

"Oh, that's an exaggeration, but he just pops up where I happen to be. I was at Schönbrunn on Wednesday—so was he. I went to the Streicher film last night: so did he. I went to the Liesingerkeller after the film, so did he—and told me so this morning, cool as brass. Said he was feeling lonely and would have liked to talk to a fellow-countryman. Then this morning he pops up again. I'm tired of him."

Stratton moved restlessly in his chair, lighted a cigarette and then added, "You're thinking I'm a snob. I'm not. I hate snobs, but I also hate the sort of aimless gossip Webster specialises in: I've no doubt he's a decent good-hearted chap, but his mind is conditioned by the gossip column. Anything does to make a caption."

"You say you saw him at the Streicher film last night," said Macdonald, but Stratton retorted:

"I didn't say so, because I didn't see him. He saw me: he said he was sitting behind me: and since he knew I went on to the Liesingerkeller and got talking with some Austrians, presumably he was there. Otherwise he wouldn't have known I was."

"What time was this?"

"The film didn't finish until eleven—it's a damn good film, you ought to see it—and I stayed in the Liesingerkeller till it closed, which was around midnight, or a bit later. I was talking to a chap I met in the Albertina: one of these students of the Fine Arts you come across so frequently in Vienna and so seldom in London. He knows a damn sight more about the contents of our National Gallery than most Londoners know, to say nothing of being able to discuss the important films of Italy, France, Russia and Japan. Quite a chap."

"How did you get back to Hietzing at that hour?"

"Schneider—the chap I was talking to—had a motorbike: he gave me a lift on the back as far as Gunzendorf and I footed it the rest of the way, with some assistance from a patrolling policeman when I got lost."

Stratton suddenly grinned, and his dark saturnine face looked quite different for a moment. "Well, I've done my best for you, Superintendent: you've heard the family history, my occupation and address, my dallyings with Webster and my doings yesterday evening. Isn't it time I had a turn at asking questions?"

"Ask away."

"Have you any substantial proof that either of Vanbrugh's guests was deliberately attacked? You see, I mistrust melodrama. Why on earth should anybody have attacked that girl? She's only a kid, isn't she?"

"You've asked if I have any proof: the answer is no: but I think even a person who distrusts melodrama has got to admit that there are too many coincidences about these accidents. Incidentally, while I realise you are short-sighted, I still think there's a chance you might be able to recognise some of the other passengers on the Viscount if you saw them again. Will you look through these photographs and tell me if you recognise any of them?"

Macdonald had collected some photographs from the *Polizeiamte*, among which was Walsingham's, and Stratton looked through them casually. The only one he paused over was Walsingham's. When he came to it, he gave a sudden exclamation: then he pushed up his glasses and in the manner of the short-sighted held the picture close to his eyes.

"Good lord!" he exclaimed. "That's odd."

"Then do you recognise this one?"

"I've seen him—but not on the plane. Was he a passenger?"

"He was, yes."

"Then who the hell is he?"

"Neville Walsingham. I've no doubt his picture will be in all the evening papers. Where did you see him before?"

"At my job—the Tutorial place—but he didn't call himself Walsingham on that occasion."

3

"As I told you, our main job is teaching languages and coaching," said Stratton. "Any standard from Finals down to classes for tourists, and any language which is asked for. Obviously we have a lot of rum chaps teaching on what you might call 'piece work terms.' Japanese, Chinese, Hindus, Koreans—you can get men who'll teach any language under the sun in London. And because all is grist that comes to the mill, we arrange for translating to be done—also in any language. Well, about a month ago I'd just finished an hour's grind with a moron who was studying Spanish and I went out—it was latish and the office girl had knocked off—I found a bloke at the door saying he wanted a translator for a short script—Czechoslovak into English. I told him if he'd leave it it'd be dealt with. But that wouldn't do: he wouldn't leave it. The translator could come to him or vice versa, but he wanted it done at once. Very urgent. Well, to cut a long story short, we'd got a hard-up Czech ex-professor who didn't get much work, one Stanislas Karillov, and I gave his address, mentioning about twice the fee that's usually paid for the job, and the bloke with the script trotted off. He gave a commonplace name—Bond or Bourne or something like that—though he didn't look commonplace himself. Rather the reverse. And this," said Stratton, picking up the picture of Walsingham, "is Bond or Bourne. I remember people all right if I see them close to: I'm only sunk when they're a few yards away. I remember thinking that the Bond/Bourne merchant looked a personality—he'd got something authoritative about him, and I wondered why he came to a small commercial undertaking like ours."

"Did you ever hear any more about the translating job?"

"Oh, yes. That's why I remember the incident. Karillov is a very honest chap: he came in next morning to offer to pay the office the usual ten per cent which is the rake off on jobs like that, and to thank me for putting him in the way of an extra fee. I asked him if the work had been interesting and he said 'Very interesting.' He then told me, in confidence, that he had an idea the script he'd translated was an official paper of sorts, probably pinched. He wasn't allowed to type the translation out in the usual way: he was asked to translate it verbally. And then he said, 'If there's anything phony about it, I think I shall forget it. Just not know anything about it. I've had trouble enough one way or another without asking for any more'—or words to that effect. I agreed with him." Stratton broke off and lighted another cigarette: then he went on:

"If a Czech, or any other foreigner for that matter, had brought an official-looking English document for translation into another language I might have thought it my business to draw somebody's attention to it, but the man who wanted this translating done was an Englishman, and he looked a responsible person. So I left it at that. But it struck me as odd—the sort of incident one could boil up into a short story."

"Didn't you ask what the gist of the script was?"

"No, I didn't. Quite deliberately. Damn it all, do you imagine I wanted to go to Scotland Yard or the F.O.—or wherever one might go—and say, 'An Englishman named Bond or Bourne or Bone, address unknown, got hold of our hard-up down-at-heels Karillov and got him to translate a document which may or may not have been honestly come by'? I just said to Karillov, 'Sure you're not imagining things?' His sort do, you know. They've seen so many preposterous things that their norm is twisted. And he said, 'Yes. I expect I was,' and we left it at that."

Stratton picked up the photograph of Neville Walsingham again and said. "This is the same chap—Bond or what-have-you. I wish I'd known. Come to think of it, it's not so surprising—the translation incident—now I know it's Walsingham. He's written a lot about '*Mittel Europa*,' and I expect he talks French and German and maybe Italian, but he's sunk when it comes to Czech. So am I. I've started in on Russian, but the other Slav languages still have me beat."

"Well, I'm interested in what you've told me," said Macdonald. "It may have a bearing on my present job—just possibly. It seems a bit uncertain why Walsingham came to Vienna at this juncture."

"Why did you come to Vienna?" demanded Stratton. "After Walsingham?"

"No. I didn't come after anybody—I came for a holiday."

"Perhaps he did, too, poor devil," said Stratton. "Incidentally, where was he sitting on the plane?"

"Right forward—according to Webster."

"Didn't you see him yourself?"

"No, I didn't. You don't see many of the passengers unless you get up and walk down the gangway. The backs of the seats are too high."

Stratton grinned. "Quite true. It's only chaps like Mr. Nosey Webster who spot everybody. Has he told you about his auntie?"

"He has. He also begged me to go to see her."

"That's a nice touch: all open and above-board," said

Stratton. "Well, I'm sorry your holiday's been translated into a job of work, Superintendent—all because somebody's brakes weren't up to standard. Though whose brakes were at fault seems to be a matter of contention in the local beerhouses."

"It will probably continue to be a contention for some time to come," said Macdonald. "You have answered all my questions very patiently, Mr. Stratton. Will you round your evidence off by telling me where you were between four and five o'clock yesterday afternoon?"

"I was here, in this house, playing chess with Vogel. I beat him because he got rattled over the storm. I didn't go out until the rain left off, when I went into Vienna and had supper and went to the Apollo cinema. And Schneider works at the Kunstbeilage Printing Works if you want to find him." Stratton suddenly grinned. "Did Webster tell you about his pictures?"

"He did," replied Macdonald.

"What a damned odd life you must live," replied the other, "always learning about the lives of total strangers."

XIII

1

"ALL CASES ARE THE SAME AT THE BEGINNING," SAID Inspector Nauheim. "You collect information all in a rush and get an access of blood to the head trying to sort it out: then the next stage is distinguished by complete lack of information and you decide it's a stalemate."

"Perfectly true," agreed Macdonald. "Let's hear the sum total of your researches this morning."

The two police officers were sitting in the small bare room which had been put at their disposal by the "Polizeileutnant" of Hietzing, and Nauheim reported as follows: "First, the autopsy on Walsingham. He was dead when the car—or cars—ran over him on the Wattmanngasse, but he'd been in an accident earlier. There are two sets of bruises on his body, one set made while he was alive, the other after he was dead. The doctors think that he was run down, receiving injuries which caused his death, and that his body was then moved.

I won't go into the details—you can talk to the doctors yourself—but it looks as though Anthony Vanbrugh is clear. I can't see any object in his moving the body in order to run over it somewhere else: can you?"

"Well—I might. But we can leave that for the moment and concentrate on facts."

"Right. I've got the list of arrivals on your B.E.A. plane on Monday. Here it is."

He handed Macdonald the list. There had been twenty-five passengers on the Viscount when it landed at Vienna: twelve British, eight Austrian, two American and three French. Of the British passengers, five were already known to the investigators; Macdonald himself, Sir Charles Bland, Miss Le Vendre, Ernest Henry Webster and Charles Stratton. The remaining seven were made up of two Embassy officials returning from English leave (John Prestwood and Guy Vincent), two English ladies visiting friends in the British Council (Mrs. and Miss Woodthorp) and two architects from the Ministry of Housing (Patrick Tindale and John Tomlinson), who were staying in Vienna as the guests of Herr Schwarz, a noted Vienna architect.

"They all seem respectable enough; I can look into them later and see if their powers of observation help us along at all," said Macdonald. "The B.E.A. list of passengers from London will give us the names of those who left the plane at Zürich."

"Next," said Nauheim (who was intent on passing on his information), "you may like to know about the people who have reported seeing Miss Le Vendre when she walked up to the old gun emplacement. She was noticed by several people, all of whom were hurrying home because they realised a storm was going to break shortly: Frau Pilsener, who lives on the verge of the woods, said the girl had Miss Vanbrugh's dachshund on a lead and she was talking to the dog encouragingly. A gardener who works at a house on the farther side of the woods saw the girl when she was nearly at the top of the hill. A couple of children with their nurse and an old man also saw her. They all say she was alone—and all thought she was quite mad not to be running home. They saw nobody else going up into the woods. When the storm broke with the first big flash, just after five o'clock, it seems probable that there were no local people within a mile of the emplacement—and I doubt if we shall get any further information, not until—or unless—Miss Le Vendre can tell us what happened. The storm complicated matters," added Nauheim thoughtfully. "Viennese people have no love of their woods in a thunderstorm: nobody but an English girl would have been perverse enough to go on, farther and farther away from shelter, with a sky like that."

"Which means that anybody who noticed the girl could have been pretty sure that there would have been nobody else on the ridge by the time she arrived there," said Macdonald.

"Do you think she would have walked up there by herself, with no motive at all, on an afternoon like yesterday?" asked Nauheim incredulously.

Macdonald laughed. "Yes, I think so. She was young, she was bored. She had been translating old letters and typing them all day, and it had been a stuffy day. I can well believe she went out for a walk determined to climb up to the ridge and get some fresh air. She might not have expected the thunder, but she wouldn't have been frightened of it. Well, that's as far as we can get in that direction."

"*Gewiss*," murmured Nauheim. "I am not taking you very far, Superintendent, but I don't want you to think the Hietzing police have not been trying. Every available man has been put on the job, asking about Miss Le Vendre, about the van (or jeep) described by Mr. Vanbrugh, and about Walsingham himself. So next, about the van. It seems pretty certain that no locally registered van (which could be mistaken for a jeep) was on the road at midnight last night. There are three converted jeeps owned by Hietzing tradesmen, but it wasn't any of these. However, a van with a low square body was seen by a patrolman shortly after midnight, travelling towards Vienna. It was in the Penzinger Strasse, just beyond the Hietzinger Bridge—the railway bridge."

"Travelling towards Vienna," observed Macdonald, and Nauheim nodded.

"Yes. This interested me in relation to the final piece of evidence which has come in. An old man named Glöck—a drunken old ne'er-do-well—came into the Police Station and said that just before eleven last night he saw three men in the Hietzinger Platz, near the church. One of these men he knew by sight—Hans Flüchs, the journalist: another he said, was an Englishman, in a light raincoat. Glöck knew he was an Englishman because he had seen him driving an English car with a C.D. plate earlier in the day: the third was a tall dark man who hurried across the Platz to catch a Vienna-bound tram. Glöck says that Flüchs and the Englishman parted outside the church at the corner of the Platz, and the Englishman walked on to the corner of Lindengasse—in the direction of

Trauttmansdorffgasse—and waited there a moment, until a big car pulled up and the Englishman got in and was driven off in the direction of Vienna—or at least away from Hietzing." Nauheim stopped and gave a large sigh. "And whether Glöck is telling lies in the hope of getting a reward, or whether he has been bribed to tell lies, who can say?" he said. "It is true that Flüchs and Schulze and Walsingham walked from the Grünekeller to the Hietzinger Platz and that Schulze caught the tram at the Brücke: we have witnesses to corroborate that: also Flüchs parted from Walsingham outside the church: but no one save Glöck saw Walsingham get into a car (if he did get into a car) at the corner of Lindengasse. It is a very quiet road— you may remember there are small shops on the ground floor, all along, and the shops were all closed, of course."

"And you don't think much of Glöck as a witness?"

"Ask the Hietzing men," replied Nauheim. "Glöck has been run in for begging and cheating and pilfering: he's a habitual drunkard and he beats his old wife. He's a cunning old fraud—and the devil of it is that he may be telling the truth on this occasion. If he is, the whole situation is altered."

"Meaning that Walsingham may have been killed in Vienna and his body brought back to Hietzing," said Macdonald.

"Just that—and put in a position where it was pretty certain that Anthony Vanbrugh would pass by the body—or over it," replied Nauheim. "It's known that he always drives back from Vienna by that route, and there are plenty of people to testify that he often drives as though the road belongs to him."

"Is this developing into an all-out attack on the Vanbrugh family?" queried Macdonald, and Nauheim replied:

"I don't know, but can you tell me this: had Walsingham

any particular reason for visiting Vienna just now? Did Sir Walter Vanbrugh tell you if Walsingham mentioned any purpose he had in view—people to see, information to seek?"

"Sir Walter does not know. My own impression is that he himself was surprised at Walsingham's visit. It's true that Sir Walter had given him an open invitation, but the visit seems to have been arranged at short notice: and we also do not know why Walsingham broke his journey in Zürich. But let's get back to the Vanbrugh angle: there have been three incidents connected with their household. The abortive attack on Clara, the accident to Miss Le Vendre, and the death of Walsingham. I take it the story about Clara has now been reported?"

"Yes, it has, and Greta Schwab has been questioned. Greta is almost 'simple,' as you say, but she comes of a respectable family and there's no reason to disbelieve her. When she and Clara were coming home through the woods on Wednesday evening, a man jumped out at Clara with a raised stick. Greta was a little way behind her. Clara screamed and Greta screamed and they both ran away—a silly story: the only relevant fact is that Clara was wearing Miss Le Vendre's coat—and so far we know nothing about Clara except that she is a liar. The address she gave in Wiener Neustadt is a shop whose owner denies any knowledge of her, and the woman who gave her a reference has herself left Vienna. But it must be admitted that such stories are not uncommon in Vienna. However, it's being followed up. And I think the most useful thing I can do is to see if we can get any report on the big grey car in which, according to Glöck—alas, only Glöck—Walsingham drove away from the Lindenstrasse."

Macdonald sat and considered a moment. "Does it strike you as quite out of character that a fellow like Glöck should have gone into the Police Station to report anything at all?" he asked.

"The Hietzing men say 'no,'" rejoined Nauheim. "He's not in the least in awe of the police, and on occasion he has produced some quite useful evidence over cases of car thefts and the like. He's a cunning old rogue and tries to curry favour in his sober moments. Inspector Brunnerhausen thinks there's quite a good chance that Glöck saw exactly what he claims he saw. So if you can get any information about what Walsingham was doing in Vienna, or who his friends were, it might help us a lot."

"I'll see what I can do," rejoined Macdonald.

2

"Anthony Vanbrugh didn't mention Walsingham to me, or anything else of interest, but oddly enough I have met Walsingham myself," said Sir Charles Bland. "I met him a month or so ago at my son-in-law's. I told you that Nigel is in a publishing firm—Barrards. He gives occasional parties for writers: you can guess the sort of thing—a number of small fry and an occasional big fish. On this occasion J. B. S. Neville was the celebrity. I recognised him at London Airport, though whether he recognised me is another matter: anyway, we disregarded each other. As things turned out, this was a pity, but at the time I felt I didn't want to get involved in a conversation which might have dragged on all the way to Vienna. I dislike talking for hours on end in an aircraft."

Macdonald was talking to Bland in the latter's sitting-room at Sacher's, and after his first inquiry as to whether Bland had ever met Walsingham, Macdonald went on:

"I don't know if I'm attributing to you a meaning you didn't intend, sir, but when you came and talked to me about the burglary at your daughter's, I got the impression that your story implied something more than a mere anecdote: that you wanted me to think the thing over, and possibly to give you a considered opinion later."

Sir Charles Bland laughed, a little ruefully. "You're right. I did—although it never occurred to me that the story could have any relevance to our stay in Vienna. I was thinking of the London end. You see, I can't help feeling that that burglary was a blind: the theft of the fur coat was only incidental, not essential."

Macdonald nodded. "I'm disposed to agree, but what was the essential?"

"I sat and thought over that story all the way from London to Zürich," said Sir Charles. "I'm not given to romancing, Macdonald, any more than you, but I wanted to make sense of the business. Someone broke into that house and removed a coat they didn't seem to want. Well, what did they want? If it'd been my own house, I'd have guessed 'information'—though it wouldn't have been left about to be picked up. But Nigel Villiers is an untidy chap: he leaves his letters and scripts and papers strewn all over what he calls his study. Could it be conceivable that there was anything of value there—information value..."

Sir Charles paused and Macdonald put in: "Did the sight of Neville Walsingham at the airport have any influence in prompting that line of thought, sir?"

"At first, only subconsciously—the fact that he was a well-known writer, and a writer who makes money, may have turned my thoughts to the writing angle. Then—well, it's an unworthy line of thought, but I'd met the chap: I'd talked to him, been civil to him. I'm not accustomed to being forgotten quite so easily: there you have it—personal conceit. He glanced at me and ignored me, and I admit I was delighted. You see, I didn't like him."

"Neither did I," said Macdonald. "I wish I had. I might have saved a pack of trouble if I'd taken him somewhere for a drink and got him talking. But to get back to your own reflections, sir."

"Yes. I worried away over the story—without any further consideration of Walsingham, I might add. I was wondering if Nigel had been getting himself in any of these muddles the younger men of to-day seem to specialise in, although everything in that ménage seems happy enough, thank God. Then I came and inflicted the story on you."

"With no ulterior ideas?" inquired Macdonald, and Bland gave a little shrug.

"I find it hard to answer that. The sight of you may have put ideas into my head."

Macdonald laughed. "Not only into your head, sir—but I feel you haven't finished."

"Quite true. I didn't give the writing angle, the 'information value,' another thought, until somebody, here in Vienna, told me that Waldtraut Körner was hawking some reputed Steinadler memoirs around. Then I began to wonder. You see, Nigel had got wind of that story. He actually asked my opinion of the probabilities."

"I wonder if we're on to something there," said Macdonald. "I also have heard this story since I came to Vienna and I'm very much interested to know that it is being discussed in London. Have you any idea if your son-in-law discussed it with Walsingham?"

"I've been trying to find out," replied Bland. "You may say it's a wild guess—and it certainly is—but it seems to me that there's an outside chance that it was that story which brought Walsingham to Vienna. Anyway, thinking the thing over after you phoned to me this morning, I thought it worth while to try to get hold of Nigel. I put a call through to his office, but he's out of town for the day and they don't know where he is. So apart from leaving a message telling him to get through to me here, I can't do anything more at the moment." Sir Charles paused and looked at Macdonald with shrewd smiling eyes. "Are we riding off on a ludicrous sort of hobby horse, Superintendent? I'm right out of my depth here."

"So am I," agreed Macdonald, "but the idea seems worth considering. I gather that a Vienna publisher of repute— Probus Verlag—have already made a bid for the Steinadler papers, but their bid was not high enough and was refused. If Walsingham gathered that a London publisher was anxious to do business over the matter, isn't there a possibility that he might have fancied himself as a negotiator? His command of German and his knowledge of affairs in Vienna would have put him in a good position to make an approach to the old lady."

"Yes. That's reasonable enough—but how does this theory connect up with all the disreputable jiggery-pokery which we've been discussing, and with the crimes of violence which you are investigating? I admitted that I disliked

Walsingham, but he's a writer of repute: I don't see him turning to crime for a living."

"No—though it seems probable that his life was abruptly concluded by crime," said Macdonald dryly. "Now I wish you would give me your own opinion about some theories which Walsingham put forward to me yesterday evening," he went on. Macdonald gave a brief résumé of Walsingham's comments on "tension between the British and certain Austrian nationalists," and the public apprehensions aroused in the latter quarter by the news that Sir Walter Vanbrugh was writing his memoirs. Bland listened carefully, but at the end he said:

"In my opinion, Walsingham was talking rubbish—and he must have known he was talking rubbish. I don't believe any of it, and I certainly don't believe that Miss Le Vendre was deliberately attacked because she was Sir Walter's secretary. Of course," he added, "you can get a more authoritative opinion from the Embassy people about all this. But my own guess would be that Walsingham was trying to direct your thoughts along lines of his own choosing. I may be wrong, but there was something about the man which I distrusted." He stopped abruptly, his face frowning in deep thought. Then he went on: "To use the cant phrase, where do we go from here, Macdonald? We've got this idea that Walsingham might conceivably have come to Vienna to try his hand at negotiating for the Waldtraut Körner papers: but that sort of negotiation is protected by laws of copyright and subject to contract. In other words, theft is hardly likely to come into it, because no publisher of repute will pay for a stolen script."

"Of course you're right, sir," agreed Macdonald, "but if Walsingham were trailing somebody else who was after the same prize, it's possible that the somebody else succumbed to the temptation of laying Walsingham out, and, having done so, moved his body to confuse the issue. You've got to admit that there's quite a lot of confusion around, including the fact that Anthony Vanbrugh is likely to have a very bad press. Now it's high time that I got on to headquarters to study reports phoned from London, but I should like to give you a short outline of facts and suppositions which may help to connect up some of our loose ends: the thing's a demented cat's cradle at present, but it may sort out."

At the conclusion of his outline Macdonald asked: "Have you anything to add, sir—from your own observation, that is?"

Sir Charles Bland shook his head. "I'm ashamed to admit it, but I can't help you. I spotted you on the plane, but apart from you (and Walsingham, whom, also, I knew by sight), I didn't notice a soul. At Zürich I read the papers, sitting with my face to the window and my back to the crowd."

Macdonald laughed. "Mr. Ernest Henry Webster has got us both beat: there wasn't much he didn't notice. Our chaps in London will be busy by this time, checking up on Mr. Webster and his observations."

"Yes, I think so. But the action was conditioned by Vienna, and it will be in Vienna that we shall have to work it out."

3

As Macdonald had said, the officers of the C.I.D. in London had wasted no time in checking up on the persons whose names had been telephoned through from Vienna at intervals that morning. Some of the inquiries were answered quickly enough. Mr. Webster, well known as a free-lance camera-man, was vouched for by his landlady, Mrs. Higgins of Nightingale Buildings, Clerkenwell. Mrs. Higgins knew all about Mr. Webster's flight to Vienna: she was as excited about it as though she herself had made her first flight in a Viscount. She knew about "his auntie" too. "He's a good kind fellow," she declared. "He's been planning to go and see the old lady for years. He's that clever," she added, "it's not only his pictures, he knows all the nobs and all the news." It was Inspector Jenkins who inquired about Webster, and not only in Clerkenwell. Mr. Webster was well known in Fleet Street. "He's a clever little cuss," was the general opinion. "If he says he spotted Rimmel's brother, he was probably right. He put in a lot of time on that case."

It was Chief Inspector Reeves who inquired about Rimmel's brother. A brother existed all right (the authorities knew that). Alec Rimmel had been a clerk in an export firm in Liverpool, a very respectable man and the police had nothing against him. Alec Rimmel had left his job two months ago and gone to Newcastle—and he had left Newcastle a week ago for a holiday on the south coast. His whereabouts at the moment were unknown, but no Alec Rimmel had booked a seat on the Viscount last Monday. Reeves left a painstaking sergeant to make contact with B.E.A. personnel with a description of Alec Rimmel, and Reeves himself went on to the Bloomsbury Coaching Association to inquire about Charles Stratton.

Here, as in the case of Mr. Webster, the answer seemed plain. Stratton was vouched for by Dr. Towler, the owner of the coaching establishment (a serious-looking gentleman of donnish aspect). "He's a first-rate fellow, hardworking, conscientious and exceedingly able: he's been here for six years and I've a great regard for him," said Dr. Towler. The latter knew all about Stratton's search for his mother and half-brother. "Does him great credit. He's nothing to gain by finding them—only more bother—but he's devoted to his mother, even though she abandoned him and his father." In conclusion Dr. Towler said, "Whatever the nature of the trouble Stratton's run up against in Vienna, I can assure you he's trustworthy. Some people find him unsociable and some of his colleagues dislike his flippant or cynical manner of speech, but he's a sound fellow."

Dr. Towler knew nothing of the inquiry for a Czech translator, though he said a Mr. Karillov had been employed occasionally in the office on the very rare occasions when Czecho-Slovakian was asked for. "But if Stratton told the police of this incident, you can rely on the story being truthful," said Dr. Towler.

Finally, Reeves tackled the more difficult problem of Neville Walsingham. "He's the only one of the bunch who's well known, and yet nobody seems to know anything about him," said Reeves resignedly. The inquiry started at the only address known—that of Walsingham's publishers. Mr. Walbrook, one of the heads of the firm, spoke of Walsingham with less enthusiasm than might have been expected. (It was only later and by a side wind as it were that Reeves discovered there had been "a disagreement" between author and publisher which amounted to a blazing row.) Mr. Walbrook could give no fixed address for J. B. S. Neville. "He can't be said to live anywhere," said the publisher, "except in hotels or aboard ship or in camp or caravan. He's always on the move. Last time he was in London he was staying at the Sussex Palace, and before that he was in Edinburgh and before that in Scandinavia. He's a fine writer: I might say a brilliant writer, but he's a very difficult fellow to deal with. As for what he was doing in Vienna—well, Vienna's just about the place I should expect him to go to at this juncture. We shall be having a book called *The Military Consequences of the Peace Treaty* next." He broke off and then added hastily, "I mean that's the sort of book Neville would have produced if it hadn't been for this deplorable traffic accident. Well, I'm sorry I can't help you any further, Chief Inspector. Try his bank—they ought to know."

The bank was no more helpful than the publisher. If Neville Walsingham had had any relatives, nobody seemed to know of them.

Reeves phoned through the result of the joint researches to Vienna, adding that he was going to put in the rest of the day on the Rimmel-Walsingham tracks. After that he hoped for a flight on a Viscount himself.

XIV

1

"WELL, SO MUCH FOR THE LONDON REPORT. THEY'VE done as much as could be expected in the time: and now for a few ideas of my own," said Macdonald. "I doubt if I've ever put forward a theory with fewer facts to justify it," he added cheerfully. "It's a network of supposition, mainly holes, with a few tough strands to connect the random observations."

The Superintendent and Inspector Nauheim had met for a belated lunch and were consuming rolls and cheese washed down with Lager beer. Nauheim had established one important fact: at twenty minutes past eleven the previous night Walsingham had been seen on the Kärntnerstrasse, in the heart of Vienna. This discovery had been made by a combination of hard work and good luck—those twin factors of success in detection, because all the hard work in the world can come to naught without the occasional lucky chance. Working round the different parking places in the city with a photograph of Walsingham to display, Nauheim had found one of the old men who stand by the car-parks to open car doors in the hope of occasional *groschen*: this ancient claimed that a tall man in an English style raincoat, wearing English shoes, had alighted from a car just after eleven-fifteen: that he had had an altercation with a motorist who was in a hurry to move off and that the latter—Herr Marx—could be found at his place of business in Weinburggasse, not far from the Stephansdom. Herr Heinrich Marx had obliged by identifying the photograph of Walsingham with certainty. Indeed, he had thought that Walsingham's face was in some way familiar and was greatly animated to learn that the man he had argued with was the English writer, J. B. S. Neville, whose books were known to Herr Marx.

"And that in itself is fortunate," said Nauheim, with his quick flickering smile. "Because he was a popular writer, his picture appeared on the jacket of his books: all we had to do to get copies of his picture was to buy copies of his books— and Wolframs have a quantity in their excellent book shop. Had he not been a writer, we should not have obtained these 'speaking likenesses.'"

"Very fortunate indeed," agreed Macdonald, "and the fact that he was a writer, with friends in the literary world of Vienna, encourages me to put one of my outrageous guesses to the test. I postulate in the first place that Walsingham did not go to the Grünekeller merely to pick up local gossip concerning Miss Le Vendre's accident, but in the hope of meeting somebody. Whether he saw the person he hoped to see we do not know: it is possible that the presence of Schulze, who knew Walsingham, made the latter decide to change his plans, and he walked on, to be picked up in a car at the corner of the Lindengasse, as described by Glöck, and was driven to the car-park, near the Opera House, in the Kärntnerstrasse."

"That's all reasonable enough," said Nauheim, "and it's worth considering that he did not tell Sir Walter that he was going into Vienna again, neither did he take the small car Sir Walter had put at his disposal. Which indicates that his business was something he preferred to keep quiet about."

"Yes: and I think the fact that he did not tell Josef that he expected to be very late indicates that he expected his business to be brief," went on Macdonald, "so now for my guess. Did Walsingham go to see Fräulein Waldtraut Körner, with whom he was hoping to negotiate for the famous Steinadler papers?"

Nauheim looked at Macdonald almost reproachfully. "You knew of this negotiation then?"

"No, I did not: and I do not know now. I told you I was guessing—outrageously. I did not hear this story of the Steinadler papers until I came to Vienna, although I have since heard that London publishers are interested in the matter. It doesn't seem too far off the mark to suggest that this was the business which brought Walsingham to Vienna. That, as I have admitted, is guesswork: the only fact I can put forward to support it is that Walsingham was recently a guest in the house of a young English publisher and that the latter had some information about the Steinadler papers which he may have discussed with Walsingham."

"Ah...not entirely guesswork then," murmured Nauheim.

"Well, let's get on to something nearer at hand," continued Macdonald. "According to your morning papers, Waldtraut

Körner was present last evening at the performance of Aïda in the *Theater an der Wien*. She would not have got back to her hotel before eleven o'clock. I think it would be worth your while to ask the porter at her hotel if Fräulein Waldtraut Körner had any visitors after she returned from the Opera. From what I know of old singers, they tend to be more approachable towards midnight than before midday."

"That," said Nauheim, "is a very good idea."

"We shan't lose anything by it," said Macdonald. "Now I gather that you haven't been able to learn much about the car in which Walsingham left Hietzing?"

"Herr Marx thought it was an old Benz, probably pre-war: dark grey, wide, with a Vienna number plate. He said the driver backed it into position after Walsingham had got out, thus blocking Marx's exit, but as Marx reserved his abuse for Walsingham he didn't notice the driver who was still in the car."

"It might be worth trying to find out if any patrol men noticed a car which had broken down, or had anything in the nature of a small collision," said Macdonald. "It appears from the preliminary autopsy that Walsingham was knocked out—or knocked down—and his body then moved to the Wattmanngasse. Now we know that he arrived in Vienna at eleven-twenty, having been driven direct from Hietzing. His body was lying in the Wattmanngasse by midnight, and it would have taken at least a quarter of an hour to have got him from the centre of Vienna to Hietzing. So he was only in Vienna for twenty-five minutes at most. Now I should think it's improbable that he would have been attacked in the centre of the city. Vienna is still lively between eleven o'clock and midnight, isn't it?"

Nauheim nodded. "Yes. I see your idea: there are a lot of people about at that time and the main streets are brightly lighted. You are thinking that he would have been driven out of the city and attacked in a quiet quarter where there were no onlookers."

"Yes: and I think Walsingham would not have been an easy chap to lay out: he was a big powerful fellow. But if he and the driver got out of the car to investigate a breakdown, if he bent over the bonnet or was induced to crank the car, well, that puts a man in a vulnerable position. I have known attacks engineered on a motorist by that method."

"That's a sound idea," agreed Nauheim. "Now the first thing I will do is to go to the Emperor Maximilian hotel, where Waldtraut Körner is staying, and see the porter. After that, I will worry the city police again to see if they can get any further news of the grey car, and then go to the Liesingerkeller to find if the waiters remember your cameraman and young Mr. Stratton."

"And I will go to the Embassy and see the two men who travelled in the Viscount on Monday, and perhaps I will go and see Mr. Webster's Auntie," replied Macdonald. "I'm interested in Auntie."

Nauheim laughed. "Are you hoping she has the same qualities of observation and curiosity which distinguish her nephew? Meantime, I'll report to H.Q. If there's anything in your guesswork, we might ask to be received by the Waldtraut Körner later. That will be a distinction for you, sir. She is as unapproachable as royalty."

2

John Prestwood and Guy Vincent, both of the Diplomatic Service, welcomed Macdonald to their office in the British Embassy with lively interest. When he saw them, Macdonald remembered both their faces: he had noticed them in passing both at London Airport and at Zürich. John Prestwood, the younger of the two men, fair-headed, sunburnt and lively, laughed straight back at the C.I.D. man.

"Yes, I remember you, Superintendent. I thought you might be a member of the Surgical Congress which is meeting next week."

"I'm delighted to know you're a person who takes an interest in your fellow travellers," said Macdonald. "I generally do, but on this trip I was half asleep. Say if you start by telling me how many people on the Viscount you noticed enough to remember."

It was Guy Vincent who answered this one. "There were four Austrian women and two men: two of the women are well-known buyers in a big Vienna fashion house and the two younger women were their secretaries. They'd been to some fashion pre-views in London. I think the two Austrian men were in the same line of business. There was a stout French dame and across the gangway from me two blameless-looking English ladies of the academic variety. Then there was the young lovely who was met by old Vanbrugh, and she was sitting next to a dark-headed fellow in a camel coat: there was Sir Charles Bland, whom I recognised, and behind Prestwood and me two chaps whom I guessed to be architects in government employ—brief-case of government issue, plus Journal of British Architects, plus copy of Nicholas Pevsner's latest. I noticed these details when I passed them going forward. The navigator was a pal of mine and he asked John and me to the flight deck."

"That's a pretty good effort," said Macdonald, but John Prestwood put in:

"Well he knows the fashion contingent anyway, and he got in a huddle with them at Zürich—that's the sort of lad he is—and that lot's of no interest to you, Superintendent. Neither are the two architects—if that's what they are: they're Civil Servants anyway, and as a job that's as fossilising as the Diplomatic. I'm more interested in low life: the stout merchant with the camera took my fancy. It's funny, you know, but if I'd been asked to spot the detective out of that bunch of passengers, I'd have plumped for the stout merchant. He was on the qui vive all the time, snooping round at everybody. Shows how mistaken one can be. I should have put you last in the detective stakes. You were obviously uninterested."

"Don't rub it in," said Macdonald. "Now it seems to me you two can be helpful: you say you went forward to the flight deck."

"Yes, and we saw J. B. S. Neville, alias Walsingham, sitting right forward," put in Vincent. "We didn't know who he was at the time, but I got a copy of one of his books at lunch-time, after we'd heard about his death, and the picture on the back settled it. He was sitting next to a dreary-looking chap: a pallid, unhealthy object in a drab raincoat and a depressed hat. Looked as though he might just have come out of quad and not seen the sun in years. The two were a complete contrast: Neville very well turned out, prosperous-looking, sure of himself, and the other bloke looking furtive and sickly: but they were talking away at a great rate, almost as though they were consulting over something. Oddly enough, I got the impression they were talking German—but I may have been wrong. I only noticed them as we went forward but I didn't really hear a word they said."

"Did you notice either of them at Zürich?"

"No," replied Prestwood. "Neville left the plane there, didn't he—and the other bloke, too? At least, I didn't see either of them aboard after Zürich. As for the halt at the airport, I told you Guy ganged up with his fashion friends, and we made a party at the bar and weren't doing any noticing. And at Schwechat they let us both through, more or less— diplomatic immunity, God bless it."

"You haven't noticed any of the passengers around in Vienna?" asked Macdonald, and Prestwood replied:

"I've seen the fat cameraman several times, busy taking pictures. He's a talkative bloke, he tried to button-hole me outside the Rathauskeller, but I wasn't having any: and I think I saw the camel-coat object gooping around on the Heldenplatz—but I'm afraid none of that's going to help you very much, Superintendent." He stopped a moment and then went on. "There are the wildest stories going around. In the cafés they're saying that Anthony Vanbrugh ran over Walsingham and killed him and then tried to cook it as an accident. I think that's hitting below the belt, especially as it doesn't seem too easy for Vanbrugh to disprove it. The moral seems to be don't move a body if you find one in the road— leave it to the cops."

"I know: it's a difficult problem to be faced with," said Macdonald soberly. "Well, thanks very much, both of you."

"I'm afraid we haven't done a thing to help," said Vincent, and Macdonald replied:

"I wouldn't say that. You may be able to identify Walsingham's companion if the occasion arises."

3

"Fräulein Braun—Tante Ilse, as everybody calls her," said Mrs. Edshaw, smiling across at Macdonald. "We all know Tante Ilse: she's a remarkable old woman."

In a small room at the British Embassy Macdonald was talking to the wife of one of the Counsellors who had undertaken to tell him what was known by the "Embassy ladies" of Mr. Webster's Auntie. Macdonald felt he was having a breathing space, a pleasant interim when he need not analyse every answer given to him, or seek for a possible hidden meaning in ordinary conversation. Mrs. Edshaw had beauty and poise and dignity—the attributes which every diplomat's wife should have—she had also a beautiful voice and a quality of repose, so that Macdonald found it refreshing to talk to her.

"You probably don't realise how many old English women like Tante Ilse still live in Vienna," went on Mrs. Edshaw. "Old governesses, old confidential maids, even old dressmakers and tea-shop ladies: they were just caught by the disaster of war and they couldn't even get home. They had no money, no influence and no exit visas. When we came to Vienna after the war—the British and Americans and French—all the Embassy wives formed committees to help the poor derelicts, particularly the old governesses. We give them parties and help them with necessities. I always think Tante Ilse is the most interesting character of them all."

"In what way?" asked Macdonald.

"Because she is a very intelligent woman, and always has been," rejoined Mrs. Edshaw. "When she came to Vienna as a girl, fifty years ago, she couldn't have been a well-educated girl, but she lived with a very good family: the Rothmeisters were highly cultured and informed, and all their children had to speak French and English in addition to German. Because Tante Ilse lived with them so long, and was by nature educable, I suppose, she developed her own intelligence and acquired information because she lived among informed people."

Mrs. Edshaw looked across at Macdonald inquiringly. "Am I just wasting your time, Superintendent? Do stop me if I'm only being irrelevant."

"You are not being irrelevant, far from it," said Macdonald. "Please go on and tell me in your own words about Fräulein Braun: what you are saying is giving me a fresh angle on Mr. Webster's 'Auntie.' And would you like a cigarette—or do you not smoke?"

Mrs. Edshaw smiled at him; her smile was like her voice, almost grave, yet tinged with amusement. "Thank you: I do smoke—and it will be a great help. I am not used to giving evidence…" When she spoke again, she said, "You know—you must know—a little about the history of Austria in the last fifty years: it's an integral part of your life, as it is of mine: the magnificence of the Hapsburg régime before 1914, the glitter and the brilliance of Vienna, and then the appalling collapse after Germany was defeated in 1918. Vienna starved—literally starved. Then followed the slow building up of an Austria cut off from its eastern territories, the Federal Republic with very real achievements to its credit: then the Germans again, occupying Vienna: and then another hideous collapse, with devastation and the Russians marching in. Oh dear… I'm not trying to give you a very bad lecture on Austrian history: all I want to remind you is that that remarkable old woman lived through all this history. She was here, she remembers it, she can talk about it. For all I know, she could write a book about it, because she's taught herself to use words—German in preference to English: but she really is remarkable…"

"Good heavens!" exclaimed Macdonald. "Not another book." He suddenly laughed. "I seem to have plunged into a world of memoirs, all of them fraught with significance: Sir Walter Vanbrugh, Fräulein Waldtraut Körner and now Mr. Webster's Auntie."

"Don't take me too literally," she cried. "Perhaps I can best explain my outburst by telling you that when I first saw Fräulein Braun I thought she was just another old derelict, half-starved, looking like a witch in shawls and ragged wraps, poorer than anything you could imagine in London. Yet behind that poverty was a background of experience which she could express in academic German, even though her English was commonplace. It was because she had lived so long with the Rothmeisters and learned their ways of speech. You see, my husband and I were in Germany for years and I did learn the language."

"Unfortunately I never have learnt the language," said Macdonald, "so I shall have to talk to Fräulein Braun in English."

"Oh, you are going to see her: I'm glad. I'm quite incapable of describing her properly."

"But you have told me a lot that is very valuable," said Macdonald. "Now when you describe Fräulein Braun as intelligent, doesn't that imply that she would keep up with the news, the gossip of Vienna of to-day?"

"It does, indeed. She has a host of acquaintances, many of them as old and poor as herself, but between them they are in touch with a surprising variety of people. I know that I am always very careful what I say to her, for she has that avid curiosity that old people do develop, including the intelligent ones."

"Did she ever talk to you of her relations in England?"

"Yes. I asked her if she would like to go back to England, but she said no. She told me she had kept in touch with her sister in London until the latter died, and there were one or two nephews, but she could not face going back and living in a country which was now strange to her: she also implied, with the quaint snobbery you find in her type, that her people had always been small-minded, their interests very limited, while she had been fortunate in living with the Rothmeisters. In short, the old folks at home were not up to her own social standard," concluded Mrs. Edshaw with her grave smile.

Macdonald pondered for a moment: then he said, "I know this is going to be a difficult question to answer, but I think you possess a sort of awareness about people: you appreciated Fräulein Braun's intelligence and her memory for the troubled history she has lived through in Austria. What sort of woman is she—good, bad, indifferent? Trustworthy or the reverse?"

"The Rothmeisters found her trustworthy—and she slaved for them," replied Mrs. Edshaw. "I have never had any reason to distrust her: she has never told me any lies, so far as I know: she has never cheated, or tried to get more than her fair share of the comforts we dispense, as some of them do. But if you want my own opinion, I have the feeling that she's a wicked old woman. I've no justification for saying so, and my husband would be very angry with me if he knew I'd said such a thing. I've told you she's intelligent and that she worked for years for a fine family, but I think in her old age, after all the miseries of wartime Vienna, she has gone sour. Perhaps the word wicked is too strong—but that's the way she affects me, and since you asked me, I've told you."

4

Fräulein Braun reminded Macdonald of a spider: she was so small, so shrunken, so brown, and her claw-like hands were incredibly thin. Her quavery voice spoke English with the mincing refinement of days gone by, and was oddly accented at moments by Germanic gutterals which made her none too easy to follow. "Auntie" told Macdonald her own history, sometimes putting in a German phrase when the English escaped her. "It is long since I speak English," she said. "It is easier to me now to speak German, but I am happy to have my nephew here... He has been kind to me, very kind. He is a good man."

"Wouldn't you like to go back to England again?" asked Macdonald. The answer to his question did not matter: he wanted her to go on talking so that he could get some idea of the personality behind the shrivelled brown mask and the filmy deep-set eyes.

"I could not go back to England: I have told Ernest so. I am used to life in Vienna, no matter how hard: I am used to the food, to the language. I have my own friends; they are poor, like myself, but we understand each other. To the English I would be a foreigner."

"You must have many friends in Vienna," said Macdonald, and she quavered on, telling him of Frau this and Fräulein that, of the ladies from the Embassy who brought her books and papers as well as food. "I have always been a reader and tried to follow the news," she added. "With the Rothmeisters I heard good conversation, talk of the arts, of opera and ballet. Everybody in Vienna cares for these things; in England, nobody. I cannot go out much now: in the winter, not at all. Who would talk to me in England?"

He let her go on for some time before he said, "I have told you who I am, Fräulein Braun, and my business in Vienna."

"You are a detective," she said, and her filmy eyes suddenly looked venomous. "You cannot expect me, an Englishwoman who lived in Vienna during the Nazi occupation, to welcome the police. What do you want?"

"I don't want to worry you," said Macdonald. "My questions are very simple. I want to know where your nephew, Mr. Webster, was during the thunderstorm yesterday, and what time he came in last night."

"You could ask him, Herr Superintendent. He is a very truthful man. You could ask my neighbours in the flat across the hall. They see him come in and go out. Frau Wilhov, she sits at her window all day long. She knows when he goes out and comes in. When the thunder began, Ernest was here, *Gott sei Dank*. I have always been afraid of thunder since I was a child, and now it grows worse: thunder reminds me of the bombing: but he was here. He promised to come in early and to get me an English tea as he calls it. I have told you, he is very kind: he was here before the thunder began, and he did not go out again until after the storm was over. It was late when he came in—midnight. I did not go to bed until he came in. I was listening to the radio. Ernest bought me the set, heaven reward him: it is the first radio I have ever had, and I listened until the station closed down at midnight. Ernest came in just after I had turned the knob."

As he listened, Macdonald became more and more certain that she was lying. He could not have told why this conviction grew on him, why it was that this ancient desiccated crone, with her careful speech and refined diction, gave him such a sense of unease. He remembered Mrs. Edshaw saying "I have the feeling she's a wicked old woman," and Macdonald knew what she meant. "And she'll stick to what she says and bribe and cajole her neighbours into saying exactly what she wants them to say," he thought, "and if we try to disprove it, she'll raise a wail of Gestapo, police bullies..."

"You cannot tell what a radio set means to me," went on Fräulein Braun. "I love music: I have heard the great opera singers in the old Opera House, I have heard the Philharmonic Orchestra—Vienna is like that, rich and poor go alike to the Opera..."

An idea flashed through Macdonald's mind: a ludicrous idea, perhaps, yet one worth trying. Because he believed that "Auntie" was lying to him, there must be some secret she and her voluble nephew were guarding, and her conversation about the Opera gave him his opportunity to spring a surprise on her.

"You must have heard many singers during your years in Vienna," he went on conversationally. "I expect you have seen Waldtraut Körner since her return to this city. She is a friend of yours, is she not?"

As he said to Nauheim afterwards, it was the element of surprise which took her aback. One moment she was a refined old governess, boasting in genteel fashion of her experiences in the musical world of Vienna, the next moment she was a baleful old horror, with eyes that were venomous and lips that quivered: but she recovered herself remarkably quickly.

"A friend of mine, the Waldtraut Körner?" she quavered. "You do not know what you say. No one but an Englishman could say a thing so foolish. Why should I know her, why should she know me? I am poor, I am old, of no importance... You may be a great detective, Herr Superintendent, but you should not make mock of a poor old woman."

Macdonald did not answer for a moment. He sat and considered the old woman in her bare comfortless room. Mrs. Edshaw had said she was intelligent: that in the German language at least, she was highly literate. She had lived in Vienna in the thirties with Frau Rothmeister, and had opportunities to know the Rothmeisters' friends. Was it conceivable that this poverty-stricken old woman had used her intelligence, had been a link in this story which Macdonald was trying to unravel? Of one thing he was certain, he would get no admission from her, beyond that startled glance of sheer hatred which he had precipitated by mentioning the name of Waldtraut Körner.

He got up at last, deciding not to let her know what was in his mind—to leave her to guess.

"I am very far from making a mock of you, Fräulein Braun. I have a great respect for the straightforwardness with which you have answered my questions. Thank you very much."

As he left the poor apartment house, Macdonald saw another aged face peering at him from a ground-floor window: another face which showed in its wrinkled greyness the aftermath of starvation. They were not starving now, these old derelicts, but they were very poor. Fräulein Braun had an English nephew who could buy her a radio set, a warm coat, new blankets. Macdonald guessed that it was pretty certain that the other inhabitants of that poor house would think it worth their while to keep on the right side of Mr. Webster's Auntie.

XV

1

"Your outrageous guess was right," said Inspector Nauheim. "Walsingham did go to the Emperor Maximilian Hotel. The porter recognised the photograph at once. Walsingham arrived at the hotel at twenty-five minutes past eleven: he gave the name of Herr Waldemar, and Fräulein Waldtraut Körner told the porter to send Herr Waldemar up to her suite. He only stayed for about ten minutes and then left the hotel on foot. And lest you feel too hopeful, Superintendent, I hasten to add that Waldtraut Körner can receive no visitors to-day. She has had a heart attack, and her doctor says that her health is precarious and that she must be kept very, very quiet."

"You have seen her doctor?" asked Macdonald, and Nauheim smiled.

"Yes. I was not going to be put off so easily, but the Herr Doktor Gropius, who is a physician of repute, says that this is no simulated illness. She is really ill. He was called in to see her at midday, and his opinion is that she had a shock of some kind and a collapse followed." Nauheim gave his characteristic shrug. "So we are held up," he added. "I told the Herr Doktor the circumstances, but he said that even if he gave permission for us to see her, it would be quite useless. She would not speak."

"Did she have any visitors before her sudden collapse?"

"No, Superintendent, but there is a telephone by her bed: she had several telephone calls. And I've no doubt that somebody rang her up and told her that Herr Waldemar was dead."

"Has she a maid?"

"No." Nauheim chuckled. "I had a talk with the manager. Waldtraut Körner reserved his best suite—the Imperial Suite. As you know, her name is famous in Vienna: because she was a great singer the Viennese adored her. There is no city in the world which idolises its opera singers as Vienna does. So the manager of the Emperor Maximilian knew it would not be good policy to be difficult over the lady, though he had his private doubts about her ability to pay. These hotel people always know. The manager tells me now that he believes she has no money at all. Everything has been put down to her account—everything."

"So to cut the cackle, we can assume that the lady came to Vienna to raise some ready money somehow," said Macdonald, "and her hope of raising it was these famous Steinadler memoirs."

"That, Superintendent, is a very fair assumption," said Nauheim.

"It alters the nature of the transaction," said Macdonald. "I had been assuming that the sale would have been conducted with the usual decorum in such cases: a contract argued out after examination of the script, and an advance paid on publication. But if Fräulein Waldtraut Körner is virtually penniless, she may have been trying to get a quick advance, and prepared to deal with anybody who would pay spot cash in the hope that the papers in her possession were worth a quick bid."

"So perhaps we see daylight," said Nauheim. "If Walsingham was in a position to make her a substantial offer of cash down, he might conceivably have taken the script, unexamined, against a post-dated cheque: he gave her a receipt for the script and she gave him a receipt for the cheque. As you say, the transaction is no longer in the nature of conventional dealings with a publisher of repute."

"And Walsingham may have had both the bank balance and the inside information which would have made him know the chance was worth taking," said Macdonald.

"So...and the assumption is that Walsingham was watched, that his business with her was known, that he was killed, robbed and his body left for Herr Vanbrugh to run over on the Wattmanngasse?" queried Nauheim blithely.

"Perhaps—but we can't short-circuit things like that," said Macdonald. "I refer you to the evidence—all of it. Beginning with Miss Le Vendre's accident, continuing with the loss of Dr. Natzler's keys, going on with Walsingham's lift into Vienna in a car which might have been a Benz, and not omitting that most intelligent old lady, Fräulein Ilse Braun. We have developed some ideas, but the ideas aren't going to be much use to us without evidence."

"Fräulein Ilse Braun?" queried Nauheim.

"Miss Elsie Brown, aunt to Ernest Henry Webster, the

cameraman. Auntie came to Vienna in the long ago as a simple English governess: she lived with the Rothmeisters and developed into a highly intelligent woman, speaking excellent German. My own theory is that Auntie learnt about the Waldtraut Körner papers and wrote to her nephew saying that here was the chance of a lifetime if he could get somebody in the London newspaper world to put up the money for a quick sale. That, my lad, is a theory. I think Webster has highly developed wits and Auntie has a highly developed intelligence service."

"Well..." said Nauheim, "that's a variation on the original theme."

"There are a lot of variations in this story," said Macdonald, "but let us get down to the essential facts. One of them is Webster's presence at the Liesingerkeller last night. Auntie attests that he was back at her house shortly after midnight; if he was at the Liesingerkeller until nearly closing time and back home by twelve o'clock he could not have been out to Hietzing to get Walsingham's body in the Wattmanngasse, also shortly before midnight."

"And if Webster went to the Streicher film and then on to the Liesingerkeller he couldn't have followed Walsingham to the Emperor Maximilian Hotel," mused Nauheim.

"And I certainly don't think it was Webster who drove that Benz," said Macdonald. "Someone picked up Walsingham in Hietzing and drove him to the Kärntnerstrasse."

"If he was to pay the Waldtraut Körner for her papers, she might have arranged to send a car for him," put in Nauheim.

"You have two cars to trace—the Benz and the converted jeep," said Macdonald. "The latter may have been accidental, just one of those confusing extras, but the Benz is integral to the case. Who owns it? Who drove it? There is a lot of work for you to do which I can't do anything about. I'm sorry, but there it is."

Nauheim laughed, his white teeth flashing. "You produce the ideas, sir: outrageous ideas, but they work. You leave us the donkey work—it is a fair division of labour. I have an army of patient donkeys inquiring about those cars, so let me try to sort out the motives of some of these people: the cameraman and Auntie. I am impressed by their insistence that Webster was in Vienna all the evening. If they knew that Walsingham was himself killed in Vienna, would they not have tried to prove an alibi elsewhere?"

"Provided they can produce witnesses to prove that they were in evidence at this place or that the whole evening, it doesn't matter where they claim to have been," said Macdonald. "Walsingham left the Emperor Maximilian about eleven thirty-five, according to the porter. His body was in the Gloriettestrasse by midnight: that means he was driven there. I still think it's improbable he was killed in the main streets of the city—between the hotel and the car-park where the Benz was left. A breakdown en route seems to me more probable—somewhere off the Mariahilfer Strasse or the Schönbrunner Strasse perhaps. The person we want is the driver of that Benz."

He paused a moment, thinking hard: then he said: "When I was at Schönbrunn on Wednesday, I saw Fräulein Waldtraut Körner there. She must have been driven there. You might find out who was the elderly gentleman who escorted her: he may have been a car-owner."

Nauheim sat and pondered. "You saw a lot in a short time, Superintendent. So the Waldtraut Körner was at Schönbrunn—at Hietzing... Did she go there merely as a sightseer? I doubt it."

"Mr. Webster says he was also at Schönbrunn on that day: he is a most accommodating man," observed Macdonald. "I wonder if Mr. Webster speaks academic German, as his Auntie does. He has told me very firmly that he does not speak German."

"This thing grows more and more confusing. Let us think again," said Nauheim. "A friend of the Waldtraut Körners possesses a car..."

"Perhaps," put in Macdonald. "You suggested that the lady sent a car to bring Walsingham into Vienna, that his errand might be conducted with suitable secrecy. After all, she was an opera singer: she has led a dramatic life; perhaps it is in character for her to do things in a dramatic manner—and this is Vienna, not London. But making all allowances for the operatic manner, I can still imagine no circumstances in which the car driver sent by Waldtraut Körner should have killed Walsingham on the way back to Hietzing. The driver complicates things."

Nauheim nodded, his eyes very bright and intent. "Yes. This may be wheels within wheels. I think this is very much worth while, Superintendent, to argue this thing out and see the implications. I have my own small suggestion to make, while we guess our way along. Waldtraut Körner, who was on the rocks, was conducting several negotiations: she was prepared to do business with the highest and the quickest bidder, and she played them off, one against the other."

"As an answer to some of the problems that would serve admirably," said Macdonald, "especially if she was foolish enough to inform another bidder that Walsingham was coming to see her that evening to settle the deal. That suggests possibilities. And now perhaps we had better leave our theorisings and get back to plain detection: you to contact your patient donkeys on the roads from Vienna to Hietzing, me to talk my own ideas over with the Natzlers—who are very intelligent people—and to find out from London if anything else has turned up their end."

"It is very necessary that we find out about that grey car," said Nauheim. "We are watching the railways and the airport, but it is difficult to stop every car which makes a devious way out of Vienna."

Macdonald nodded. "That's it—and if somebody does not do a bolt I shall be surprised. One last suggestion for you which has just occurred to me—practical and not theoretical: could you ask the Waldtraut Körner's doctor if he would be willing to have Dr. Franz Natzler as consultant, to give a second opinion about the patient's heart? Franz Natzler knows all about this story and he is a very intelligent man as well as a distinguished doctor. If anybody can help us in this matter of the old opera singer, he might."

"*Schon.* That is a good idea. I will approach Dr. Gropius at once."

2

Macdonald left the *Polizeiamt* and walked across the streets to the Kärntnerstrasse, to note the layout between the

Emperor Maximilian Hotel and the car-park. He felt pow-
erless in Vienna: he could not follow up the investigation
as he would have done in London—that must be left to the
Vienna police. All he could do was to produce ideas for others
to prove or disprove. But he felt again that it was common
sense to assume that Walsingham had not been attacked here
in the Kärntnerstrasse, the Bond Street of Vienna. At least till
midnight it would have been glittering with lights, crowded
with "window shoppers" who would have filled the brightly-
lighted pavements.

When he reached the impressive entrance of the Emperor
Maximilian, Macdonald chuckled. There, gesticulating and
smiling to the resplendent porter, was Ernest Henry Webster.
The moment he set eyes on Macdonald, Webster beamed.

"Well, Superintendent, it's an ill wind that blows nobody
any good. I'm sorry about the old lady—she's very bad, I
gather, very bad. The greatest dramatic soprano of her day,
I'm told, to say nothing of all these stories—romance and
that. But I reckon these should be valuable—some of the last
photos ever taken of her, and good pictures, too. Never taken
better. You have a look, sir."

He thrust a packet of photographs into Macdonald's hand,
and with his back to a shop window, the C.I.D. man studied them.
Against the background of the Schönbrunn fountains, with the
Gloriette in the distance, Fräulein Waldtraut Körner stood in
her sable cloak and picture hat, with her old escort a step or so
behind, just as Macdonald had seen her. The photograph was
more than good—it was a masterpiece: light and shade, background and foreground, all were a setting for the "Erzherzogin"
as Elizabeth Le Vendre had called her, the Archduchess.

"It's very, very good," said Macdonald, and Webster beamed.

"Look through the others, sir. I found a chap who could do some quick developing and printing—first-rate he is. I wanted to make sure I hadn't slipped up."

Waldtraut Körner outside the Opera House; on the steps of the Karlskirche; in the great open space of the Heldenplatz before the plinth of the equestrian statue of Prince Eugen; on the steps of the Emperor Maximilian Hotel—all the pictures were equally good.

"You must have followed her all round Vienna," said Macdonald.

"I did," said Webster cheerfully. "I told you I was going to get pictures of her, didn't I, sir? Architecture's all right for Tucker & Tucker, but the papers like human interest. Now what about that one? I only took it this morning, but this chap I told you of he does that quick-dry method as well as I do it myself. Champion that picture is though I says it as shouldn't. 'Student of History in the shadow of the Hapsburgs' Folly.' That's a picture to be proud of."

It was. The arches of the Gloriette soared up against the sky: in the foreground, by the pool, a young man with a dark head sat reading in the shadow: it was not only a remarkable picture, it was an admirable likeness of Charles Stratton.

"One or two enlargements—uncommonly interesting head he's got: very striking head," said Webster, and Macdonald studied the pictures thoughtfully, his face calmly interested, his mind working furiously.

"Very good indeed, Mr. Webster. You're an artist at this job."

"I've made my living at it, sir, and there's a lot of competition, as you must know. It's not enough to be good, you've got to have the eye for it—and maybe imagination comes in, too. This one now." He picked out the enlargement of Stratton's head. "Made my living," he said slowly. "You could call it my living, in a manner of speaking. That one—well, I call it my alibi."

"What do you mean by that exactly, Mr. Webster?"

"I'll tell you, sir, and welcome, but this is a poor place to talk, and if you're not careful you'll be having some of these pressmen turning their cameras your way. All agog they are—the story's just breaking. Now say if we walk along to the Cathedral, the Stephansdom they call it, though where the dome is beats me. It's nice and quiet in there and they don't seem to mind you talking—very broadminded these R.C.s are."

"Right," said Macdonald, and as they turned towards the Cathedral, Webster gave his cheerful little chuckle.

"Talking about somewhere quiet, have you ever been in the Capuchin Crypt, sir, where all the Emperors are buried? Lumme—that crypt knocked me flat! Twelve Holy Roman Emperors and fifteen Empresses; one hundred and thirty-seven Hapsburgs counting the whole lot—and Maria Theresa's governess—I like that last bit, so does Auntie! Holy Roman Emperors—and that copy of Charlemagne's crown atop of them. Beats our Abbey hollow. I mucked in with a party of Americans just as one of them monks was taking them round. I couldn't follow the lingo but the coffins spoke for themselves. I was almost jittered. There's a place for a murder, I said to myself, behind one o' them coffins. It's a big place, too: easy to slip away from the party, and the old monk, he'd never've noticed. Just across the road and be careful of the traffic, sir. I like this place. This is a church and no mistake, but that crypt turned me cold."

In the Gothic magnificence of the Stephansdom the shadows were deepening as the afternoon sun sunk lower in the west: quite unabashed by the solemnity of the vast building, Webster said:

"There's a coupla' chairs over there. Nice and peaceful here—my feet gets tired after a long day. That's better. Now what was it you was saying, sir?"

"Why did you use the word alibi, Mr. Webster?"

3

"I may not be educated, but I'm not plain silly, sir. I see how things is—you getting busy on all the passengers in that Viscount on Monday: quite right, too, seeing what's happened. But it's not a comfortable feeling. And all these pressmen, they're routing out the bits and pieces, dead on the mark they is. You reckon that Walsingham got put paid to in Vienna, sir, don't you, not in Hietzing as appeared: some of them have routed that out. You see they'll tell me anything, sir. Uncle Ernest's got the pictures. Now the long and short of it is, I was in Vienna last night—and not that far away from the Kärntnerstrasse. I told you so, sir."

"You did. You said you went to the Apollo Cinema and on to the Liesingerkeller."

"Quite right, sir—and I'd like to be able to prove it. I'm a commonplace-looking cuss myself, short and fat and shabby: dozens like me—but this Stratton's quite a different cup of tea." Mr. Webster pulled out his photograph again. "Striking, as I said. So I went to the Apollo, and I went to the Liesingerkeller, and I showed these pictures and I said 'Do you remember this young chap now?' The waiter who served us both Lagers, he remembered Stratton and he recognised me, and he knew we stayed there till closing time."

"Don't you think you would have been wiser to come to me, and let me deal with the matter, Mr. Webster?"

The stout little man met Macdonald's eyes squarely. "Yes, sir, if we'd both been in England and you'd been doing the job. We trust our police in England, sir, and by our police, I mean you. But you're not doing the whole job here, sir. No offence meant, but you're in the same box as me: you don't speak the lingo, do you?—not easy. It's these Austrians are asking questions here, sir, and I've heard a bit about the police here from Auntie. She don't trust them, and she's a very intelligent old lady, is Auntie."

"She certainly is," said Macdonald, "but if you don't speak German, how do you talk to the waiters at the Liesingerkeller, Mr. Webster?"

"Same as you, sir—interpreter. I got on to young Stratton on the telephone, just after you left. I knew he was staying with that Vogel—a lawyer, isn't he? Stratton wouldn't come and help himself, but he gave me the name of the young fellow he chummed up with last night—name of Schneider. He came with me in his lunch hour."

Once again Macdonald was impressed with the sheer calmness and aplomb of the stout little man who sat beside him in the Stephansdom: Webster sounded quite unruffled and completely certain of himself.

"Lovely bit of carving on that pulpit," murmured Webster to himself. "I'd like to get a picture of that. I wonder if you could help me to get a permit, sir—I believe they're very difficult. After all, one good turn deserves another."

Mr. Webster was shuffling his photographs again and produced the one of Waldtraut Körner at Schönbrunn.

"The old gentleman with her now: he's a lawyer—a notary is it they call them here? Auntie recognised his face when I showed her this picture. Herr Heinrich Guggenheim—real mouthfuls these names and no mistake."

"That's very helpful," said Macdonald.

"I want to help, sir. If you could only get it into your head that I *want* to help," pleaded Webster. "There's a lot of talk about some car: it was the pressmen told me about it, sir—wonderful the way these boys talk English. Mr. Walsingham came into Vienna by car last night, so they're saying. The old man at the car-park saw him—and making a good thing out of it, I've no doubt. A big grey car, pre-war model, was that it, sir?"

"You seem to know as much about it, as I do, Mr. Webster."

"Well, sir, maybe I know more in a manner of speaking. These pressmen, they'll talk to Uncle Ernest when they're not that keen on talking to their own police: that's how it is. The boys know Mr. Walsingham went to see Waldtraut Körner at her hotel—you can't keep a thing like that dark. The head porter and the Herr Ober, they're careful enough, but there are the pages and the floor maids and all the rest: anyway, you can take it from me that the press boys know about where Mr. Walsingham went. And about that car, sir. I haven't said a word to none of them. I reckoned I'd be seeing you around. I told the boys straight, if you think you're a jump ahead of our Macdonald, I told them, you think again."

Had he not been in the grave shadows of the Stephansdom, Macdonald would have laughed aloud. The stout little man was surpassing himself.

"And you was quite right when you said I'd been chasing the old dame all round Vienna, sir. I've paid good money to get in a position to take some of those pictures," said Webster. "I got that picture outside the Opera House on Wednesday— three o'clock it was—and I saw the old dame get in a car with the old Guggenheim gent. I took a taxi, sir, reckoning there might be another picture to come. That's how I got to Schönbrunn, following the grey car with the old dame in it."

"Was Herr Heinrich Guggenheim driving the car?" asked Macdonald.

"Bless you, no, sir. I reckon he's eighty if he's a day: not that the shuffer was a chicken—old chap, he was, but smart enough in his regimentals—brass buttons and that. I was alongside when they pulled up at the Schönbrunn Palace entrance: come to think of it, I've got a picture with that car in, just as the old lady was handed out. And I heard the old gent talk a lot of gruff to the shuffer—shouted at him about something. I don't know what it was all about, but I heard the shuffer's name—at least I reckon it was his name."

Mr. Webster paused: a good melodramatic pause, giving Macdonald time for another guess. After all, his guesses had been founded on probabilities as well as information received. And he was right.

"If I heard aright, sir, the name was Pretzel—funny sort of name: stuck in my mind, somehow. And that's about all from yours truly at the moment." Mr. Webster sighed, and then mopped his forehead, though it was cold in the great church. "I'm not used to all these excitements," he said. "I've taken pictures of any amount of characters in crime stories, but I've never got muddled up with the story myself. But I do reckon I've got a scoop here, in the picture line. It'll be front-line news in London, too, this about Mr. Walsingham going to see the Waldtraut Körner just before he was laid out— and I don't want to miss the bus." He looked at Macdonald pleadingly. "Anything against my getting home, sir, on the first plane that's got a free seat? Then I could place my pictures to advantage: getting in first's everything in my job."

"I'm sorry, Mr. Webster, but I'm afraid you can't do that. Your evidence may be essential—and your photographs, too."

"As you say, sir. But I've told you all I know—and I thought maybe you'd stretch a point. Anyway, could you help me by getting my pictures on the plane, sir, so that they could be picked up by a friend of mine at London Airport? I reckon the pilot or navigator might oblige, especially if you put it to them…"

Macdonald studied Webster's round candid face: was this simplicity or the reverse? Again Webster spoke.

"If you're asking yourself 'Is he phony?' I ask *you*, sir— haven't I been straight with you since I first set eyes on you at Schwechat? Haven't I given you the dope as I picked it up? I reckon it's a bit hard to be looked at like you're looking at me."

"Detection's a hard trade, Mr. Webster."

"Maybe. Oh, well—no use crying over spilt milk—and if you'd like these prints, sir, you're welcome. I've got others, and I know you won't do the dirty on me getting them published without leave—as some might."

He got up and looked about him. "Light's going—but I might still get a shot or two. 'Sunset over Schönbrunn.' Wonderful effects you get with those clipped trees—like a rampart against the sky, they are. One thing I've thought of—'Moonlight on the Gloriette.' Now that'd be a picture—and the moon's nearly at the full. They turn the public out at sunset, but if a chap stayed put, behind them hedges, well, they can't search the whole blooming grounds, could they, sir? The place is too big."

"You can't expect me to encourage you to break local by-laws, Mr. Webster—and thank you very much for the photographs, and for trusting me with them."

"You're welcome," beamed Webster, "and as for trusting, you're English police. That's good enough for me. I'd trust you right through—to the end of the road, as the old song has it. And now I'll just hop on a tram and get to Schönbrunn. I can just make it if I'm slippy."

XVI

1

PRETZEL. MACDONALD REMEMBERED THE NAME ALL right: while he was worrying out the complexities of this case, he had wondered if Pretzel would appear again. In Macdonald's experience, the supers in a case did often make another and inglorious entry before the case was finally finished off. Herr Pretzel was the patient who had been to see Dr. Franz Natzler before his keys had disappeared and Macdonald had wondered whether he himself, Dr. Natzler's guest, had provided reason for the theft of the key-ring. "Did somebody think life would be simpler if I were removed and that possession of the keys of the Natzlers' house might facilitate my removal?" he had thought. But it was Pretzel himself who got "removed." Even before Macdonald and Nauheim had had time to go out to Gaudensdorff to interview Herr Heinrich Guggenheim, the Vienna police had fished Pretzel's body out of the Danube Canal. The canal is a loop of the Danube, connecting the heart of Vienna with the mighty river which flows south east along its flood plain, not through the city itself (though antiquaries say the line of the canal was the main course of the river in prehistoric times).

It was near the Franz Josef Bahnhof, below the bridge which connects Alserbach Strasse with the Wallenstein Strasse, that Pretzel's body was found, not a mile from the Ringstrasse itself. There was nothing on the body to identify it, but Macdonald and Nauheim were both mindful of the driver who had brought Walsingham from Hietzing into Vienna.

"I think this will be Pretzel," said Macdonald. "Webster has a knack of being right. Pretzel saw too much, so Pretzel was disposed of."

Herr Guggenheim was a very old man, and a very frightened old man. He was so old, his face so livid with fear, that the detectives dared not press him too closely. He looked ready to pass out into a world where no detectives could tackle him. The story he told was simple and innocent: The Waldtraut Körner was indeed an old and a well-beloved friend: he had known her since her debut in the *Staats Oper*, over fifty years ago. He had, during his professional days as notary, given her advice about her contracts and other business matters. "I did not see her for many years, alas," he went on. "After her retirement she left Vienna. I was overjoyed when I heard she was coming to stay here again. I went to her hotel to greet her, and finding she had no car, I begged she would make use of mine." After a pause (for his voice was shaking and uncertain), the old man told of the visit to Schönbrunn.

"I walked round the gardens with her, but I am no longer

strong enough to walk very far. She wished to see the State Apartments—the great gallery where she had sung for the Emperor Franz Josef himself. I went and sat in the car until she returned. As you must realise, she is much younger than myself, and she insisted on doing the arduous round of the State Apartments." Herr Guggenheim was unable to tell them if the lady had met or spoken with any friends at Schönbrunn. He had put his car at her disposal each day, and yesterday evening she had rung him up, before going to the Opera, to ask if the chauffeur could bring a friend—Herr Waldemar—out from Hietzing to see her at the Emperor Maximilian Hotel. It was agreed that Herr Waldemar should be picked up at the corner of the Lindengasse. "And that is all I know," wailed the old man. "I gave orders to my chauffeur, Humpfinger: I know he took the car. I know the car is now again in the garage, and that Humpfinger has not come to work to-day. I can tell you no more."

"You say your chauffeur's name is Humpfinger," said Nauheim. "Did you always call him by that name? I am told you called him Pretzel."

The old face grew more livid, but Guggenheim answered with an effort at contempt. "Pretzel? Yes: an old nickname: he has served me since a boy. We used to call him Pretzel then, and the name stuck, as such foolish names do."

Macdonald wondered very much if the old man was capable of standing up to much more questioning, or if he would collapse on their hands, but Nauheim went on, quietly and persistently.

"You knew that Fräulein Waldtraut Körner came to Vienna to transact some business, Herr Guggenheim?"

"I knew that, yes. Everybody in Vienna knows it. She had some valuable literary property to negotiate. But I, alas, was too old to advise her. I have retired from professional work long since."

"Do you know her present legal adviser?" asked Nauheim.

"I cannot tell you. Indeed, I did not ask. It was better so. I knew—for she confided in me—that she no longer had the means to instruct a lawyer of note. Costs are very high to-day…and life is hard." He mumbled uncertainly for a moment, then he added, "She was conducting these negotiations herself: against my advice, I might add. But I am too old to deal with these things."

He sighed and leaned back in his chair, closing his eyes. "I am very tired, Herr Inspektor. I cannot talk any more. It has been a shock to learn that my old friend is so ill…she who was the pride and ornament of our *Staats Oper*, the greatest of them all."

Nauheim was very persistent: he went on, "I think, Herr Guggenheim, that you must be aware that Fräulein Waldtraut Körner employed an intermediary in this matter," but his persistence was useless. The old man's head leant back feebly against his chair and his jaw dropped. He was still breathing, but he looked terrifyingly old and frail. Macdonald got up.

"It's no use—he's on the verge of collapse. I'll get his servant."

As they went through the hall Macdonald said, "I think we can see the way things went, and sort it out for ourselves. Proof will be forthcoming eventually."

As they left the gloomy hall and the front door was opened, the faint evening light shone on their faces. The western sky was still a glory of fading rose, dappled clouds changing to grey even as they watched.

"Sunset over Schönbrunn," murmured Macdonald. "I wonder if he got his picture." Then he turned to Nauheim. "You've got plenty of jobs to do—jobs I can't help you with, not in Vienna. I think I'm going to back my fancy and see the full moon rise over the Gloriette. If I get caught, you can bail me out to-morrow."

Nauheim looked horrified. "You're not going alone. I'll send a couple of men with you."

"No, don't do that," said Macdonald. "I'll take Karl Natzler with me. He'll be back from Zürich by this time. After all, if an Englishman is taking liberties in the precincts of Schönbrunn, it's picturesque justice for an English policeman to deal with it. All you need do is to give me a *laisser-passer* for the man in charge."

"I don't like it," said Nauheim. "I've got a man tailing all of them—"

Macdonald laughed. "I shan't be at all surprised if Ernest Henry Webster has evaded his shadow. He may be simulating a grizzly bear in the Tiergarten by this time: but I have an idea he'll be there to shoot his coveted picture, 'Moonrise over the Gloriette'—and if he is, I'm going to see him do the shooting."

2

"I'm going to back my fancy and see the full moon rise over the Gloriette." So Macdonald had said to Nauheim, and an hour later Macdonald chuckled silently to himself as he remembered his own words. In England he seldom had a chance of

"Backing his fancy" as he was doing now; back home he was responsible for handling the routine work, for giving orders to his men. The responsibility was all his—in England. Here in Vienna there were many things he could not do: it was the business of the Austrian police to marshal their own forces, to shadow the suspects, to watch the roads, the railway stations, the airport: to check alibis, to interrogate minor witnesses. How good they were at the job Macdonald had no means of judging: he knew he could not get the "feel" of a foreign police force after working with them for only a few hours. He hoped they were good—as good as he knew his own men to be in London: as tenacious as Reeves, as patient as old Jenkins. But now he had left the Vienna police to their own methods, and he, Macdonald, was standing in the deep shadows of the clipped trees which rise like forty-foot box hedges flanking the approach to the garden front of Schönbrunn Palace.

Macdonald and Karl Natzler had been admitted by the Tiergarten: it was the wisest entrance, for in the Tiergarten there were always keepers on guard at night, and comings and goings did not attract attention. Karl was now on the far side of the gardens prowling silently on his own.

As he stood in the darkness Macdonald could hear some of the animals calling in their cages: nocturnal animals to whom the night brought their time of greatest awareness. It was a bit like being in Regent's Park at night, where the call of lions and the howl of wolves mingled with the rumble of the London traffic. Here, as in London, there was a glow in the sky, a glow which had replaced the afterglow of the sunset. In the eastern sky, the myriad lights of Vienna were reflected up to the misty clouds, and Macdonald knew that when his eyes grew accustomed to the gloom, he would be able to see the open arches of the Gloriette up there on the hill, opposite the garden front of the palace. Had the players in this most un-Viennese melodrama used the Gloriette as a rendezvous? Macdonald remembered Mr. Webster's hopeful voice saying "They can't watch the whole blooming grounds... If you got shut in after the gates were closed..." Was that an invitation, a bait? A hope that even a London C.I.D. man would lose his head in the atmosphere of Vienna? "Perhaps I am in the process of becoming light-headed," thought Macdonald, who knew he was far nearer to laughing than was customary to him when he was on duty: it was the effect of being free of routine: free to prowl, like a nocturnal animal, in the fragrant shadows of the Hapsburgs' gardens—"in the shadow of the Hapsburgs' Folly"—but no one who hasn't been in Vienna will ever appreciate Ernest Henry's caption, thought Macdonald.

He began to move at last; he could see the arches now, up there on the hill, dark and beautiful, a serene shadow against a sky which seemed pale only because his eyes were conditioned to the night. The Gloriette was to the south of the palace: the moon would come up over Vienna itself and shine athwart the arches, across the pool at their feet.

"Well, even if this proves to be empty folly from the point of view of detection, it'll be an experience to remember for the rest of my days," thought Macdonald. "Moonlight over the Gloriette, an experience once reserved for the Hapsburgs, Maria Theresa and old Franz Josef...and perhaps the Waldtraut Körner in her prime."

He intended to outflank the Gloriette, to get behind the

colonnade on the Fasan Garten side, where the shadows would be deepest, away from the reflected lights of Penzing and the Hietzinger Hauptstrasse. He walked very slowly, mounting the hilly tree-shaded paths on the Tiergarten side, and so up to the Tiroler Garten at the top, hearing the ululations of wolves and the murmur of distant traffic, the wind in the trees—but no other sounds.

3

Lying prone under the colonnade, his head resting on his arms, so that he could hear any echo of footfall from the telltale ground and so that his dark head should be all of a piece in the shadows with his dark suit, Macdonald had an odd feeling of satisfaction. He believed he knew exactly what had happened since he left England on the Viscount: he believed he could prove his case—but the business of arrest (barring unexpected fireworks) was in the hands of the Vienna police. A solitary C.I.D. Superintendent whose German was negligible, could not issue orders to the rank and file of a foreign police force, but he could back his fancy. He was here because he believed that Ernest Henry Webster still had an ace up his sleeve, "and even if he hasn't, I shall still see the moonlight on these arches and on the Austrian eagle up there," he thought.

That was Macdonald's last tribute to what might be called the aesthetics of the matter for some time, for he had heard a footfall. Quietly and steadily someone was coming up the hill.

It was some moments before the new arrival reached the top, and he was panting by the time he got there. He came to the front of the Gloriette, and it took Macdonald some careful squirming to get himself into a position where, by raising his head a little, he could just make out the bulk of a man's figure, seated calmly on the long seat between the colonnade and the formal pool, facing towards the palace. In the gloom it was difficult to distinguish the figure at all, but such impression as Macdonald could get suggested bulk rather than length, a fat man, with round-shaped hat, a bowler perhaps, but its shape was indistinguishable. It was hearing rather than sight which identified the newcomer: under his breath, in a sibilance not quite a whistle, the stout man was producing a very old tune, an English tune which Macdonald remembered hearing in his early teens.

"*You are my honey-honey-suckle, I am the bee,*" breathed out ludicrously from the Hapsburgs' Folly.

This, then, was Mr. Webster: surely nobody else in Vienna could be whistling "The Honeysuckle and the Bee." The tune faded out and was followed by words: very softly, Mr. Webster was talking to himself—or was it to himself?

"It's a fair old mess-up: no mistake about that. I knew there was some hanky-panky all along. Not that that worried me, not at first. Stands to reason there'd be a bit of funny stuff, seeing what we was all after, and I was game to do a bit of play-acting meself. Just one of those things, wasn't it? And I'd've helped you out and gone shares over the doings—fair shares, mind you—but you gone too far. It's all U.P. and I'm throwing me hand in. I never bargained for sharing the business end of a rope."

The voice was the voice of Ernest Henry Webster, talking undiluted Cockney: but he wasn't being funny: he didn't sound funny, he sounded oddly impressive. He was putting all he knew into his soliloquy. A warning phrase flashed through Macdonald's mind: "Anything you say can be taken down and used in evidence," but he didn't formulate it. He wasn't asking any questions, he was listening to a recital, surely the oddest recital ever produced at the Gloriette, no matter what strange confidences those stones had heard.

"I wanted the doings: a cool coupla' thousand old Ike offered if I pulled it off, and I knew there'd be others after it. Stands to reason—too much talk there'd been. Ike knew, bless you: good as warned me to watch out for you. And I'd have gone fifty-fifty with anybody who played straight, seeing I hadn't the technique to work it single-handed. I tumbled to it you was the snake in the grass, young fella-me-lad. I saw you make up to the old lady in the Porcelain Room as they calls it, in the Palace there, Wednesday it was. Watch? Blimey, I watched like a cat over a mouse hole, tailing of her all round Vienna. Tailing you, too, come to that. But I didn't realise how bad it was, not till to-day. There's been too much of it and I'm through. I tell you so straight. So you might as well come out and talk business. I know you're there. You're sunk without me: you know that."

There was a moment of dead silence, and then Mr. Webster went on, "I said I'd go fifty-fifty. I would have, too. I've got the cash—and I reckon you needed it. Your flash friends'll want some of the needful before they get you out of Vienna in a wine barrel or whatever it is."

"You talk too much: that's your trouble," said another voice. It came from the shadows, under the colonnade. "You had a perfectly good idea: cook an alibi, for both of us. You put that one over as neatly as anything I ever heard. Passed it to me as slick as a conjuring trick: we both needed it and you pulled it off. What are you losing your nerve for?"

"I'm not losing me nerve. I tell you I've had enough. I know when to stop," said Webster. "And it's now. I'm not playing ball any longer, all I want is to quit. If I'd known the sort of party this was going to turn out, I'd never have touched it—never. And I'm telling you you'd better beat it while you can—the faster the better. Better for you and better for me. I'm through."

"Sure of yourself, aren't you?"

"Pretty sure," said Webster. "Not that I know everything, though Auntie helped me a lot. Got contacts everywhere, Auntie has, in that hotel and out of it. It was a case of all watching one another: though I wasn't on the spot when that car stopped in the Mariahilfer Strasse. Just past the West Bahnhof it was: eleven forty-five, I'm told. Funny thing that, a friend of Auntie's saw it happen—accident or something." There was a moment of dead silence, then Webster went on, "One thing I can prove, and half a dozen witnesses to swear to it, no hocus pocus or funny stuff: I was still in the Liesingerkeller at a quarter to twelve last night. I could have carried you through with me, too, and saved you a lot of bother, only you went too far. Too far altogether. Accidents may happen, but you've got to draw the line somewhere."

"Oh lord, don't you love talking," mocked the faint voice from the shadows. "You asked me to come here because you said you'd got something urgent to tell me. As I see it, we're in the same boat, but there's no need to get in a panic over it. If we stick to the same story we're safe enough, and we'll share the proceeds later."

"The same boat," murmured Mr. Webster. "The same plane's nearer the mark. Well, I'm not arguing: I'm telling you. There's no proceeds to share. I know that. I'm not plain silly. But things have got to the state when you can land me in the mess you've made yourself, and I'm not sharing the rope you've earned. I've not earned it. So you quit. Got that? It's your last chance."

"Why the hell d'you think I'm going to take orders from you?" demanded the other. His voice was low, but it was dangerous now.

"Because I know: I've tumbled to it," said Webster. "I was slow enough, wasn't I? but I didn't get a chance of a real look at you—not till Zürich. If a chap keeps his nose in a book and his hair flops down over his horn-rims, you don't get much chance of seeing his dial." The Cockney voice was slow and steady, almost ruminative, and it went on with maddening persistence. "I sat here on this seat beside you—only this morning, was it?—and I still didn't tumble to it. But I've been thinking since I came up here: very nice and quiet it's been since the gates was shut. Funny how you can tumble to things, and I suddenly saw it all plain. I reckon that's what happened to the young lady: something suddenly clicked in her head, same's it did in mine: and that Walsingham, did he suddenly look at you when you stopped that car and say 'But you're not the chap I saw at London Airport'?"

Macdonald was creeping forward now: he didn't want to miss a word of Mr. Webster's meditations, but the fat man was asking for trouble and Macdonald sensed that trouble was not far away. It wouldn't be a shot: a shot would bring out the wardens from the Tiergarten, the night watchmen from the palace—and a shot can never look accidental. Macdonald guessed that another "accident" would develop, and he suddenly visualised Webster's rotund form floating in the ornamental pool there...found drowned at the Gloriette.

"You should never have trusted that Vogel," went on Webster, as though he were trying to make certain of the trouble that was certainly coming to him. "Vogel's a twister—Auntie knew that. He was only using you to get the doings..."

The trouble materialised when Macdonald was only a yard from the fat man. It was very dark under the arches, very dark on that seat, and the unseen man sprang just as Macdonald stood up: sprang straight at the fat man who sat slumped on the seat. Macdonald never forgot the sound which followed: it was not the thud of a rubber cosh on an unprotected head, it was more like the sound of a cosh on a London policeman's helmet. And then the fat man moved: with a power which Macdonald would never have suspected, the fat hands and short arms gripped the assailant behind him, and lifted the body over his head and flung it down, on to the stone verge of the ornamental pool. It lay there for a split second and then slipped into the dark water and was still.

"You might not think it, but I did strong man in a circus once," said Webster, panting a little. "Weightlifting...and that's my crash helmet. Thank you, sir. I reckoned that was how he'd do it and I came prepared, spine pads and all. I put my money on your being here to see the grand finale—seeing's believing, as they say—and as for believing, I always did believe in our English police."

4

Charles Stratton was dead. Karl Natzler told them that at once.

"And a good thing, too," said Webster calmly. "It'll save a lot of trouble: and if you want to charge me, sir, well, if I hadn't been nippy it'd've been a quick right and left for you and me, too. He was a quick worker. Self-defence my bit was—and I like to think I had a Yard ace for a witness."

Karl Natzler had gone to get the police and an ambulance. ("It seems my métier in this case," he said resignedly.) Mr. Webster spoke to Macdonald almost appealingly.

"It'll be a few minutes before they get up here, sir, to arrest me, I suppose…but can't we sit here and talk it over. I'll tell you all I know—and if so be you'd tell me if you rumbled him, and how, it'd be a privilege."

"Say if you bat first, Mr. Webster."

"O.K., sir. I've nothing to hide. The only one I tried to put over you was about the old lady's sparklers and there wasn't much harm in that. You see, this story of the Steinadler memoirs was known in London. Vogel'd been over, trying to get a fancy price, and Ike Levi heard of it. (He owns the *Sunday Blast*.) I'd heard the story, too—Auntie put me wise. I contacted Ike and he said O.K. You try to do a deal with your fancy friends in Vienna and I'll pay up—a cool two thou, he offered. But he warned me—there's other folks on to it, he said. That young Stratton who's working for the New English Agency, he's after it. He's got contacts in Vienna, too. I expect you tumbled to that little lot, sir, though it's the hell of a mix-up."

"Say I did a lot of guessing, Mr. Webster. You were in a better position than I was at the kick-off, because you had the basic facts and you were on the look-out. I wasn't. I came here for a holiday."

"If you say so, sir. Well—I did look out. I spotted young Stratton on the plane. Not that I looked at him carefully, I didn't get a chance with his nose in that book: not till after Zürich—and that was a different story."

"You're right. It was," said Macdonald. "I ought to have realised it at once, because of the suède shoes. He left London in suède shoes and arrived in Vienna in leather brogues."

"I never noticed that," said Webster regretfully. "Changed places at Zürich, did they? Auntie got one of her buddies to ring Zürich for me—on the spot, she is. Matter of accident in the gents', wasn't it, sir? Cunning, that. And on with the camel coat and pinch the passport, etc., and leave his own duds for poor Charles. Brothers, was they? Very much alike they were. You know, sir, I reckon Charles must have been using his brother as contact man in Vienna to see how the old lady was getting on marketing those memoirs—and bro. did the dirty on Charles."

Macdonald laughed: he couldn't help it. "I thought I was a good guesser, Mr. Webster, but you've got me beat."

"Not beat, sir. Call it equals: after all, it was mostly common sense when you thought it out. Now he'd pulled it off, this cosh-boy had, but he was nervous. That's why that young girl got hers—she'd had a real look at Charles: she sat beside him, didn't she, and I reckon he saw her looking at him a bit too sharp, up in them woods."

"Yes, I think that's about it," agreed Macdonald. "Any theories about the attack on Walsingham, Mr. Webster?"

"Same story, sir. Leastways, that's my bet. Maybe you'll get a bit more evidence from the London end, some of those airport girls are pretty snappy, noticing things. I wonder if you could call it to mind. We waited around a bit in that lounge, just before they took us out to the plane. You were sitting near the door, doing *The Times* crossword, wasn't you—that's when I first spotted you. Stratton—camel coat—he wasn't a yard from you. I'm trying to see it as a picture, the colours and all. Walsingham had that light raincoat on: you wore a grey herring-bone tweed, and there was the camel coat... I reckon Walsingham and Stratton had a word together just then. Likely they knew one another: Stratton—the real one—was working up a bit of a business with translation rights and that. If you look into it, I reckon you'll find there was a connection. Then, as I see it, Stratton senior as we might call him, got his stooges to watch the Emperor Maximilian Hotel and heard Walsingham had seen the old duchess. So Stratton senior and one of his pals stops Walsingham's car on the way home—to chat business. It didn't turn out that way, because Walsingham rumbled Stratton senior wasn't the lad he'd seen in London. Come to think of it, Stratton senior couldn't risk a show-down, not after that game at Zürich." There was a little pause and then Webster asked innocently, "And Rimmel, sir? Any news of him?"

It wasn't often that Macdonald felt like digging a rogue in the ribs: Webster was a rogue all right, in a jovial fashion, but not, Macdonald was convinced, a murdering rogue.

"It wasn't Rimmel—and you know it," he said.

"Well, you *do* surprise me, sir," said Webster. "I don't often make a mistake over a face."

"I'm sure you don't," said Macdonald. "Would it be a good idea if you told me just what you were up to, Mr. Webster?—and leave me to sort it out. You're not out of the wood yet, you know."

"I know, sir. But I'm trusting to you to see me through: after all, I tipped you the wink about this evening, didn't I? It was a fair old mess-up. I'd heard that Walsingham had been done in, but I didn't know the time-table. I reckoned you'd be out after all of us who was on that plane, and you'd tumble to it that I'd been after those Steinadler papers, same as Walsingham himself was. And I didn't fancy the set-up, not at all I didn't. I said to meself, 'Why not fix a good alibi, for the whole of the evening?'—and when I saw Stratton sitting on this very seat, after he'd been in that beerhouse with me yesterday evening, I thought I'd just offer him the idea—palm it, so to speak. He took it: just what he wanted, it was." Mr. Webster sighed. "It wasn't till I thought it all out I realised what he'd done, sir. Then I tried to put matters right my own way. I tipped you the wink about coming up here, sir. I thought he'd give himself away by going for me. That's why I put my crash helmet on. And I'll tell you this, sir: if I hadn't done it, you'd never have got him. I reckon he knows Vienna backwards, and he's got enough pals here to get him out of the place easy. I may have tried to be clever over that alibi, but I tried to square it up my own way to-night. After all, it was my head what had to be coshed as a demonstration... Glory, sir, that's the moon coming up. Look at that... I'll get that picture after all."

The full moon rose above the mists of Vienna and shone athwart the Gloriette: on the serenity of the classical arches, on the golden Imperial Eagle: on the formal pool; it shone across the clipped trees, making black shadows on the grass, and touched the formal front of Schönbrunn Palace: Maria Theresa yellow no longer, but misted white under the moon.

"By God," said Ernest Henry Webster. "That's a picture…"

"By God, it is," said Macdonald—and he meant it.

XVII

1

"A DISTINGUISHED PUBLISHER ONCE WROTE A BOOK ON 'The Marketing of Literary Property,'" said Macdonald. "It is a form of property which is habitually negotiated with dignity and decorum, subject to careful safeguards against misunderstandings. In this case, it wasn't the problematic sale of the still more problematical Steinadler Memoirs which caused all the trouble: it was, as usual, one criminal—a rogue elephant—who ran amok while trying to force events to his own advantage."

"I sense a feeling of gratification in that preamble, Macdonald," chuckled Karl Natzler. "You are glad to keep your convictions about the probity and respectability of the publishing profession. You do not wish the book trade to be turned into a free fight."

"No, I don't think I do," agreed Macdonald, "but every profession has its seamy verges, including law and medicine. In this case, I think the literary property was the catalytic agent, for without it the events would never have occurred. It was the Steinadler memoirs which brought Stratton, Walsingham and Webster to Vienna, all hoping to do business in their own peculiar ways, but it was Stratton's brother—a criminal known to the German police under a variety of names—who caused all the trouble. Let's sort it out into its simplest form."

"When it comes down to brass tacks, most difficult cases have the same basis," put in Inspector Peter Reeves (who was having his chance to see Vienna). "Some bloke goes off the rails and tries to score by a foul: he tries it for profit, or from fear, or from plain hate: but most often profit."

"In this case it was fear first and profit second," said Macdonald. "Wilhelm Moritz, half-brother to Charles Stratton, was wanted by the German police. He managed to get into Switzerland on forged papers, but he was pretty hard up. Having heard the story of the Steinadler papers, he got into communication with his English half-brother, Charles Stratton, and the latter decided to come to Vienna to try his chance at negotiating with Waldtraut Körner. Reeves got this sorted out eventually by interrogating Stratton's friends in London. That was Act One, Scene One. Moritz then made up his mind to try to change places with Charles Stratton at Zürich. Karl had better tell the next bit. He knows more about it than I do."

"This is the part I want to know," said Sir Charles Bland. "It was done under my nose, so to speak."

"Under mine, too," said Macdonald.

"It was a cleverly thought out affair," said Karl. "Moritz, in alpine kit—shorts, windjammer coat, boots, beret and rucksack, reached Zürich Airport by car, was booked in for the Swiss plane to London, and went to the Toiletten about fifteen minutes before the B.E.A. Viscount touched down. Moritz did his act tumbling down stairs, recovered and asked for a shower. The next stage is surmise, but it seems quite clear he waited till Stratton came to the lavatories, the probability being that he'd arranged to meet him there. Stratton was then coshed—a perfectly calculated blow on the base of his skull which stunned him and set up cerebral hæmorrhage. Moritz stripped Stratton, put on his clothes, including the famous camel coat and horn-rims, left his own kit in the shower-room with the unconscious victim and re-emerged into the main hall of the airport the replica of Stratton, possessed of his passport, plane and luggage tickets and all the rest. These two half-brothers resembled each other markedly, but what made the exchange easier was Stratton's habit of wearing his hair too long and letting it fall over his forehead, and the big horn-rims helped. The only thing which defeated Moritz was the suède shoes—they were too small for him. He had to wear a pair he'd brought with him in his rucksack. He had plenty of time for everything: the B.E.A. plane put in over an hour at Zürich."

"Well, I'm damned," said Sir Charles. "It was a matter of boldness paying. If he'd only left it alone, Moritz could have got clear away on Stratton's passport."

"I don't think that was his intention," said Macdonald. "Having turned himself into Stratton, he intended to carry on with Stratton's business and collect the Steinadler papers. Remember he had Stratton's brief-case, with all his papers in, his cheque-book and travellers' cheques, and letters of recommendation from the perfectly reputable Literary Agency Stratton was representing: also letters from Vogel, arranging to meet him at Schwechat. And neither Vogel, nor anybody else in Vienna, had ever seen the real Charles Stratton."

"But didn't Vogel tell you he had seen Stratton in London?" put in Dr. Natzler.

"As he hastened to remind me, Vogel didn't actually say 'met': he said 'made contact with,'" said Macdonald. "He now says that the business with Stratton was done by phoning. Undoubtedly Vogel went to London to see if he could find a buyer for the Steinadler papers, and put in an inquiry about a late client in addition, as cover to his activities. The ancient Herr Heinrich Guggenheim has since admitted that Vogel was 'advising' Waldtraut Körner on her literary property. How much Vogel knew—or guessed—about the Stratton-Moritz affair we shall probably never know. Herr Vogel is fully occupied at the moment in explaining various awkwardnesses which have come to light, including his association with Pretzel, the chauffeur."

"Ah," said Karl Natzler, "this is the piece which concerns me."

"This is where we bring Ernest Henry Webster into the story," said Macdonald. "Webster is a mixture of considerable shrewdness and surprising stupidity: he threw a spanner in the works all round. Webster knew Stratton was after the Steinadler papers, and Stratton was staying with Vogel. It was the easiest thing in the world for Webster to call on Vogel on the pretext of asking advice about permits for photography, in reality to 'take a dekko' as Webster puts it.

And quite gratuitously Webster told Vogel that I was on the Viscount—a Superintendent of Scotland Yard on business in Vienna. Vogel was puzzled: he didn't know if Webster was putting over a fast one. My own belief is that Vogel bribed Pretzel to play the part of a patient, call on Dr. Natzler, and steal his keys if opportunity arose. Then Vogel might organise a little espionage in the house where I was staying to find out if Webster was right and Scotland Yard indeed had an emissary in Vienna."

"I'm willing to believe that," said Karl Natzler. "Vogel is a bad one: I've known it for years—but he's never been caught."

"He's caught now," said Macdonald. "When we searched his flat, we found your key-ring: he hadn't time to get rid of it. In my own mind I have no doubt at all that Vogel knew 'Charles Stratton' was bogus: that was why Vogel was worried about the possible presence of Scotland Yard in his own locality."

2

"Well, that was the set out when we all arrived in Vienna," went on Macdonald, after Karl Natzler had refilled their glasses. "I expect the bogus Stratton—Moritz—considered he had been lucky—everything had gone according to plan. In only one way was he unlucky: Vogel lived in Hietzing and Elizabeth Le Vendre was staying in Hietzing. She saw Moritz three times altogether: once in Schönbrunn, when Moritz went to meet Waldtraut Körner: once in the Tiergarten, and the third time up at the old gun-site. She saw him face to face, and she suddenly knew that he was not the man she had sat next to in the Viscount. He must have suddenly realised the awareness in her mind. She says she remembers staring at him—and then nothing: he struck her down as he had struck his half-brother, but the blow was less competent— she wasn't killed."

"He was a complete criminal type," said Natzler. "He probably learnt his trade with the Nazis. Any young man with criminal tendencies got a liberal education in Germany during the Hitler régime."

Macdonald nodded. "Yes. That's only too true. Now I think that Moritz made up his mind that it was time he got out of Vienna: he had friends to help him there—he had been in Vienna several times of recent years: he could get news of what was going on, and he had all the information which Vogel could give him. Vogel knew (through Pretzel) that a Herr Waldemar was being taken to see Waldtraut Körner, and Moritz must have made up his mind to try to have a word with Herr Waldemar on his return from the Emperor Maximilian Hotel. What Moritz did not know was that Walsingham had met Charles Stratton in London. Reeves found that out."

"Good old routine," chuckled Reeves. "You can find out anything if you've only got the time to do it. You can run a chap's friends down and get talking, here a little and there a little, but it takes time."

"I'm tremendously interested in all this," put in Bland. "You often see a headline in the papers, 'Security leakage suspected.' In my own sphere, there's always the chance of some operative talking when he shouldn't about some new process which is still on the secret list. It happens in every human activity because it's the hardest thing in the world to stop people talking. This business of the Steinadler memoirs started as Top Secret: yet the repercussions got all round Europe. Hitler's Generals are still news."

"The story certainly reached London," said Macdonald. "It was debated by reputable publishers and proprietors of not so reputable newspapers: the Steinadler Memoirs could be treated as serious history by a writer like J. B. S. Neville, or as headline sensationalism by the *Sunday Blast*. Doubtless Walsingham thought it was just his line of country, and got into touch with Charles Stratton to see if he knew anything about it."

"Moritz's little story of the Czecho-Slovakian translation was just a red herring served up to explain away the possibility that Walsingham had been seen at Stratton's place of business," put in Karl Natzler, and Macdonald nodded.

"Yes—and to make Walsingham appear to be involved in some business which might lead to a sticky end in Vienna. Webster produced another variation on the same theme— the Rimmel story, and Webster did it most convincingly: but let's finish with the Moritz angle first. Wilhelm Moritz, half-brother to Charles Stratton, may be said to have been conditioned to expert thuggery in the Nazi régime. He killed his half-brother at Zürich, took his place on the plane and determined to get hold of the Steinadler papers. One crime led to another: Moritz coshed Elizabeth Le Vendre—but did not kill her. He coshed Walsingham, and did kill him, thereby making it necessary to kill Pretzel—the witness of the murder. He took the car, put Pretzel's body in the Danube Canal and Walsingham's body on the Wattmanngasse, hoping it would be assumed that Walsingham was killed in a traffic accident."

"But why bring the body back to Hietzing, where Moritz himself was staying?" asked Bland.

"Because he had to return Guggenheim's car to its garage," replied Macdonald. "If the car had been missing in the morning, Guggenheim would have reported to the police, and Moritz did not want attention drawn to that car. Moritz then made his way back to Gunzendorf and told a patrolling constable he was trying to find his way back from Vienna to Hietzing. Moritz had Schneider as an accomplice to swear to his presence at the Liesingerkeller—and Webster came in as an unexpected ally."

"Which brings us to Ernest Henry," chuckled Franz Natzler, "a cheerful rogue, I gather."

"He's not a bad bloke," put in Reeves in his tolerant way. "Webster's lived in London and earned his living without getting into any trouble, as far as we can make out. I reckon Vienna went to his head—plus his Auntie, of course. She's gone real wicked in her old age."

"Webster's not a criminal: he's an opportunist," said Macdonald, "and an opportunist is often a criminal in the making. Webster works for that section of the press in which the ends justify the means—any lie, any intrusion on privacy, any twisting of the facts is permitted to get what's called news—pictorial or otherwise. Webster was shrewd enough to know he might be involved in trouble when trouble broke out which involved the Viscount's passengers. He had Auntie to swear to an alibi for him—any time, anywhere, but he thought some reinforcement might be useful. Thereby he showed his sixth sense: he picked on the one passenger in the plane he sensed might be glad of an alibi in his turn—Stratton."

"Set a thief to catch a thief?" queried Karl, and Macdonald nodded.

"I can't tell you why, and I'm sure Webster can't, but he thought Stratton was a twister. Very well, offer him an alibi, for the whole of the evening when Walsingham was killed, and that alibi involved Webster's presence in the same place. It was very subtle, and Webster fairly palmed the suggestion like an artist. It was an interesting situation," added Macdonald. "Webster had been following Waldtraut Körner round Vienna with his camera: he had contacted Vogel, he had chatted to Pretzel—Webster talks very passable German—and he had been in Hietzing and had seen Stratton hurrying home in the thunderstorm. Webster was more than a little afraid."

"Then it *was* Webster who worked the flashlight when Brunnerhausen was talking to us?" cried Karl.

"It was—as I always believed," said Macdonald. "Webster went up into the woods with the instinct of the newshound—anything in this for me? He moved very slowly and cautiously, and eventually he heard voices and snaked his way up until he got within distance for a long shot. Then the voices ceased—yours and mine, Karl—and Webster still didn't know what it was all about. He made sure he had a quick get-away down a steep path behind him—he's a very quiet mover, he says he's had to be in his job: he waited, and at last he took his courage in both hands and risked his flashlight shot, knowing his subjects would be momentarily blinded. He got away and hurried home to Auntie. Now Auntie could swear an alibi for him if there were need for that afternoon—but he considered it was advisable not to put all the onus on Auntie, so he went fishing after Stratton, with two motives—'one good turn deserves another' and 'is there anything in this for me?'"

"Do you think he sensed the change over at Zürich?" asked Karl, and Macdonald nodded.

"I think he was aware of some 'hanky panky' as he called it, but it wasn't till later that he realised it might have been murder. And in spite of the fact that he's an unblushing and unrepentant liar, there are two things to be said in his favour: he had no hand in the attack on either Miss Le Vendre or Walsingham—Nauheim really has substantiated his alibi for both those occasions—and he did stick his neck out for me up at the Gloriette. He sat there and baited Moritz until Moritz went for him with the cosh, and though the crash helmet and spine pads were a beautiful idea, Webster still took a thundering risk to prove his point."

3

"It is a very dreadful story," said Ilse Natzler. "Never have such things happened in Hietzing before, but I must ask one question: What about pretty lazy Clara? She was the first of all to be attacked: was Clara innocent, or a 'baggage,' as Sir Walter said?"

"Undoubtedly a baggage," rejoined Macdonald, "but Nauheim is satisfied that the 'attack' on Clara was no more than a threat of reprisal from a disappointed swain—a would-be lover, as one might say. But investigation of pretty lazy Clara brought a very interesting fact to light: good characters for not very good maids have been supplied by Fräulein Braun—Webster's Auntie. In her beautiful governess's hand, in either English or German, Auntie would oblige with a suitable recommendation for a girl whose character was not what Auntie said it was: and Auntie is very well up in the names, styles and residences of Austrian notables from whom an answer about a maid's character might not be immediately forthcoming. In return, Auntie received a small fee and such news as the maid could supply from the post thus obtained. Clara had told Auntie all about Sir Walter's memoirs, and about his new English secretary, for instance."

"But what a shocking story!" exclaimed Ilse indignantly.

Sir Charles Bland began to chuckle. "That's a very nice postscript, Macdonald—but even pretty lazy Clara could not make Vanbrugh's Memoirs sound very sensational."

"Ah…" chuckled Karl Natzler, "and here is a second postscript for you, Sir Charles. These Steinadler Memoirs, believed to contain revelations which will astound Europe: I have read them: at the old lady's bedside I read them, for she kept them under her pillow. No wonder Probus Verlag declined to make a good offer: no wonder Walsingham went empty away—to meet an undeserved fate. I tell you the famous Steinadler Memoirs are no more sensational than those of Sir Walter Vanbrugh: indeed, they resemble one another, being the family history of a period no longer inter- . esting to the pundits of to-day."

"I like that," said Reeves. "It shows what mugs some of these smart-Alecs are. But the thing that interests me—if I'm allowed to ask a question myself—what'll the Austrian authorities do with Ernest Henry Webster?"

"That is for them to decide," said Macdonald. "My guess is he'll be let off with a caution: he didn't really behave any worse than newshounds are trained to behave by those who demand sensationalism in their newsprint, and he behaved like a hero when he trusted his crash helmet to save his skull. I think Auntie will be deported, though. The false character racket is taken seriously, so Ernest Henry will have to take Auntie back to London—and neither of them will really enjoy that."

"Final sentence—support Auntie in the style to which she is accustomed," murmured Franz, and Macdonald turned to Bland.

"The only part of the story we haven't sorted out is the mystery of your daughter's mink coat, sir. Was there by any chance a cameraman outside the house when a party was given for distinguished writers?"

"My God!" exclaimed Bland. "Webster?... 'taking a dekko'—and chancing his arm later to get information?"

"I wouldn't put it beyond him," said Macdonald. "It's like him—because you see he didn't steal the coat. Ernest Henry is all on the side of the angels. But we shall never prove it—never. That will remain one of the unsolved mysteries of the case."

"And that is quite enough," said Ilse Natzler firmly. "We will have no more talk of crime. It is not suitable—not in Hietzing."

Karl Natzler rose to his feet. "This evening, Macdonald, we take you out to the heights of the Wienerwald, to Cobenzl. You shall at last enjoy a *Heurige,* and we will drink the local vintages—Grinzinger and Gumpoldskirchner, and your holiday in Vienna will really begin."

"*Gott sei Dank,*" exclaimed Ilse, and Macdonald added, "*Und Lob.* Amen."

If you've enjoyed
Murder in Vienna,
you won't want to miss

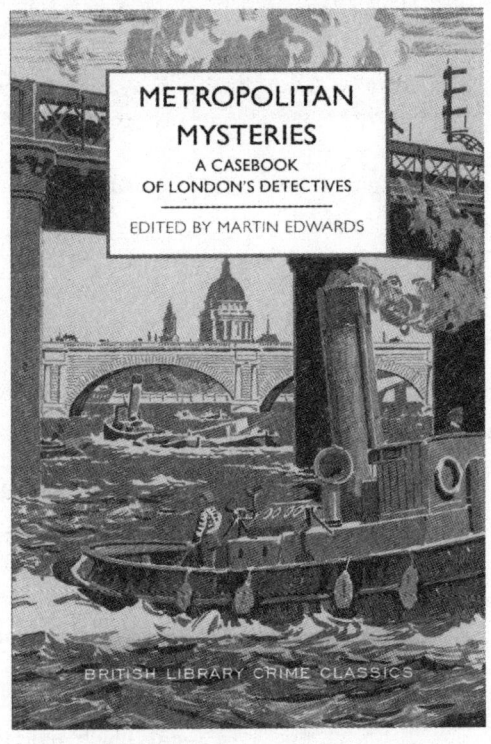

the most recent BRITISH LIBRARY CRIME CLASSIC
published by Poisoned Pen Press,
an imprint of Sourcebooks.

Praise for the
British Library Crime Classics

★"Carr is at the top of his game in this taut whodunit... The British Library Crime Classics series has unearthed another worthy golden age puzzle."

—*Publishers Weekly*, STARRED Review,
for *The Lost Gallows*

★ "A wonderful rediscovery."
—*Booklist*, STARRED Review, for *The Sussex Downs Murder*

★ "First-rate mystery and an engrossing view into a vanished world."

—*Booklist*, STARRED Review, for *Death of an Airman*

★ "A cunningly concocted locked-room mystery, a staple of Golden Age detective fiction."
—*Booklist*, STARRED Review, for *Murder of a Lady*

"The book is both utterly of its time and utterly ahead of it."
—*New York Times Book Review* for *The Notting Hill Mystery*

★ "As with the best of such compilations, readers of classic mysteries will relish discovering unfamiliar authors, along with old favorites such as Arthur Conan Doyle and G.K. Chesterton."

—*Publishers Weekly*, STARRED Review, for *Continental Crimes*

"In this imaginative anthology, Edwards—president of Britain's Detection Club—has gathered together overlooked criminous gems."

—*Washington Post* for *Crimson Snow*

★ "The degree of suspense Crofts achieves by showing the growing obsession and planning is worthy of Hitchcock. Another first-rate reissue from the British Library Crime Classics series."
—*Booklist*, STARRED Review, for *The 12.30 from Croydon*

★ "Not only is this a first-rate puzzler, but Crofts's outrage over the financial firm's betrayal of the public trust should resonate with today's readers."
—*Booklist*, STARRED Review, for *Mystery in the Channel*

★ "This reissue exemplifies the mission of the British Library Crime Classics series in making an outstanding and original mystery accessible to a modern audience."
—*Publishers Weekly*, STARRED Review, for *Excellent Intentions*

"A book to delight every puzzle-suspense enthusiast."
—*New York Times* for *The Colour of Murder*

★ "Edwards's outstanding third winter-themed anthology showcases 11 uniformly clever and entertaining stories, mostly from lesser known authors, providing further evidence of the editor's expertise… This entry in the British Library Crime Classics series will be a welcome holiday gift for fans of the golden age of detection."
—*Publishers Weekly*, STARRED Review, for *The Christmas Card Crime and Other Stories*

Poisoned Pen
PRESS

poisonedpenpress.com